A Twilight Celebration

MARIE-CLAIRE BLAIS

ALSO BY MARIE-CLAIRE BLAIS

FICTION

The Angel of Solitude

Anna's World

David Sterne

Deaf to the City

The Fugitive

A Literary Affair

Mad Shadows

The Manuscripts of Pauline Archange

Nights in the Underground

A Season in the Life of Emmanuel

Tête Blanche

These Festive Nights

The Wolf

Thunder and Light

Augustino and the Choir of Destruction

Rebecca, Born in the Maelstrom

Mai at the Predators' Ball

Nothing for You Here, Young Man

The Acacia Gardens

NONFICTION

American Notebooks: A Writer's Journey

A Twilight Celebration

MARIE-CLAIRE BLAIS

Translated by Nigel Spencer

First published as *Le festin au crépuscule* in 2015 by Les Éditions du Boréal
First published in English in 2019 by House of Anansi Press Inc.
www.houseofanansi.com

House of Anansi Press is committed to protecting our natural environment. As part of our efforts, this book is made of material from well-managed FSC®-certified forests, recycled materials, and other controlled sources.

23 22 21 20 19   1 2 3 4 5

Library and Archives Canada Cataloguing in Publication

Blais, Marie-Claire, 1939–
[Festin au crépuscule. English]
A Twilight Celebration / Marie-Claire Blais ; [translated by] Nigel Spencer.

Translation of: Festin au crépuscule.
Issued in print and electronic formats.
ISBN 978-1-4870-0248-0 (softcover).—ISBN 978-1-4870-0249-7
(EPUB).—ISBN 978-1-4870-0250-3 (Kindle)

I. Spencer, Nigel, 1945-, translator II. Title. III. Title: Festin
au crépuscule. English

PS8503.L33F4713 2018   C843'.54   C2017-904745-0
C2017-904746-9

Library of Congress Control Number: 2017947369

Cover design: Alysia Shewchuk
Text design: Laura Brady
Typesetting: Sara Loos

Canada Council for the Arts   Conseil des Arts du Canada

We acknowledge for their financial support of our publishing program the Canada Council for the Arts, the Ontario Arts Council, and the Government of Canada. We acknowledge the financial support of the Government of Canada through the National Translation Program for Book Publishing, an initiative of the Roadmap for Canada's Official Languages 2013–2019: Education, Immigration, Communities, *for our translation activities.*

Printed and bound in Canada

For Patricia Lamerdin

With thanks to Peter Gillis,
a faithful and generous friend

Thanks to Sylvie Saint-Martin

Thanks to Sushi, a remarkable artist

It would be under the sign of immensity, said Mère to Daniel, she looked so incredibly young, everything that happens will be signalled by immensity, she'd said to Daniel in his dream, like when you feel overwhelmed by the enormity of mountains, by dizzying heights or vast oceans, she said, offering Daniel a glass of rosé, everything was of the same rose hue, Mère's woollen clothes, her face, Mère's wrist beneath her woollen sleeve, the wrist Daniel kissed, saying, you are cured, how much better you look, then you must tell Mélanie, said Mère, so she'll no longer worry, promise me you'll tell her, Daniel, that aside from the crushing vastness of this place, too much for me, too many mountains and rivers, such savage immensity so unfamiliar to me, though aside from all of this so like the immensity of the universe I inhabited before, not so different, really, aside from my being so bewildered at not knowing quite where I am, yes, aside from this mystery I cannot grasp, tell Mélanie all is well with me, I really couldn't feel better anywhere other than in this abandoned and gigantic space, for I was never a believer, and yet they say it is God's place, tell her again and again I couldn't feel any better than this, when all at once, after swallowing the pink liquid that, smiling warmly, she held out to him, Daniel heard himself saying, Mère, Mother, tell me is it really you, oh, you know I'm a creature of airports who's so tired of flying, said Daniel waking alone in his hotel room, for after such long trips he always fell promptly onto the bed, suitcase and all, tomorrow was soon enough to unpack in rooms which always appeared so unfriendly at first, though so very comfortable that he usually managed to come to terms with them, first stunned into a fitful sleep as though tumbling into a fog and swallowed, like the restless sleep of a plane crossing the Atlantic, or was he already there, in that limitless desert of anonymous hotels, stretched out as though his unfolding legs and arms were too long for him on a grim bed in a grim room and repeating to himself that maybe he was the first one to arrive so no one here was expecting him, this claiming of a home without smells that was not his own, to be followed by plummeting down in an overpowered elevator, so fast, everything was going so fast, though he could barely keep his eyes open as if, stiff and practically sleepwalking, he had taken a twenty-storey jump, for as Mère had told him in his dream, all manifested itself as immensity, the vast hotel, a void just as vast, and this quality of silence, this silence reaching so far it echoed from room to room, floor to floor, corridor to corridor, for such are the hotels travellers frequent, he thought, frequently on the edge of a highway, buildings ugly in their massiveness, denatured, no park, no grass, just concrete and steel and this grey sky weighing down on the tops of buildings, yet they say for our meeting, our conference, we'll be in the heart of nature, and there in the mountains all will be so grandiose, so huge, that we, all of us, gathered from fifty or more countries, we worn-out, rumpled, and disillusioned writers, that we'll be dazzled by our hosts and the majesty of these locales, though, as Mai said, thought Daniel, you, Papa, no, you're not like them, you're not worn out and disillusioned, Papa, in fact you risk life and limb for what is new because you love me so much, me, your daughter, or that which is like me and changes from one moment to the next, and besides it's an international writers' conference, and maybe you'll bump into Augustino because you're always searching for him, my dear Papa, for my vanishing phantom-brother, and Papa, maybe you'll find him, he who writes books here and there then disappears into the crowd, who knows, maybe he'll be hiding in the melee of writers discussing peace, we don't know how, whether together or singly, each with their own language and thoughts, in such a babble of voices and faces, yes, who knows, Augustino might even show up and retreat to some corner, though Mama says he may still be in India, but this is me, Mai, talking, and I know when you're off it's always in the hope of finding Augustino, you who don't like meetings or conferences and for whom, Papa, so far from your home and garden, departing for other continents it's always for him, Augustino, that you go, oh, I know, said Mai, this voice Daniel thought he was still hearing on his telephone, Mai, who was wiser than her father and knew it all, first the smooth sliding of the elevator, the taming of deserted spaces, Daniel heading to the bar, similarly deserted, out of which a vapid music emerged, bland but soothing, so would they all just surge in at once out of nowhere, where were all these writers, artisans of the word and avid readers, not one, there seemed to be no one at all in the hotel, thought Daniel, yes, you're the first to arrive, said the waiter appearing suddenly in white coat and black tie, they'll not be here for the festival until tomorrow, we're celebrating its tenth anniversary already, they'll be coming here from all over the world so welcome, sir, to our town and villages, there will be booksellers strolling in the streets, houses set up for book signings and rest breaks, festivities in the woods, in our forests, you'll see, it's going to be quite an experience for you, especially tomorrow evening's Twilight Celebration, our custom these past ten years, yes, ten years already, and yet it will be the first time that writers, poets, translators, and publishers will express in their lectures and seminars their desire for a more peaceful world, their own fervour must be recognized, they say, for writers are often thought of as not very useful, their lessons too personal and of no benefit to society, what's your opinion, sir, me I'm just a waiter in a bar, Eddy's my name, said the young man, and he shook Daniel's hand, and here's your vodka with lemon zest, sir, of course I'm visiting Scotland myself, like a lot of nomadic servers I'm here in Scotland learning about the world, so much to discover, next year I want to go to New Zealand, like I said, there's so much to learn about the world every day, and listening to Eddy, his talk a little monotonous, Daniel's mind turned to Augustino, easy enough to spot because he stood tall among the young men of his age, awkwardly too, his discomfort, thought Daniel, having an impetuous edge, as if the anger he projected ahead of himself was propitious but always a little off-target, Augustino definitely not one to charm or please and said by his critics to write with vitriol, quite unlike his father, so distanced from dour thoughts, it was clear, thought Daniel, that he took after none of his father's habits, even if they shared the same genes, no, they were wholly dissimilar, and yet, despite the years he would know his son right away, one thing I know, one thing I'm sure of, said Eddy, is that writers are serious drinkers, fine by me, because as you know life isn't easy for us, us waiters, I don't mean they're all alcoholics, no, though some do die alone in their rooms, which makes me sad for them and for all the books they've written, works all of a sudden left in their wake, as if they no longer remember having written them, oh, that pains me, said Eddy, what I mean to say is they aren't all sober like you, sir, you seem to be a light drinker, you wouldn't ask for a second vodka after fifteen hours on a plane, no, don't get me wrong, I'm not saying booze is a sickness with writers, no, though there are those who might, psychologists would say so, but seriously, might it be a path to inspiration, for aren't all kinds of addiction a trajectory to knowledge and complete sobriety a denial of life, you don't learn, you don't live, I'm not one who thinks ill of them, you know, not someone who sees alcoholic writers as demented, in fact I'd say we live more fully in excess, what do you think, Daniel? I can call you Daniel, right, because we'll meet many times over the bar like this, you and me, and Daniel said, at your age what is great is the feeling of invincibility, I'd love to feel the way you do, but I don't react well to excess, I have to accept a disciplined routine I don't much like, but a person gets used to it, you'll see one day, Daniel said, realizing he was being a bore, or was he in effect talking to Samuel or Mai or Vincent about their own excesses, boy, what a pompous know-it-all he was becoming, and he had been for quite some time, well, said Eddy dryly as he rinsed glasses under the tap, no two lives are the same, I'd like mine to be an awesome voyage, yes, totally awesome, he said again, I'm closing this bar, the Celtic Tavern, at midnight, and then I'll go dancing with a girlfriend, well, a few of them, he added with a smile, and since you're my one customer, Daniel, maybe I'll be closing early, oh, no rush, you have plenty of time to relax by the fireplace and warm up by the embers, fall's coming on and it's already cold and damp, they gave this place a country inn makeover recently, tomorrow you'll see our landscape of hills and sheep, far as the eye can see, yes, this inn has too many large and chilly hallways, too many rooms to get lost in, will you be visiting the north of Scotland for the ruins and castles, at least the architect didn't forget to put in an elevator for the lazier guests, of course I don't mean you, Daniel, but we do have guests who barely leave their rooms, annoying, because they demand room service all day long when the countryside is so amazing with its fjords and mountains and forests peppered with lakes, them with meals in their rooms calling us up incessantly, they're the richest ones, of course, regulars they are, they travel the world without ever leaving their luxury suites, maybe to take a dip in the pool or watch the snow come down or the fog roll in over the glass roof, the roof we sometimes open up to a summer sky full of stars, though summer's short here, see it's already nearly over, honestly, without the wool industry I don't know how these deprived areas would survive, I really don't know, he said skeptically, looking at his watch because it was nearly midnight, too early for the ladies yet, he seemed to be thinking, and this writer, Daniel, still around, staring at the fire and chewing over his thoughts, now I just bet he's going to sink into one of those armchairs next to the humming fire no more than glowing ashes now, no way Eddy was going to add another log and stoke it up again, but, a conscientious worker, he said to Daniel, you know, sir, let me say that we, the hotel staff and waiters and bartenders, we're at your service these next three days what with the great cause you are serving so diligently, you and your colleagues from all over the world who speak so many languages, why, can you just imagine what an event this is for us humble townsfolk, it's an occasion never to be forgotten, isn't it, and when I'm in New Zealand next year, I'll still remember it and meeting you, Daniel, especially with a memory for detail like mine, my mother used to say it's a hardship remembering so many details, but for a waiter whose duty is to his clientele, it's better to forget none of their preferences, none of their tastes in beer and alcohol, am I right, but, said Daniel abruptly, what is the grand cause we are serving—writing books, is that it—my son Augustino would say the writer working at home and surrounded by his wife and children, as I've always been, is dedicated to no one but himself, is egotistical, oh, but I wouldn't say that, said Eddy, he's someone who, all the time he is writing, for months and years, forgoes the joys and pleasures of ordinary folks like me, Eddy the Epicurean, enjoying ourselves all the while, while you live the austere life, yes, thought Daniel, but what if my son is right and it's a sterile life or even a wasted one, meaningless even, an absurd and irresponsible choice, these were the thoughts he kept to himself and did not share with Eddy, whistling as he closed the bar before midnight, soon he'd be dancing with the girls and forget all about doting on this writer, thought Daniel, yet Eddy, though consumed by his sensual desires, could still appreciate authors and their drinking habits, the drift of their discourse, he knew better than anyone these clients who did not quite resemble others once they'd had a few, because of their manner, their tendency to poetic language, and a rancour in their remarks that was sometimes astonishingly severe, to him they were originals, often of refined intelligence, not like those drinking boors who had nothing to teach him about the art of living, and Eddy, whether travelling or tending bar, always wanted to learn or at least to rise above the condition of the dead-enders he served, not at all like the writers passing through, people from whom it seemed he had learned a lot, believe me, Daniel, I learn so much from listening to the lot of you, the world offering itself up to me at this bar every day, isn't that the truth, but Daniel was still thinking of Augustino, he felt as if he was engaged in combat and his adversary was taunting him, especially with his silence, Augustino, who knows, perhaps he had left India for Egypt, hadn't he emailed his brother Vincent that he was always so preoccupied by the fate of women in countries devastated by all the turmoil and violence of aborted revolutions, or in other countries that were incubators of incomprehensible barbarities, for a revolution at its height often leads to a kind of rapture, Augustino had written to his brother, and this delirium can be more murderous than the revolution itself, what with its experimentation with new weapons, unanticipated ones, and Augustino wrote to his brother of a woman facing a bulldozer with arms folded to keep her little children from being crushed and screaming, enough, enough, one of them already lying on his side with his arm outstretched, as if he'd been wounded, reaching for an empty Coke bottle and an empty jerry can as the bulldozer plowed through garbage bags and broken bottles, a landscape ravaged by insurrection, by war, and this woman, her arms raised, crying, enough, enough, was an icon amid the carnage, this mother standing in fields of garbage trying to save her last son was woman as protector, an image of dignity Daniel also carried inside himself but could never convey in the way his son could, Daniel still separated from the world as it was by some diaphanous veil, or was it a corrupted slide through which passed only the most distressing realities of the world beyond his gaze, so that he felt at a remove and in a mediated peace, and without it would he have had the strength to write all that he was feeling, but Augustino, thought Daniel, Augustino did not benefit from this remove or the solace of a break from his thoughts, he was immediately enraged by what he saw, judge and victim both, as if this heartbreaking sight of a woman and her wounded son were a part of him, suffusing his blood and nerves in a cauldron of torment he could not push away from his soul, yes, thought Daniel, this was Augustino alright, he who at the same time seemed indifferent to his doctor brother despairing that polio vaccination was banned in Pakistan and Afghanistan, where thousands more children will die, wrote Vincent to Daniel, where there will be more of the epidemics by which the soldiers of tribes at war are forever punishing children, children and animals, thought Daniel, because don't we ignore the number of animals, also victims exterminated in the wake of men and their bulldozers and their weapons slicing through the sky in all directions, wind-fed fires chasing birds from buildings, from homes, blowing piles of flame and ash before them, this, yes this, thought Daniel, is what he would like to talk about at the conference, as he would about this mother protecting the children still left to her too, she who stood before the bulldozer rolling toward them through the street's unfathomable chaos, its accumulation of discarded mattresses the two sons had probably tried to use for cover or as ramparts against the enemy, beside which one was now lying on his side with a head wound, seemingly asleep in the street, his hand releasing the empty Coke bottle that was likely his only weapon, that's what Augustino told his brother, Daniel too could see the truth and describe the scandal and pain of it, and Augustino warned his brother about working too many hours given his frail condition, but Vincent assured him he was living healthily by working hard, his episodes fewer and farther between, though deploring to Augustino that in this era in which men walked on the moon, still there was no practical cure for children who suffered from acute asthma, still no radical therapy to ease their pain, Daniel revisiting a dream he'd often had in which he was like a mother bird on a branch trying to teach her little ones to fly, but the branch was too high up, so was the top of the wall, yes, her fledglings were lined up beside her in this dream and in the distance were the white sands of a faraway beach, Daniel and his kids had needed to reach it, this beach, but none of them had any experience of jumping into the void, Daniel would go first, if with a feeling of dread, but they were still young and stayed on the wall and watched as their father leapt alone into the emptiness of sky spinning like a black cloud, yet he knew his feet would touch ground, that he'd feel them graze the white sand, or was he just hoping not to die? Well, Daniel, I'm going to have to close up, said Eddy in the Celtic Tavern, emboldened because he was about to meet up with the girls and dance, anyway, we'll only be dancing for a few hours, said Eddy, because tomorrow it's work again, every night I'm at La Mer du Nord, I could take you there if you like dancing, even though the music's electronic and loud, or you can unwind here, sit by the fire for a while before it's completely out, this morning I put on some branches damp from last night's rain, I figured you'd like the smell of the sap, the walls of the inn also smell like the branches burning in the hearth, it's like a warm bath, comforting if your body's not hurting, but it can be depressing, don't you think, these days I feel a bit down when I think of the poets who were here at the festival at the end of the season but won't be with us again, we're missing a few every year though we can't say their passing is a sad thing because they have joyful funerals, yes, that's when we waiters have our work cut out for us because poets, all these bards and writers, love a party, they want us to celebrate them at parties that can be hard going, and to do so with gravity and panache, yeah, that's when the whisky flows freely, we try to make it happen the way poets like even when they're no longer around, for we celebrate their renown, trying not to think of them as dead poets, that's the power of youth it seems to me, not liking death, yes, do you know what I think, Daniel, said Eddy as he guided him over to the sofa chair in front of the fire in the brazier emitting its dying sighs and murmurs, yep, I think each year the souls of deceased poets drift off to join a fraternity, must be huge too, all of the bards and poets who've wandered the woods and forests of Scotland and Ireland finally together again, telling one another stories through the centuries, maybe some of them saying how several times they escaped execution, punishment for their liberated verses, oh man, they'd have stories to tell, the heretics, I bet a bunch of them were hanged, and as they wandered about the woods and forests, who knows if they did not gather for a secret banquet of celebration in the mountains and pastures where sheep graze, or some clearing where one can lie down on beds of greenery and all the while chant mystic spells, incantations to the joy of living, who knows, there was a red-headed poet who came to the festival each year from London, what a pleasure it was for him to recite his verses, surrounded by his red-headed daughters, when I brought them drinks on reading nights I was lost in contemplation, the elegant minstrel apologizing for being a little drunk, I believe his poem was concerned with the stitches of eternity that gradually fray between our fingers, yes, said Daniel, stitches of eternity, I remember now, or maybe, said Eddy, it was the cloth of eternity that wore out, yes, I remember the poet, said Daniel, we called him the Poet of Gentle Decadence because he sprinkled words of Latin through his poems and resisted violent political opinion, yes, he'd mellowed a lot, will he be joining us this year, asked Daniel, no, I must disappoint you, said Eddy, he won't be with us, his red hair suddenly turned white, I was at his funeral a few days ago and glad to see his daughters, yes, he was fêted, truly celebrated, almost as if he were still here among us dancing and whooping it up and had organized the whole thing himself ahead of time, drink and dance and think of me, that's what he ordered his wife and daughters to do, for a poet shouldn't get mixed up in politics as in the past I was, ah, such a fine man, how we'll miss him this year, like they said in the papers, a man who knew how to honour the beauty of life and who, over time, stopped judging people, yes, said Daniel, with the passing of time how do we judge a man, Daniel was somewhere else, his eyes closed to the fire's dying heat, and in some undefined place a stranger came toward him saying, do you see this house before you with all its windows open, they're like black holes, pools of shade, come with me to the far end of the corridor, your son is waiting just to the left, so Daniel followed the stranger to the house and down the hall, knowing Augustino was in one of the rooms, it was as if he could hear his breath, his footsteps nearby, and yet Augustino did not come out to meet his waiting father, and Daniel felt a leaden heaviness crushing his chest, he said it again, Augustino, are you there, Augustino, I know you're here, and the thought of his son not loving him was a lead weight in his chest and all he felt made him weep, but then unexpectedly Eddy tapped Daniel's shoulder, sir, said Eddy, I think you fell asleep, I guess it's time for you to go to your room, I have to close the Celtic Tavern, oh, said Daniel, yes, I must have nodded off, there's so much to do before the conference and there's something in particular I must not forget, I'll go there now, thanks, Eddy, said Daniel as he rose, you've reminded me of my duties, have you seen our pictures of the hunt, Eddy asked, real masterpieces, aren't they, the hunters, just like the dogs, are especially well portrayed, so realistic you practically hear the shooting and barking, isn't that the truth, said Eddy, but Daniel had disappeared and Eddy heard the old clock strike midnight. I remember it all, thought Lucia, yes, everything, so maybe the gaps in my memory are all gone now, because I can see them just the way they were that night in the street, the mother with her child, nameless they were, or their misery was so objectified that you could give them any name you wanted, later I found out they were Jill and Jonathan, though his mother would call him Jono as she led him by the hand, a little boy just four years old whose head appeared too closely shaved, and Jill, the young mother, was wearing cut-off jeans but you could sense traces of her former vanity, and as I passed by with Night Out on my shoulder, she stopped me, I can't say what state she was in, I think she'd just done heroin, anyway, I can't be certain, they weren't far from the poor people's Salvation Army Store, I figure they hung around there a lot, that's what I told Bryan the first time I spotted them, and Bryan said she's not allowed to panhandle in the street after 8 p.m., that if she doesn't go to the Shelter with her son, Social Services will take him away from her, and I thought oh no, they can't be separated, and that's how it all began, yes, I remember recounting this to Bryan and he was amazed at how good my memory was, how clear things have been since I moved to the Acacia Gardens, in my memory the mother said, your parrot sure is beautiful, and I answered that we were inseparable, Night Out and I, he never leaves my shoulder, then she asked if I was also spending the night at the Shelter and I told her that some time back my sisters had taken my home from me, and now, thanks to Bryan, whom I love like a true son, my own son being a mean good-for-nothing who deserted his mother, Bryan has taken his place and no regrets, Brilliant is what they call him not least for the light that inhabits his heart, a brilliant, warm light we see shining in his full, brown, luminous eyes just like his dog Misha's, no, I said, I told her I had an apartment in the Acacia Gardens and was very happy there, and as I was saying all this to a woman on the street whose name I did not yet know, and to her little boy, I realized this was the day of my transformation, that the Other Lucia was no longer a part of me, I don't know where she'd decided to go but I could feel myself reborn as someone else, as someone who had never been forced to sleep in the prickly bushes of her garden in the middle of winter after my sisters slammed my own door on me, that landscape of humiliation had vanished like something disappearing in a fog at sea, oh no, I said, he's not a parrot but a budgie that Mabel, the lady who sells roses and ginger lemonade, gave me one day, it's his red tail, yes, that's what I told these two when they asked, a mother and son with plenty of other things to worry about, wandering the streets with no idea of where they were going to spend the night, the mother faint from her journey and her son clinging to her, saying no, don't go with Rodriguez tonight and don't go see Dad in prison, he'll beat you again, look at your red cheeks and the scars on your forehead, soon even the Shelter won't take us anymore, and remember, I have to go to school tomorrow, I got a place in kindergarten, I'm gonna be first in everything just like I promised you and Dad, in prison he kissed me yesterday, he said you've got to come first, always, so Mom, you have to take me to school tomorrow, don't worry, said Jill, I'll take you on the seat of my bike, Mom, Rodriguez stole that bike, we're better off walking, then walking is what we'll do, said Jill, Dad's eyes were weird and he'll hit you again if you see him, repeated the young boy, and if he beats you, Mom, then you'll go back to hospital and I won't be able to see you at all, Social Services will come and take me away, and this, thought Lucia, was how it began, they had nowhere to spend the night, it's happened to me to have to sleep in the streets, but I'm talking of that Other Lucia, the Lucia despised by her sisters, not this changed Lucia, the one with an apartment in the Acacia Gardens, I looked at them, Jill and her son Jonathan, knowing the Other Lucia would have extended a hand but from a distance, not wanting to walk the way of humiliation again, but it was necessary to extend a hand, if only symbolically, because they were so alone, and my mind went back to Brilliant who'd begun his studies and was working at the clinic of Dr. Dieudonné and aspiring to be a nurse's aide, then a nurse, that was Brilliant's dream, though for now he was only a volunteer on Sundays, bringing meals to the convalescents of Acacia Gardens, and almost every day he took Misha to visit Angel, really it was a shame for me that Brilliant was back on the straight-and-narrow with his head in his books and not going out in the evening anymore, nor reciting any of his prodigious oral masterwork late into the small hours, in bars, in taverns, this story he'd certainly never write down, it seemed to me, I mean where would he find the time to write with all the different jobs he had, he who was always so busy, well, answered Brilliant, you can do anything in life, you can sing, you can write, you can write in your head most of all, you can learn to be a nurse's aide, there will always be people to heal and comfort, time to waste and win back again, yes, you can do anything in life, anything, that's what Brilliant said, and he told me as well that they won't get into the Shelter after eight o'clock, this mother and child, it's not allowed, no drugs either, of course, nothing, they'll be watched, is it true Rodriguez stole the bike, they were looking for him, this Rodriguez, the thing is this young woman only falls for bad boys, for thugs, Brilliant told me, and it was the little boy who said it was him, Rodriguez, I saw him steal the bike, this boy had seen everything and without complaint, how each day his mother sat on the sidewalk waiting for her fix of heroin, saw them all, the ones she sold herself to, saw everything, saw every one of them and kept watch, standing in front of his mother as if he were shielding her from prying eyes, from the police, said Brilliant, the Shelter and rehab were their last chance, if not she would lose the boy she apparently adored, yes, this was their last chance to make it to the Shelter before eight, and suddenly there I was before them, Night Out on my shoulder and wondering what would become of the two as it was late already, past ten, and they still weren't back at the Shelter for women, mothers and children, and I thought of the police who'd be making their rounds soon, seeking them out and chasing them like miscreants, it was closed, the Shelter was now closed, and I wondered how many women and children there were in all the refuges, in all the towns, in all countries, how many children and mothers in separate dorms, nuns sometimes coming by to comfort the children, they're well fed, the kids especially, but sometimes there are just too many, too many haggard mothers pledged to sobriety with their children, or else, or else, yes, Jonathan had seen Rodriguez take the bike, same as he had seen everything else and never let out a murmur, I thought how ashamed he must feel, the way I used to be as the Other Lucia, ashamed of being poor, but the boy was saying nothing, the eyes below his shaved head were expressionless, his mother always holding his hand and repeating, yes he would go to school tomorrow, she'd even bought health insurance for him so he'd be like the other boys and not stand out, no, I thought, Jonathan seems not to know what shame is, his confident hand in his mother's, and as for that Rodriguez often at Jill's side, the troublemaker, the one who stole the bike, he belonged to a family of which his was the third generation to face charges of theft and possession of stolen goods, his brothers, parents, uncles, all of them in jail, their campers and tawdry trailers seized on the outskirts of town in old hangars and yards with incredible amounts of cocaine and crack, but also illegally purchased lobster tails, the whole family set to appear before a judge on drug trafficking charges, and it was this Rodriguez who was hanging around Jill, the man they called a public menace, his entire family incarcerated and Rodriguez sure to follow in no time, Jill often looked at him, admiring his lips, his eyes, she needed a guardian and maybe he was the one, this arrogant petty criminal, certainly she needed someone, needed a man, this woman alone with her child, afraid, panicked, no longer knowing what to do with herself, yes, life is a senseless and terrifyingly bad joke for so many of us, luckily I made it out, I have my dignity back, a home to go to and sleep in at night, I really wanted to help them, Jill and her son Jonathan, I really did, but there was always this Rodriguez she loved in the way, Jill growing weak at the knees under his gaze, she loved this man, was trapped between a thief and a husband who beat her even when she came to visit him in prison, her face marked all over, once I had a job in a store selling jewellery, she said, but they let me go after a few days, still I managed to put a little money aside for my boy and for a while we ate well every day, and I never arrived late at the Shelter for Women and Children, no no, I didn't do anything wrong, I don't want to go to jail like my husband, okay, we're in the street, Jonathan and me, but is this a crime, no, we'll find a place, but days went by and still they were out there, and I thought, me, the Other Lucia, about the great exodus of thousands of homeless people in countries never resolving their conflicts, women and children, mostly, forced into flight as the men go on fighting, it's always the mothers and children who go hungry, I thought, and of Jill and Jonathan too, not knowing where they would sleep that night, or what schemes and secrets she would need to hold on to him, Rodriguez the provider often insisting that she spend a night in a hotel with complete strangers, which she could only do with her boy by her side, and who never handed over the money she earned, he kept it all, and I'd come to tell Jill that as it was raining, the two of you, mother and child, should come home with me for a night, Bryan will fix you a hot meal, and little Jono tipped his head to indicate he wanted to, and not to spend the night on the beach, clinging to his mother and his eyes lacklustre and drained by fear, I could reach for the phone on my belt and call Brilliant at any time of day or night to tell him to come get them in his car, that was our agreement, that he'd pick them up in his car, and now he was no longer pedalling a rickshaw-taxi, he had a slightly ramshackle car that he drove too fast, Misha thrusting his wolf-head out the open window, eyes open and teeth bared, Misha totally revived, as if at last all the catastrophes and conflagrations of the past were out of mind, except that he still barked uncontrollably, always for no reason, and Bryan had to say, shush, be quiet, Misha, the whole town can hear you, sweet Misha, don't bark so much, so here we were, all of us at the Acacia Gardens, just for one night, so the mother and child might get a meal and some rest and put an end to their wandering that night, unlike the others, I thought, unlike the thousands of others in warring countries waiting for aid workers to bring them water, bread, and a tent, the shelter that would be denied them another night, though maybe not the morrow, yes, I could see them, a multitude of mothers and children waiting in the rain or snow, could see them clearly as this mother and child gorged on their food, the child with empty eyes looking at no one, fixated on the food in front of him, then asking all at once if there was fruit, I'd really like to eat some fruit, like they have at the Shelter, I watched and thought how well his mother had brought him up despite everything, that he had good manners, that Jill wanted him to be polite and well behaved, a thoughtful child, though I also knew this wasn't going to happen as long as the villain Rodriguez was around, and Brilliant needed to leave because he was employed as the nurse's aide in Emergency, there were nighttime car accidents, and I lent my room to Jill and Jonathan, said Night Out and I, inseparable as always, were used to sleeping in our hammock out on the veranda, we even had a tarp to protect us from the rain, a precarious construction of Brilliant's, and finally they managed to sleep peacefully, until Rodriguez burst in out of the night and said come with me, Jill and Jono, get on my motorbike, we're outta here, I gotta be off of this island tonight, they're right behind me, the bastards, come quickly, Rodriguez slapped her and she hurried out of bed, quick, come on, and off they all went, her face turning red in an instant, so many cuts and bruises, Rodriguez's slaps as familiar as kisses, this the only treatment she had known from men, never rebelling, never protesting, it made me ill to see them leave in such a flash of violence, thank you for the orange, said the boy as he left, are we coming back, Mom, yes yes, said the mother, maybe tomorrow, thank them for the cake said Jill to her son, and the child said thanks, thanks for the carrot cake, thank you, and egged on by Rodriguez's brutality they descended to the street and left me, his motorbike roaring, and I knew all this was far from over, yes, of course it wasn't, that I know, thought Lucia. And even though he knew he was dreaming, Daniel could not shake off the avalanche of nightmares along which his body was sliding, telling himself to wake up but unable to, the dark corridors of his dreaming stretched out before him, enemies and persecutors ready to attack, and at times he was transported into the hunting scenes he'd seen on the walls of the bar downstairs, he was the deer, the fox, the boar, braced in the face of traps and bows pulled back and at the ready, panting, he could only hope the hunter would finish him off quickly, that he wouldn't suffer too much, and then suddenly he was a man pursued, struggling in the mud at gunpoint, begging his enemy to forgive him or finish him off at once, he was awake a few seconds and then fell right back into the same dream, but these were not his dreams, he told himself, in those he would see Mélanie, Mai, or Augustino, but in these ones, sad and apocalyptic, the faces of his children were absent, no, no doubt he was recycling someone else's dreams, it happened at times and they made him feel low, crushed and oppressed by the wreckage of thousands of other people's dreams seizing control of his memory, he couldn't pull himself out of this muddle, this nightmarish fusion of hostile images, none of which appeared to relate to his own destiny, and then suddenly Mère would appear in her pink knits, walking alone and apparently unaware of Daniel, still, feeling her presence nearby comforted him, and then suddenly Daniel was in a clearing, an oasis, he was jumping from a moving train, he was in Spain, in a station in the countryside and he could hear canaries singing, and Rodrigo welcomed him with open arms and said, do you remember me, I'm Rodrigo, the Brazilian poet, on a retreat in this old Madrid monastery, do you remember, amigo, like you I believe in the return of impenitent souls, the damned, but alas, what with wives and children I have so many financial worries that I haven't written a single poem in a very long time, come, amigo, the others are waiting for us in the woods, I wanted to write about them, these youngsters, these adolescents of the New Order, the Bloody Order, still we see them on the streets of Buenos Aires perpetrating their Nazi propaganda, come, come on, and Daniel was delighted and relieved to see them all, Rodrigo, the poet from Brazil, and Mark and Carmen, New York punk artists who called themselves The Debris because they only worked with ruins and detritus, fashioning them into installations, sculptures that were typically intimations of grief, at last, they all said, Daniel has come back to the monastery in which, in his cell, he'll write and reminisce like the rest, artists and writers, all of them in close proximity, and he'll finish volume three of *Strange Years*, peering through his window he'll see the young couple Mark and Carmen as he used to, hustling toward their studio with paint, with sculptures, with bags of filthy odds and ends on their backs, with everything they'd been able to extract from ruins and from garbage piles, yes, Daniel would once more see the farm geese and the ducks, the dog Heidi, he'd see it all again, and putting a hand on Daniel's shoulder Rodrigo said, amigo, let's go meet this year's fellowship winners, come, friend, you know I can't write a single word of my long poem, I'd like to ask your advice, you see I never felt marriage, family, or any of that was for me, except that men, more so than women, have no idea how to resist the turmoil of the senses, yes, that's what I wanted to say to you, amigo, but Daniel was wondering why the canaries had stopped singing and Carmen took him by the hand and led him to a meadow, see Daniel, she said, I've set up my installations on the lush green grass of this field, and what met Daniel's eyes were a hundred tiny, tidily ordered graves, more than a hundred of them were killed this week, she said, I've got to wake up, thought Daniel, I've got to, only here in this hotel so far from home I can't hear the song of the turtledoves, and the golden canary song is all but gone, I'm like Balzac, said Rodrigo, so unlucky with women, come sit in the shade of this cypress, amigo, and let me tell you of my defeats, most of all of my inability to write a single word since last we met in that monastery where you and I had come to write in retreat and where me, I did nothing, all I did was sit on a bench and listen to the birds singing, Rodrigo's black hair fell like a mane over the back of his neck, how little he had changed, Daniel thought, the couple Mark and Carmen too, weren't they all immutable, when he woke up he'd have to address, in his book, the suppleness with which dreams repeated themselves, reappearing in fresh hues, with perhaps a patina of black or grey or pink, there was a suggestion of eternity in miniature, particularly if one had ceased to age or had been arrested in some youthful guise, and likewise he would need to analyze the prodigious impact of living several lives in fluid simultaneity, time as fluid as water and the unravelling of several lives taking only seconds, time no longer measured as it is when we are awake, would not this limitless state of being, this immensity, resemble an infinity in which the perpetuity of time traps each one of us in ennui without end, unless, as Mère said, God's country made us feel at ease a little bit, a tranquility she did not seem to possess despite her serene façade, she in her pink woollens and so understanding of the torment of Daniel's restless nights, as if she were saying to him, come, child, this will pass, when he is no longer a child but a fellow in a writers' and artists' colony, resident for several weeks, maybe months, in the Spanish monastery where he had vowed to write, write, of course, only here was Rodrigo the Brazilian poet incessantly distracting him with his petty confidences, his failure with women, his rage against the unwritten word, had he really come this far to listen to writers whining this way, whether Rodrigo or any of the others, Daniel shutting himself up in his cell and only leaving it come evening, oh, lamented Rodrigo, why aren't I the bachelor I used to be, do you remember the library and the refectory where we'd meet at night, tell me, how are your kids, amigo, let's go listen to the musicians, do you hear them, Daniel, Schubert, yes, can you hear the music, Daniel preparing to follow him to the musicians' studio but instead finding himself in snow-covered woods with bear cubs emerging from the dens where they'd hibernated, Daniel had always loved bears, even captive ones, so he leapt at the thought of being able to stroke one of the little things plodding toward him in the snow, massive for a cub, only suddenly he was enmeshed in a world of bears large and small and beyond his control, too many, there were way too many, tomorrow, he thought, he should write about this burgeoning overabundance that provoked such anguish in his dreams, yes, thought Daniel, when I wake up I must, only he could not, the flesh and memories of others, the lacerating actuality of their presence, like something he might see on morning television, all these sensations of an uncertain world he was unable to grasp, thrust into scenes of massacre in which he was both killer and victim, and someone called to him from the woods, was he at the trial of disloyal soldiers in the Central African Republic, or was this just a recollection from newspapers he'd read the day before, of soldiers in uniform and red berets, no treason that Daniel could recall and impossible because he knew neither the country nor the militia standing in judgement, there was only a poor, emaciated black man in front of him, soon to be lynched without due process and in wretched clothes, shorts and a filthy shirt, he'd been stripped of his uniform, everyone applauding his imminent execution, though not before youths dragged him by his feet, no sentencing beforehand, no, just the steel-toed boots of his assailants kicking at his head, if he still had a head, if he still had a cranium at all, his torturers delighting in doling out one death blow after another, and there was a woman with them too, the only one among his executioners, she alone was not applauding, nor was she laughing, she seemed devastated, might she be the sister or mother of the condemned man stretched out against his will on the parched grass, he wondered, Daniel waiting for it all to be over, the woman turned her merciful gaze his way, he was going to die, perhaps he'd been decapitated already, but in the last instant Daniel opened his eyes, he was free and intact, and the words of Rodrigo the poet echoed in his head, I believe in the return of the impenitent and the condemned, that's what Rodrigo had said, but his poet companion with the jet-black hair, his long-time friend, was no longer by Daniel's side, and who knows, as Daniel wrote in one of his books, if the souls of the condemned and all those who made them so, all those who killed others daily and without compunction, are unable to force their way into our dreams, the earth beneath us laying a shroud of silence over this river of the executed, then, Daniel thought, would not poets succumb without warning to some venom-tipped needle and wake no more, like the poet from London whose memory Eddy invoked, the great man whose hair had suddenly turned white, falling as quickly from the pedestal of his life, at the height of his glory, yes, this is how it was, wrote Daniel sitting at his desk in the early morning, whispers rising from the hotel corridors, he was no longer alone, already the arriving writers were being celebrated in the breakfast room, and Mai wrote, I am already getting my photography exhibition together, kisses, Papa, don't forget I love you, I know you didn't want to go all that way to the conference, just tell yourself it affects our future, Papa, unless you are like Augustino, do you have doubts, do you, who knows, thought Daniel, perhaps unrepentant souls are constantly with us, taking advantage of the innocence of our sleep, yes, disrupting the blithe impartiality of sleep in which we are exposed to all sorts of acts, good and evil, at any time, so that as we sleep, these impenitent souls, never to be pitied, these torturers and executioners, distill their poison in us, yes, thought Daniel, in this way do not our nights slowly kill us, shortening the days of our being, truncating our lives as we live them with our eyes shut tight, all these dramas of uncertain derivation, that are not our own, insinuating themselves bit by bit into our unconscious, eating our flesh, drinking our blood? Lou, not used to getting up so early, watched her father Ari, who had summoned her to his studio early and before school so she knew he meant business, there he was with his gigantic unfinished sculpture draped and set against the wall behind him like a ghost, thought Lou, his hands, trembling with anger, held her school report, no A's this month only C's he said, even in science, you disappoint me, Lou, you have no idea how much you disappoint me, said Ari to his daughter, even this early in the morning his voice was in possession of all its vibrancy, she thought, while Lou, barely awake and who detested mornings, all she wanted was to tap away on her tablet before her father took it away, he'd almost certainly take her cell phone too, so she wouldn't be able to talk interminably with her mother who was volunteering at the Episcopalian church, Lou would phone, several times a day or, what with the church where her mother Ingrid offered her services to the community being near her school, cycle over to give her mother a hug, saying, Mama, I never want to leave you, I want to live with you in your apartment, all Papa does is criticize me, and Ingrid would answer, Lou, be kind to your dad, you know how nervous he gets when he's finishing a sculpture, so be clever about it, Lou, we'll be together next week, but Lou asked, why must I be one week with him and then one week with you, Mama, I want to be with you and my brother Julien always, I know Papa doesn't love me the way you do, said Lou to her mother from whom it was always so painful to tear herself away to go to her dad's, no, said Ingrid to her daughter, you're mistaken, your father loves you in his way, I'm afraid he just doesn't really get teenagers, but I'm sure he really does love you, try and be a bit more obedient, less rebellious, my sweet, you know how easily you react to him, he's just a man, moreover he's an artist with troubles of his own and he wants you to love him too, I'm sure of it, but Mama, said Lou, there are too many women in his life, if I could be with you all the time I know I'd get straight A's and not C's, I got a C because he's so grouchy, oh Lou, don't hold it against him, you're often surly yourself, some days there's almost no talking to you, said Ingrid, you can be quite a difficult kid, even the most patient of mothers wouldn't always be able to figure out what's going on with you, your crises, your rage, Lou, you know that, but Lou had already put her cell phone in her backpack, and now she could feel the silence around her in the church as her mother, divorced and with two children who also volunteered but in schools, prepared to take up a collection for destitute families telling her daughter, when the father is out of work we have to do something, but why, thought Lou, why did she spend so much of the little time she had on charity work rather than on her, why was she dispersing her attention so liberally among people who didn't really need help, thought Lou, they don't deserve anything, these people, and the thought rolled around in her head with its canopy of blue hair, a strand of which she was twirling with her finger as her father repeated, yes Lou, I'm really disappointed, you have no idea how much, this thought of people's unworthiness diverting her attention from what her father, so self-assured, was telling her, as was some electronic music she wished she had composed herself, who knows, maybe one day she would come up with music as stimulating and iridescent, such an exuberant tumult of the mind, but right now all she did was play saxophone in the school orchestra, nothing like what Dead Mice had dreamed up, nothing like it at all, though she could draw pretty well too, so maybe later she'd do that, and suddenly all these thoughts receded and disappeared as the voice of her father repeated oh, how you've disappointed me, Lou, how you've disappointed me, the litany unbearable, even the bitter shape his lips took on when he said it was not attractive, nor the grey beard he'd not been tending to lately, no, the deplorable situation she had found herself in so early in the morning moved her to think of a person far away who had written to say he loved her, he'd even written Ari to say your daughter is a real treasure, and when the universe sends you such a gift let nothing harm it, but where, asked Ari, was her godfather Asoka now, grunting as he read the words, for they'd touched a nerve, a treasure, he says, what on earth is that monk Asoka talking about, he's never had kids, has he, and he said again, her father did, that Asoka knew next to nothing about Lou, what would he say confronted by her blue hair, Lou wearing her brother's clothes, her tie loosely knotted over a grungy t-shirt, and the winter boots she had worn in the tropics, whatever could Asoka, this virgin monk, really know about bringing his daughter up, asked Ari, and suddenly Lou interrupted the sermon asking, coyly, where is my godfather Asoka, am I ever going to see him again, and her father replied as though he'd heard nothing, I hope you showered this morning, you should every day, not once every two weeks like you do at your mother's, okay, so I'll shower once a week, Lou thought and she asked again, do you know where in the world my godfather Asoka is, because one day I'd like to join him in Sri Lanka or wherever he is, yes, I'd go to Sri Lanka, she muttered as she fooled around with her tablet, sure I will, in fact it's easy to find him, even write to him, though seeing her godfather again would not bring her closer to her father at all, to his early-morning rancour, his bitter words, the whole of him morose, grating, nagging, and her own stomach knotted, yes, Juliette and Emma are waiting at the door for me on their bikes, helmets pulled down to their ears, and my godfather Asoka is in northern Sri Lanka, he'd written her to say it was his country once, he'd built a school over there and the monks were to be the teachers but one night it was burned down, see, he wrote, that was the north of Sri Lanka for you, the chance to study at a school if it's not burned down overnight, Lou, that's your lot and it's a privilege, did they burn the children too, asked Lou, no, wrote Asoka, they fled but were never found again, people who burn schools deserve nothing, thought Lou, better to think of the blues, the electric blues, or of the Youth Film Academy where she wanted to study one day, far away in California where there was no one to scold her in the morning, she'd invent brilliant video games and make films of them, she had so many ideas for games but couldn't talk about them in front of her father who ranted about how passively people sit at their tablets for hours on end, eyes fixed on screens, busy fingers doing nothing of consequence, why, he asked, instead of this pointless, indolent activity, did you not take up dance like your friends Emma and Juliette, my, they are attractive, said Ari, so slim, such slender legs, perfect girls who make their parents proud, and Lou, irritated, thought of her friends' legs that went on forever beneath frilly skirts, floral tops stretched tight over their tiny breasts, why, she wondered, were they so into men already, and besides, they're so health-conscious, they like the salads and veg their mothers feed them, that's why they're so tall and graceful, Papa, she yelled, mortified, I'm taller than them, I'm the tallest in my class, but, said Ari pitilessly, you're not the thinnest, and Lou thought again and again, my father hits me when I'm down like it's never enough, he's a monster and I want out of here, I want to stay at Mama's and never have to see him again, but there's still one more day of punishment to be endured in this house where we're never on our own, him and me, always his mistresses, his women, early morning is our special time, when he lets me have it, but there's no discussion, he deserves nothing, thought Lou, most of all he does not deserve me, Mama says I'm not like anyone and being different is a charm, she actually said that, thought Lou, retreating behind a silence that was like an icy wall, her father was determined to get through it and make the wall crumble so he'd say, sweetheart, I know you're really gifted, you see how proudly I display your drawings and paintings in my studio, especially your most recent picture in which you painted a green sky, even if the colour of the trees and fields looks a little tawny beneath it, still I admire it, you know that, well, I learned to paint all by myself, said Lou, but I did teach you few things, said Ari responding to her show of pride, no, I did it all on my own, said Lou, I learned everything by myself, alright then, said Ari, let's get back to your report card, I know you can do better in science, so much better, why, weren't you saying you wanted to be a chemist, here I am hiring a private instructor for your singing and your voice teacher says you don't pay attention, couldn't you at least be attentive in class, and Asoka had written to Lou, when I was very young I went begging in my own village, it was an apprenticeship, that was how a young monk learned humility, my dear Lou, I'm sorry your father no longer sends me his articles about art and spirituality for my journal, *The Evolution of Consciousness*, my readers used to love what he had to say, but Papa keeps saying he no longer believes, as he used to, in art and spirituality, now he says art is to be found in sensuality, or that sensuality impregnates art, that's what he says, it's quite novel, but what Lou understood from this was that her father was stepping away from the influence of his friend Asoka the pure, and of course, her father's curt skepticism of Asoka was just like him, she thought, that he should allow a shadow of suspicion to fall between him and his friends, all to abet some non-existent solitude, thought Lou, because the truth of it was that many women visited him, and unexpectedly he would exclaim the need to be alone, to see no one, to suffer nothing that might interfere with his natural impulses, in life as in art, geez, what a game, thought Lou, for he had none of the conviction that the solitude of an artist requires, always needing to be surrounded by women indulging him, but she, Lou, she would have the courage of her convictions, yes, later she would, though her destiny still seemed obscure to her, as if she were a novice mountain climber who could just about spot in the distance the snow-covered peak she had to reach, and suddenly, maybe it was because she'd been thinking of her godfather Asoka, such a virtuous man, she wondered if she would ever have the impact her father did when he used such flagellating words, callously comparing her to Emma, to Juliette, girls so perfect, always at the front door astride their bikes with their helmets on, waiting for Lou so they could head off to the Starfish School, those slender girls, lean as blades of grass, in floral shorts, skirts clinging to their long thighs, they're not like me, thought Lou, they're true young women, Emma and Juliette, but Lou, Lou could be a thug like her father, and she had once, long ago, in the cabin of her father Ari's boat, pulled Rosie's hair, Rosie, who was too small to stand up to her bullying, Rosie, whose childish deference Lou adored, Rosie yelling, enough, enough, while Lou yanked on the hair her mother had so carefully tied in ribbons that morning, as she'd done for all her little sisters, Lou needed to get at Rosie, why, because at the time Ari had been courting Noémie, said he was very much in love with her, and Papa had to be punished for forsaking Lou and instead spending so much time with Noémie in New York, this in the period of his sculptures *Open Corridor* 1 and 2, the huge works he was intending to install in a New York park effectively his means of seducing Noémie, a novice art critic much too young for him, this no doubt the reason they separated so quickly, thought Lou, her father was too impatient and temperamental and no woman, said Ingrid, could stay with him for long, so it was because of Noémie, for a time so fervently the object of her father's desire, that Lou had tormented and humiliated little Rosie on the boat that day, pulling her hair until she cried out, enough Lou, enough, and it must be said that hearing the soft moan of Rosie's voice, as beseeching as a tiny bird's, vindicated in Lou a taste for power she knew she could not assert, what she had done that day to Rosie was her secret, something to be ashamed of, and Ari looked at his daughter thinking, I must change my attitude, maybe I'm too hard on her, I wonder what Asoka would say, probably that kindness was first among virtues, and he imagined the monk as an adolescent rising at dawn in his orange robe to beg for food from the villagers, wasn't this striving for humility a little phony for a monk who was already spending his days in prayer and privation, so why the need for any further humiliation, wondered Ari, and furthermore Lou's report card really was a disappointment, it was his duty to crack down on her, her mother was indulging her far too much, Lou was headstrong and a rebel, Ari of course forgetting how contrary he himself had been for so long, to the point of breaking the law, had he forgotten taking off in his sailboat with a cargo of hashish and Panama Red under the bridge, had he, in becoming a father, erased for convenience's sake memories of bold sorties that might have landed him in jail, and did he not have friends still incarcerated in Mexico and Peru for similar follies, now there was a secret he was not about to share with anyone, no, better to pack it up in the vague baggage of the artist, recollections of experiences that might well have cost him his liberty, yesterday's consumption of drugs diffused in the sensuous colours of a picture, in the exaggerated form of one of his sculptures, or even in the pleasure he derived from sexual conquest, in the excess that was pushing an adventure to extremes, dodging the coast guard, dodging the law, but if yesterday Ari had been, like the surrealists, an adventurer without scruples then it was also the case that today he believed in the commitment of the artist, and that he was asking a host of questions about the necessity of that engagement and what end it had served, really, what benefit it had brought him to chisel the words *justice* and *peace* into calcite blocks in solidarity with other artists against apartheid when the forces of evil were insuperable, and then through the chaos of his thoughts, Ari heard Lou's voice saying, Papa, the girls are waiting for me to go to school and you don't want me to be late, and he saw Juliette and Emma, the studio door opening onto a forecourt of sunlight partly shaded by the new silver palm he'd planted after a storm had uprooted several others, a palm that had endured the elements and grown substantially, and the girls were a part of the tree's new growth, mounted on their bicycles and so different from Lou in her mismatched clothes, as usual, dragging her feet as she followed, her bag so heavy it hung almost to her ankles, why is she carrying so much, Ari wondered, though of course tonight she'd be sleeping at her mom's, such an upheaval for her every time, Lou sulking to her friends and saying, it's because of Papa, it's my papa's fault that we're late, thinking to herself, it's always because of him that I'm so unhappy, yes, it's his fault. And Daniel was considering the strangeness of his hotel room, yet more pictures of the hunt on his walls, all these deer and foxes and boars that haunt my nights and stick to me by day, it was as if he'd been seized by unspeakable timidity at the thought of soon having to join a crowd of writers that had disrupted, during the night, the remarkable stillness of the inn and all the other hotels in the town, known now as the Writers' Village, writers who were populating his dreams alongside Rodrigo, the statuesque Rodrigo, Rodrigo the poet of Brazil, beret pulled down over his jet-black hair, the friend he'd made some time back at a residency for writers and artists at a Madrid monastery, he of the *return of impenitent souls*, yes, Daniel remembered now that, last night, in the crystal-clear oasis of his dreaming that was so often tormented, he'd found Rodrigo again and followed him from one workshop to another, listening to his inchoate plans, and that with him he'd heard the music of a pair of angels passing by one of the studios, does this music not come from heaven, Rodrigo said to Daniel, it's come to us from far behind and long ago, from the mystery of bygone centuries, for as I have often said to you, amigo, the sum of what we know may be no more than the communications of disparate souls, good or bad, lofty or base, and Rodrigo said to him, two children rehearsing for a concert in that studio, the boy is the son of a farmer and the girl is a Korean orphan who was adopted soon after her birth by a couple from Vancouver, and they are the vessels of talents passed on by musicians of the past that leave even those two breathless, though it may be, my friend, that they are too naive and ingenuous to wonder how they were born with such astonishing gifts, so that they communicate their gifts in deference to their destiny, perhaps I should say in deference to the sacred, for they're here to bring us peace with their music without necessarily understanding just what the purity and splendour of their music might mean to us, no, they have no idea, they play music as if it were a game, an exhilarating one, without any idea of what is the source of their exaltation as they stretch their infant fingers across the keyboard or the strings of a violin, fingers of such virtuosity and suppleness that the instruments they manipulate as they bear such childlike expressions, and smiles of seeming insouciance light up their faces as they play, and if their smiles appear nonchalant, amigo, it is because their aim is not to please, as would be the case with adult virtuosos, no, amigo, but to embrace in healing melodies a world that has lost its way, and such desire comes not from them but from the communication of musicians' souls distilled in their own blood, and is it not possible, amigo, that while this farmer's boy from Alabama is playing Bach's sonata to perfection, he is carrying inside of him one of the composer's disinherited sons, the one who died in misery after selling his father's manuscripts, and, amigo, as for me, I am not merely a caricature of the poet Pedro Lopez who, in 1379, wrote far better than I, please do reread his *Cantar a la Virgen Maria,* it has the tenor of my own poems, yet pitifully I have been the recipient of neither the slightest iota of his soul and talent, nor a shadow of his faith in God that might have lit my way, no, not a modicum of anything, alas, despite our having the same occupations, of translator, of world traveller, all I have done is borrow from the poet Pedro Lopez de Ayala, borrow the beauty of him, yes, there it is, thought Daniel, the prerogative of souls communicating their sublime or rapacious gifts is to seize upon whomever they choose, and the crystalline oasis of the children's music he had experienced with Rodrigo spilled over into his waking hours even as he repeated again and again, I must face the day, I must face all the writers, I must, I must, but now his computer screen shone like a night light and illuminated his daughter Mai, pierced ears and all, with a gentle halo, her face appearing alongside other hastily written messages that had come in while he was sleeping, one from his son Samuel explaining a newly choreographed piece finished while Daniel was asleep, and in this fashion, thought Daniel, his children were with him after all, Samuel developing his choreography as his father rested, for in the same hours that Daniel was sinking into his disturbed traveller's sleep, day persisted for others, Samuel writing his father in the twilight of a New York afternoon, the end-of-day light filtering into the studio where he directed his dancers, or before lunch, as he worked at his desk with a cascading mess of notes around him and his son Rudie nearby, this, wrote Samuel to his father, a quiet moment at last, perhaps because the last fugitive rays of the sun that might have faded more quickly had it been raining or snowing, were still shimmering on the windows and outside amid the streets and trees in the torpid humidity of the day, here is my choreography or something of what it will become later on when you're able to see it onstage in San Francisco, because we're going on tour, Veronica, the dancers, and me, the name of the piece is *China, Slow Movement*, for its slow movement, you see, like a gradual dissipation of white smoke, like the release of carbon fumes, I'll tell you how I see it, the dancers surge out of a white night of noxious vapours riding bikes and wearing gas masks that hide their faces, the masks signify stifled protest, oppressed dissent, free speech silenced by tyranny, for aren't these the real causes of toxic destruction, and the bicycles look as if they've been impeded, suspended in an atmosphere of soupy grey snow, the dancers can barely move their arms, yet still they gradually come downstage toward us with movements like swimmers fighting through thick, gummy water, and in this slow movement the dancers' bodies suddenly vanish, we see only the gas masks and the carbon-black bicycles rolling on by themselves, we see nothing else, wrote Samuel to his father, and Daniel closed his laptop thinking of the disillusionment of his children's hearts, he would have preferred Samuel to have talked about the choreography of his daughter-in-law Veronica's most recently conceived piece, or of his grandson Rudolph, who was also studying dance, but the only impression he'd been left with was of Samuel's exhaustion, the fatigue that fell upon the artist knowing he is consumed every day by his art, by the fleeting transformation of a world he dislikes, by his slow movement toward extinction, toward night, and his son's inevitable shipwreck on shadowy portals, Daniel responding with his habitual good humour to Samuel's words very quickly, answering dear, dearest children, I send you hugs and kisses, my lecture on peace is still not finished because I cannot stop adding details, sad ones, I'm afraid, so hugs to you and tender kisses to my dear Rudie, who Daniel remembered was not especially disciplined in his dance studies with Mom and Dad, his real dream, Rudie had announced, was to become a pilot, and he was already drawing pictures of the planes he'd like to fly one day, the model planes he built with his agile fingers flying around the apartment all the time, into the furniture and onto Samuel's work table, covering it completely, was Rudie aware that Samuel had unconsciously communicated with him, that his view of planes had been integrated into the trauma of the boy's interior life, that they could ferry the archangels of death from heaven to earth, that the gods of the sky could be every bit as destructive as those of the earth and scatter suicidal armies, kamikaze children whose flesh would be burned along with our own, and Samuel recalled a tableau of the filmmaker Hiraki Sawa, a kind of self-portrait of the artist we see being painted as planes take off from his kitchen table and land on the bed, leaving a scorched trail of destruction in between, the sky outside and inside one and the same, all intimacy breached, even the intimacy of the domestic we think inviolate, was it through assembling planes that Rudolph overcame his anxiety about the future, Samuel asked his father, Daniel putting it down to the inventiveness of the boy, to his irrepressible nature and lightness of being, like Samuel himself when he was young, Daniel saying that for a long time children are merely children, unencumbered by the surfeit of reflection to which we are beholden later on, for self-consciousness is born in an awareness of who we are and are to become, thought Daniel, and little Rudolph was still a long way away from thoughts that amount to our first realization of infinitely more serious, even imponderable, realities, though what purpose does it serve to lose oneself in the imponderable, thought Daniel, when for every one of us the sole reality is in this very day, this very hour, this very instant in which Daniel turned away from the face of Mai on his computer screen, her ear-piercings and their pearly hue, what a bizarre picture it was going to be seeing all the writers bent over their breakfast downstairs, Daniel could already hear the hum of the conversation he was about to join, or, as usual, would he stay put for a long time, the lone wolf he so often was in meetings, scenes of his arrival coming to mind again, of rabbits racing through the grass near the runway before he falls asleep during a stopover, of golden-brown chicks followed by their mothers as the cocks spread their colourful tail feathers and make a racket during his walking of Mai's dogs on Bahama Street an hour before his flight, and when, the dogs having tipped him off to someone's presence, what he had seen between two hedges was the face of a seated woman, the restaurant behind her not yet open because it was dawn and the woman seated under a frangipani tree gently dropping its white blossoms onto her, she was wearing makeup and jewels and suddenly she grasped one of the chains around her neck and gazed at it for a long time and Daniel, out of modesty, pretended not to see her and she said, good morning, sir, how are you, sir, you know I have amnesia, she said politely, so it could be that you're my brother whose name I have forgotten, or had she merely articulated the words and Daniel used them to create a portrait, as if he already had the intention of telling her story in a book, and suddenly the delicate rosy skin of her exquisitely made-up face, her head crowned in the blooms of the frangipani tree, infused the moment for Daniel, the sapphire-blue gaze of the unfamiliar woman imploring and seeming to say, my friend, don't forget me, don't forget me, because I'm not the only one like this, not the only one, and Daniel wondered how he could he possibly forget her or the rabbits or the golden chicks and the cocks, how they were part of a mercurial landscape rendered more ephemeral by their unlikely association, Daniel revisiting a similar conflagration of images, of a gang of boys prostituting themselves at night on the streets of Bogotá, standing in a muddled ring as cars with windows tinted to conceal the bigwigs inside circled around them, perhaps they were municipal or federal officials, their faces shielded by their hats, their identities secure and protected by the chauffeurs of air-conditioned vehicles cool as glaciers while, outside in the park, in the streets, the ring of boys discharged an excited and exciting heat, not only hot, but sweating in their immaculate white Sunday shirts, these skinny young men, who, much as they had an appetite for sex and the money they would take home to their families, were suffering a tenacious hunger in their empty bellies, and Daniel could see them again, all of them, their pallid faces in the light of the street lamps, Daniel had been studying at university in South America when he came across these young boys, black hair flowing in the warm breeze, performing their nightly ritual dance in anticipation of millionaire clients, a circle of starving bodies saying to Daniel that they knew no shame because hunger supersedes it and any such humiliation of the self, and why had he forgotten them, them and their bodies offered up and so quickly exploited, but nevertheless rising above the subservience they were forced to endure, why had Daniel forgotten them for so long, and why had they suddenly come to mind in his travel-weary state, perhaps, he thought, it's because everything in the world shifts, everything moves with us, whether we like it or not our ties to others are inalienable, how stirring it had been, that particular night, Daniel wandering the streets of Bogotá and hardly able to cope with the sight of emaciated dogs hungrier even than the circle of young boys, the dogs, the poor dogs, were stretched out on the sidewalks and barely able to move, their eyes pivoting in a melancholy without respite, and here's a little girl of seven selling pancakes and coming over to ask if he's hungry, and Daniel wants to know why she is alone in the streets at night, where her parents are, and she points with her finger at a kitchen beneath a tent where her parents are selling food to passersby, but it's late for a seven-year-old wearing only a blue camisole to be out on the streets, really, it's late, and he thought of Mai in her bed and sleeping at this hour, yes, he'd thought it too late for this child to be up, really too late, and as the circling of cars around the ring of boy prostitutes continued into the night, it seemed to Daniel that he was no more inured than his daughter was, that barbs pierced his heart, the barbs of young boys with empty stomachs and of dogs too famished to stand, and that a man of his age cannot endure the trauma of such feelings wounding him like a volley of darts, if this is what being a writer amounted to, then was this not too much for one man, thought Daniel, placating himself by taking the little girl by the hand and leading her to her parents' stall, to the smoky street-kitchen where he collapsed into a chair expecting to burst into tears the way Mai did so frequently, as the little girl's family surrounded him with welcoming smiles, but it was time to forget all these faces, yes, it was time, the furtive flashes of other memories occurring like the lightning of a summer storm that surges unexpectedly when moments earlier the night was starry and without menace, he remembered how on a beach in Mexico where he had taken the children on holiday, leaving Vincent and Mélanie at home so that Vincent, who'd been hospitalized again after another of his episodes, could rest in his mother's company and without the rambunctious children disturbing his convalescence, he'd seen four or five white dogs gathering by the sea as the sun fell, they were a good distance away, at the far end of the beach, a deserted and isolated spot that might as well have been reserved for dogs no one thought about, strays rejected by everyone, though in the silky light sweetening this short interval in their wanderings they appeared strangely intent and happy, look, Daniel said to Samuel and Augustino, see how satisfied they seem, maybe they're here every evening, and it was Augustino who was the first to cry out, Papa, Papa, look at those men in the jeeps chasing them down, the dogs are too fast for them, look, and it was true, the dogs were suddenly up and running, running so fast, the men were chasing them off so they wouldn't bother the tourists, said the drivers of the jeeps, no one wants to hurt them, there are a lot of them and they're everywhere, but yeah, we're chasing them away, getting them out of here, that's all, and Daniel and the boys never saw the dogs again, where could they go to escape such cruelty, except further and further toward the horizon, melding into the crimson sky that for a moment had alleviated their fears, though wasn't it more consoling to imagine them regrouping come evening on some distant Mexican beach, huddled together in the light of the setting sun, isn't that better, thought Daniel, if only for his conscience not to be assailed by cares he could do nothing about, for him not to struggle, so yes, of course they gathered this way every evening under the guiding hand of some divinity, their moment of rest transitory and fleeting, before, thought Daniel, the jeeps and yelling men chased after them again, and then Daniel's mind turned to the conference, he would begin by referencing a work of art, it always dissolved the tension in the room to cite a work of art, and the one he had in mind was a modern version of *Noah's Ark* he'd seen in an Australian gallery, the artist Cai Guo-Qiang inspired by the Bible though not interpreting it narrowly, embedding his vision in a landscape he'd expanded to comprise a whole world, scenes of Australia, scenes of Queensland spread over vast stretches of white sand, their immensity divided by a river of unworldly translucence at which the most unlikely animals were drinking in harmonious coexistence, the lion and the lamb, the tiger and panda, the camel and deer, all species of animal reconciled at a watering hole consensually shared, what better dream was there, thought Daniel, than one of rival nations sharing their riches as they did their differences, it was only one artist's vision, of course, but what majesty there was to be found in this dream so brilliantly conceived and expressed, at the very least in its effort to substitute day for night, in its obliteration of the enmity of men, how impressive it was to know how to eliminate in a work of art all that is dark in us but also to reveal an entirely new order, one of compassion restored for the common good because no ark can ride perilous waters endlessly, except that such an opening would surely be considered puerile, even infantile, and wouldn't it be more effective to invoke Augustino's rage at the sight of a woman standing in front of a tank, her two sons lying at her feet, for wasn't Augustino's wrath to be admired, his outrage so concrete, the fury of his activism tireless and indignant, his first book, *Letter to Young People Without a Future*, had been addressed to twenty-somethings, and his next challenged the complacency and indifference of thirty-somethings, that's how he wrote, using words like a whip and allowing them no respite, rebuking the children of technology for being a generation hooked on material goods and soulless and indifferent matters of the spirit, for being a generation without humanitarian goals thinking only of itself, a calculating and money-minded generation, this was what Augustino wrote of fellow students who'd chosen careers in law and finance, paths he'd abandoned after travelling to India and living among Calcutta's poor, would the next time he encountered his peers be in their private clubs, he'd written, their success such that they'd have become indolent, a pampered generation with no sense of social responsibility, yes, he'd called them the vapid generation, he'd see these handsome young swells again, always with a woman, elegant couples out for an evening of smoking hash in some exclusive nightclub, entering two by two and settling into armchairs screened by white curtains revealing no more than a glimpse of their tanned faces, brown legs extending out from chic shorts and aspiring to nothing because they were so invested in their own well-being, so comfortable in their inertia, and it was this that incensed Augustino to the point of his censuring them as an emperor would, categorically, as if they'd never been friends, forgetting, thought Daniel, that he was born of the same privileged milieu and might so easily have resembled them, who was to say that he did not possess the same arrogant manner, even if he wrote about them so cuttingly still he could not escape where he came from, these young adults snorting coke on their sailboats seemed to Augustino to be leading an existence of sophisticated decadence, a lifestyle that was egotistical in its exclusive engagement with the self, vapid, even, but how could he ignore their despair, was it not written in the weary and disillusioned expressions on their faces, was not Augustino forgetting that there is a desperation in such excess, in the satisfaction of their rarefied thirst and hunger, a sadness these young people were experiencing despite themselves? The Nowhere Generation, wrote Augustino, aspired only to accumulation of wealth often tied to the fortunes of petroleum companies, regardless of the havoc their refineries and chemical plants wrought on the oceans and along the coastal plain of the Gulf of Mexico, nesting birds, turtles, the lot of them dying in oil-poisoned mangroves and lagoons, while they, they made the most of their privilege, not caring the least about the future of the planet, the massive extinction of birds and turtles didn't matter to them one bit, Augustino wrote, the fate of humanity not in their filthy hands, his fury with them was unrelenting, though could it be that with Augustino it was always thus, that everything had to bend beneath the weight of his anger, before his indignation and uncompromising tones, it must be understood, wrote Augustino, that one day we'd find thousands of men, women, and children in the slick of oil spills covering us as they do the birds and turtles, and that mountains of oily mud would crush our houses, yes, this was the doom Augustino invoked in the rage of his prophetic writing, thought Daniel, and thinking again of the young thirty-somethings Augustino lambasted in his work, Daniel remembered the visit he had made to Charles and Frédéric's former house before departing, and having seen Stephen, who had extended the term of his residency there in the house Charles had bequeathed to emerging writers and poets, no, Stephen did not want to leave, to go back to New York, because he could feel the fervid spirits of Charles and Frédéric at his side and they were returning him to the discipline of writing, he said, especially now that the influence of the diabolical Eli was operating at a remove, what with Eli having been incarcerated for trafficking offences, though his sentence would be short, less than twelve months at the sole prison in town and reserved for juveniles, Eli's innocent demeanour having fooled the judges once again, that's what Stephen told Daniel, who, during his visit, thought he heard the melody Frédéric used to play at the piano when he came here in the past, vague, distracted notes floating on the air of the silent room, disturbed occasionally by the sound of the fans, Stephen said, now at last I can write in peace, this summer, with no distraction from Eli coming in like a thief through the window, I will finish my book, such a thief he is, troubling me incessantly, said Stephen, his is such a clandestine life, and yes, I've even given up drugs so I can write better, so what are you working on, asked Daniel, I'm writing to rid myself of Eli, said Stephen, doesn't an author always write to this end, to be free of his obsessions, the author is in search of repair, of healing, that's the truth, because writing is simply another kind of healing, isn't it, Daniel, on Saturday I intend to visit Eli in prison, take him some fruit and cigarettes, more out of pity than love and also because my subject is Eli and his delinquency, how he ended up there, he's pretty well left to his own devices, and in order that he and younger delinquents just like him are re-educated, they have a zoological park in the prison gardens for abandoned animals and birds, some abused, some hit by cars or casualties of some other injury, and the young prisoners are obliged to take care of them, this is very instructive for Eli, Stephen told Daniel, he's mostly busy with the pelicans, egrets, and iguanas, all of this will be good for him, I'm beginning to feel confident about him again, you'll see, we'll make a responsible man out of this boy yet, he's not always going to be a lying crook, no, he won't, said Stephen as if Eli were the protagonist and hero of the book he was writing, an amoral marionette in which Stephen would instill, through the miracle of his imagination, a sense of good and evil, concepts that of course had never crossed Eli's mind before, and Stephen said, I must remember he's in detention, already, so early in his life, reduced to wearing the humiliating yellow prison uniform, you see what pains me is knowing the words PRISONER NO. 4 are written on his back, but still, if Eli refrains from getting into fights with the others, refrains from confronting them with violence, he'll be let out soon and embark on a healthier life, start over again, that's what I tell myself, Stephen said, and Daniel was sorry Stephen was so sure of Eli's rehabilitation because he believed that Stephen's credulity would be his downfall, Daniel also worrying that Eli, what with his ability to seduce those around him, would be released too soon and Stephen would end up suffering so much at his hands again, so suddenly Daniel said to Stephen, my dear friend, and was he not talking to him as he would to Augustino, Stephen, we must all fight off the devil that can kill us just like that during the night, yes, really we must, but Stephen was not listening and Daniel knew he was like that, he didn't want to listen, not another word, he was intent on the writing, on making Eli the hero of his novel, saved and born again, Stephen had given up drugs for gin and white wine, already a little drunk and drowning in dreams this morning, and he was going to write the story of Eli, of his magnificent rise and fall, this book would be a masterpiece, Stephen told Daniel, that's what's going to happen, and still thinking back to Charles and Frédéric's house, Daniel could see Frédéric with his fist against his cheek, sitting as he used to on the sofa and staring anxiously at the headlines of natural and political disasters scrolling across the screen and then, suddenly, between black borders, the names of the executed, terrified that he would see the name Christophe, or that of Désiré Lacroix, whose staging of *The Black Christ of Bahama Street* was still being performed by young Blacks in the ghettos, it said that Désiré Lacroix, accused of several crimes against a California bank, deserved the death penalty, that's what they say, Frédéric demanded of Daniel, and Daniel felt helpless and unable to console Frédéric when suddenly old Grégoire appeared on the doorstep, tipping his cap and saying that today we go to the races, Mr. Frédéric, you must revise your views of this scoundrel who'll have his turn on the scaffold because they can't let every criminal run free, heh heh, you've more clemency than even the Good Lord, yes, you do, why, said old Grégoire, I read in the papers some poor woman somewhere is going to be the first female prisoner executed in sixty years, I think it is, and now I'm full of compassion and very sorry she'll get the electric chair, I sure am, but you see the poor thing plotted to kill her husband and murder is murder, what can you do, you can't just let her go free now, can you, I'm even sorrier for her because she's a woman, she probably had her reasons for doing him in, but your own sympathy is excessive, Mr. Frédéric, I mean, in our humble town, graduating from Bahama Street to the nobility of the gallows, you know that's not going to happen, no, he'll languish in jail for a good long time and that's all, heh, so don't you worry about him, anyway, he wrote me, he needs a bit more money, you watch, he's going to escape as he did that other time, capable as he is of slipping armed and hooded into a bank, a real daredevil eh, so no, don't you worry about him, Mr. Frédéric, get dressed and we'll go out to the dog races, you and I, and once again the piano notes were in Daniel's ear, that faraway time still so palpable it would never be resolved, as Daniel had left Stephen, descending the green steps to the malodorous street, he'd thought this is where Charles, reciting a poem or humming music as if he were alone, used to park his bike, he so loved these dawn rides along the shore before shutting himself up in his room for a day of writing and invariably, at the tail end of night and the first luminous glow of dawn, Frédéric would stumble in, joyous and the worse for wear, and meeting him on the stairs, Charles would ask with an ironic smile where he'd been, had it been another all-nighter listening to jazz, my friend, or sometimes they would meet and not say a word, as if they knew everything there was to know about each other and words were superfluous, a look sufficed. And in the lounge of the hotel, more like a refectory really, all the invited bent over their breakfast, the heads of the writers and poets were baffling to Daniel, much as he would have liked one of his colleagues to turn and look his way, not one seemed to be interested or to see him, so intent were they on the priority of their morning meal, and Daniel, having done without his habitual breakfast outside in the garden, was aware of his own voracious appetite after the long trip, what creatures of habit we are, he thought, realizing all of a sudden that he could not bear being away from the scent of the trees, the flowers, the perfume of acacia and jasmine at its most insistent in summer, and the scent of cornflowers so heady after a night of rain it was almost intoxicating, and despite the murmur of so many voices Daniel found himself eavesdropping on a conversation at a nearby table, one of the speakers saying that from the sick ward, without even leaving it, he completely renewed our experience of the written word, one could say he was not so much a novelist as a philosopher transforming the literary into something metaphysical, yes, one could say that, said a man, his voice the placating one of an intellectual, thought Daniel, someone who felt empathy for others despite being cerebral, and then someone else, his voice curt and unrelenting, it could have been Adrien's, responded archly, this sort of sensitivity to body and soul that moves you so much makes me shudder with disgust, my friend, I mean what is the benefit of this author's relating of all things right to the very root of his misery? What this writer expresses is an abnormal capacity for imbibing all the dregs of the earth, that's true, but as much as he describes his world with refinement, precision, and elegance, you have to admit as I do, dear friend, that his books are redolent of the sickening stench he was incapable of restricting to his room, his is the work of a gravely ill person suffering from a disturbing confinement, that's all, and it infuriated Daniel to have to listen to the brazen pronouncements of a literary critic that so reminded him of Adrien, what this man objected to in Marcel Proust, thought Daniel, was a sensibility that the critic, incapable of absorbing anything of the secret lives of others, did not possess, it was often this way, thought Daniel, those who do not suffer enough to write are put off when a superior sensibility feels on their behalf what they cannot, whether due to a lack of feeling or simple incapacity, certainly this was true of Adrien writing about Augustino's work, his stupid analyses, were one to consider them all, amounting to an author's several small acts of murder, the murderous acts of an author in his youth especially, though Daniel had to admit Adrien was no longer as sardonic as he'd been when Suzanne, his radiant wife, was still by his side, a writer of keen intelligence but who could be so arrogant, though after Suzanne left, the laughing, teasing, unflappable Suzanne, so magnanimous and philanthropic she was too, the arrogance of his tone had become subdued, Adrien had been shaken by the gravity of her absence, of this new and intolerable void in his life, writing and translating were no longer enough and he distracted himself by going out in Charly's limousine as she went on errands or to meet old Isaac on the terrace of the Grand Hotel, this bond with Charly, she who consoled no one, this bond of a young woman and a much older man was odd, thought Daniel, and not without risks, had Adrien forgotten the curse that befell Caroline once Charly wormed her way into the household, once Caroline had appointed Charly his chauffeur, Adrien must have been oblivious to all that as he sat daydreaming in the deck chair Isaac had reserved for him at the hotel with a bunch of books open on his lap, Adrien appreciating that his friend Isaac, so wealthy, tended to his needs, not that Adrien was without means but he was living on his savings, his professor's savings dwindling day by day, for in truth, he told Daniel, given that he was more than ninety years old, he shouldn't even be around, he should quietly fade away from a planet where he'd fulfilled his role but he was still alive, enjoying himself and in good health, which is why he had to make economies, my dear boy, and Daniel, listening to him on the beach, realized Adrien had over time learned to be critical and was now as hard on himself as he'd been on others, so yes, he felt Suzanne's absence profoundly but was composed when Daniel arrived at his house to tell him he was being honoured, that he was to receive the Poet of the Year Award, and in his distraction Adrien had forgotten he was the current year's laureate and instead saw himself inviting Charly to dinner by the sea and giving her presents, he had, for a long time, these late afternoons on the beach, among the birds, surrounded by books as he tapped away at his computer, let himself be seduced by the beauty of the days he was living, waiting for Charly, and so foolish was Adrien's daydreaming on the beach with his books, that under his wide straw hat his brow was suddenly furrowed, overcome by a sullenness that washed over him like the song of the waves lapping at his feet, he was no more than a frail old man, he thought, an old man who might go to bed at night never to rise again, and where was he in his third volume on Faust, how would he ever finish it if he continued to spend his evenings with Charly, did she not say she liked their intimate evenings, and he reflected on the freshness of her complexion and his old writer's hands, though still, he thought, his writer's hands had a certain elegance, they were refined and slender, yes, how he would have liked to caress the face forbidden to him with these cajoling hands, how much he would have liked to do that and more, and it was this image of a frail Adrien that rendered Daniel more forgiving despite his being no less conscious of the destructive efforts of that other Adrien delightedly mocking Augustino's books, distorting the surfeit of sensitivity that was the source of Augustino's comprehension of the nature of pain, all pain and all forms of pain passing through the filter of a sensibility capable of feeling anything and everything excessively, no, this Adrien, so like his neighbour at the next table now discussing literary influences on great minds, was it vanity that impelled him to include his own, he wondered, this Adrien, thought Daniel as the coffee in front of him chilled, was one he could never forget, and suddenly a clamour possessed the hall, young people with placards climbing up to the refectory windows and banging on them with their fists and signs, some demanding their hijacked country be returned to them, others denouncing unequal wages, and yet more who'd written on their placards, TOMORROW OUR CHILDREN WILL GO HUNGRY, tomorrow, this was the generation of thirty-somethings Augustino had accused of complacency, but here they were, militant and angry, knocking, knocking on the windows, yet apparently no one but Daniel could see them, they'll smash the windows and trample us all, Daniel thought, and then he wanted to leave the hall in which the other writers, impervious to the brouhaha, were nonchalantly eating their breakfast to join the protesters, I'm with them, thought Daniel, I think like them, I'm revolted by the injustices they're forced to endure, how is it that my colleagues in the room don't see it, that these youngsters are calling on us, the "thinkers," the clamour is rising to the windows despite the indifference, do you hear that, do you see them, Daniel asked those around him, I know all of you hear them, but no one responded to Daniel's questioning, even when he cut a path past the tables, and as he did so the sight of the young people hanging on to the windows of the hotel was eclipsed and the ruckus died down, and Daniel, perhaps intending to find some succor in his discomfort, remembered having saved some little chicks on Bahama Street as cars and trucks surged around them, little brown chicks streaked with yellow and looking for their mother and crossing the street alone, with the help of a few students passing by Daniel had saved them all, led them back to the mother hen in a park of palms, he'd felt the soft weight of their feathers between his fingers and also a sudden admiration of the students, no more than schoolchildren, running alongside him in the street and saying, oh look, there's another one here, and another over there, carefully picking them up one by one, we know the fate of chicks in this world, thought Daniel, but one more day is one more day and one of these days they'll proceed triumphantly to their animals' paradise, better than mankind's, and each one of these chicks will be grateful to him, yes, of course it was only a dream, and all the animals sacrificed in vain and for profit would also be in this paradise, and Daniel clung to this dream of a place from which people were banished and piglets and lambs no longer under the shadow of knives, no, but under the wing of some Master Overseer and apprehended no longer, this Master Overseer might be a lion or an eagle, some unfamiliar semblance of God whose intentions no human being could possibly fathom, Daniel had often told such a story when Mai was small, a story of an animals' paradise in which she believed as passionately as her father did, the only justification of such an elaborate fantasy, thought Daniel today, was that it was impossible to live without powdering one's existence with fairy tales, how else could one possibly live, and what was more affecting than the thought of these chicks turning their heads up toward him in the gloomy hour, these chicks with their yellow stripes joining him to chase away the darkness, and just as had happened with Mai's smile or the morning sun on the sea, despite his awareness of all the writers surrounding him in the hall and of the shouting of the protesters at the windows clamouring in his ears, his reminiscence of the plump Bahama Street chicks in his hand was joined by another more fleeting image, one of many affecting recollections that teemed in his memory, this one of Mélanie arranging Mai's hair, her still long hair that reached unevenly past her shoulders to her back, perhaps it had been before school, or when the entire family had come together to accompany Mélanie to one of her conferences, the tableau shape-shifting in time, the place hard to determine, but in which many others were waiting with them, where perhaps several other mothers were also tending in deep concentration to the hair of daughters navigating the distant lands of video games, everybody seemed to be awaiting a departure or a return, time seeming to stand still as Mélanie's hand surfed gently through Mai's hair, what a shame, thought Daniel, that it had been cut so soon and so short, all this, it had to be said, in some irretrievable moment when she was still a child, when like her mother she had seemed so pensive, but what they were contemplating together, the two of them, Daniel could not possibly know, they were an entity to themselves, a mother and daughter fiercely independent but each possessing an inner vitality that nourished the other, this was how Daniel recalled the figure of Mélanie leaning over her daughter Mai, her knees gripping the girl so she could not flee, the chaste moment belonging to a time suspended, when Manuel and his father had not yet summoned Mai to join them by the ocean on beaches where the older man peddled drugs to his son's underage friends, a time when Mai was far too attached to Manuel and the boy's father also, when, in the course of a few months Daniel was transformed into an enraged and devastated parent searching for his daughter everywhere, believing that Manuel had dragged her to the edge of the abyss, wondering if in her meandering she would prove as devious as he had been so long ago, before Mélanie had caught up with him under a bridge in New York, his back broken in an accident, when it came to the worst kinds of drugs his sons had never given him cause for concern, why had Mai, he needed to back up to that moment in the terminal when Mélanie was pleating the hair of the combative little girl only her mother knew how to manage, and did so expertly, with such patience, what good did it serve to get worked up now, Manuel's father was in jail and his son was in Lebanon, where no doubt he was carrying on the father's illicit trade, and Mai, what was she feeling when she sent her father online kisses, how could he ever know, he who was responsible for the fissure in her soul, he who had separated her from the boy she was sure she loved, who was he, Daniel, to have judged the love of a pair of teenagers, this Romeo and Juliet he had torn apart, even if his selfless motive was simply that he wanted to save his daughter from pushers, was it right for a father to act this way, and then in a more brightly lit part of the room Daniel saw a young man with straight hair, glasses, and a blasé expression who, seated at a table piled high with books, was coolly signing innumerable copies, a considerable number of young girls were gathered around him, as were savvier women who appeared to be there for promotional purposes, treating their author with a protective manner they accorded only to him, they were fawning over him so intimately you'd have thought he belonged to them, mothering him excessively and annoying the author whom Daniel handed a book for him to sign for Augustino, they think of me as a commercial author but I'm not that, I just want to go lightly, to make the writing easier for my readers, it's about being deft, really, making the most banal things sexy, it's all in the eroticized power of suggestion, today's readers don't want to be troubled or to be made uncomfortable in any way, don't get me wrong, I'm not performing for the public as these nice ladies around me seem to think, I simply want to make literature entertaining, musicians are like that, so why not writers hoping to distract us with their made-up stories, to amuse us, to entertain, to put distance between us and this suffocating present, a reality that is often so horrible people don't want to confront it, certainly not in books, my fictions present dreams to those who no longer have any, that's the cause of my unexpected success, said the young man in a withering tone, we must lead to the light those who live in the dark, we're still mired in it but dark is no longer the fashion, mine is a theory of *trompe l'oeil* in the void, I suppose, my books have a light insolence, the young man said, adding that he had to go, he had a heavy schedule of television appearances before embarking on a publicity tour of Scotland, splendid landscapes in store, the row of girls behind him nodding approvingly, his suitcase was ready, said one of the girls, she seemed to be his assistant and was gently stroking his neck, he dresses so lightly, she said, just a shirt and jeans, and Daniel took the copy he'd signed for Augustino out of the young author's hands and said, my son's a writer, I wish he weren't quite so grave and disconcerting, yes, that's the word, disconcerting, but the author of erotic novels wasn't listening, he was already out the door joking with his laughing entourage, the expression behind his glasses defiant, and Daniel thought, who knows, Augustino might have envied the young man's refusal to be anxious about the world, his delight in writing simply to entertain those for whom the planet was not a place beset by intense suffering that spread like a contagion, though he'd probably have overwhelmed him with sarcastic comments too, Daniel would have liked to spend more time with the young novelist, for them to have talked more profoundly than their too-easy banter permitted because, he mused, who knew what tremors of mortal anxiety hid beneath the writer's apparently carefree exterior, yes, what rumblings, Daniel asked himself, though seeing the young man busily signing books had rekindled his desire to see Augustino, to hear his son's caustic voice and sardonic remarks about the state of the world, to search his eyes for his son's thoughts constantly in defiance of everything, against everybody, did he still have curly hair he never took the time to comb, wondered his father, was he still the young man Mélanie could not bear to be without, his mother keeping pictures of him everywhere, would he have changed so much that only she might recognize him now, her most troubling thought not the fear that he might no longer be alive, but in what state he was living and where, the world so vast, Mélanie often saying, as a mother does, I'm worried he's not eating enough, he always used to eat so little, my ascetic and altruistic son, he's burning himself up too fast, and I'm worried he's on his own too much and doesn't have any friends, and in a concert hall in Rome, Fleur was listening to his *New Symphony* being conducted by a new orchestra leader who, like Fleur, was a very young man but, unlike him, enormously erudite, though didn't the writing of music, as his mother Martha told him many times, in fact depend on unlearning and instinct, and without Franz, the old composer and conductor who'd awarded him the Young Composers' Prize and a subsequent tour of Europe, would Fleur not still be on the streets with Kim and her dog Damien, playing the flute even as his head ached from the sun, playing, playing, yet never heard or noticed in the cacophony of the city, his throat dry, his stomach knotted with hunger, yes, nobody can know what it means to be hungry without living it, his mother insisted he come home for a decent meal once a month, but who can imagine being in such dire straits, succumbing to a body wracked with anemia and to fits of dizziness beneath a leaden sun, had he not put into music what he'd lived through so often, a thousand sirens wailing in his ears, a thousand hectoring voices assaulting him, was his symphony not the operatic story of his shipwrecked youth, of Kim and their friends, of Jérôme the African, of the Old Salt murdered on his boat by heartless bandits for the sake of an empty strongbox, these were cries of the dispossessed, but you had to see the maestro whose striking profile Fleur so admired, his hands too, tense hands hovering over his music and the orchestra and directing his symphony, and you had to see the musicians, thought Fleur, the heads of the musicians, among them several elderly violinists who appeared to understand the virulence of the score better than he did and to take pleasure in it, was it the fissure with traditional music, the systematic pandemonium of these high notes that pleased them, yes, thought Fleur, that must be it, though the conductor Claudio said he'd selected the piece for its energy, for its power and spirit, he'd promised to pour all of his striving for excellence and perfection into it, though he was too elegant, appealing, and sophisticated for Fleur, or was this an encounter destiny had intended to further his growth, there's a hidden design in the music which must be brought to life, said Claudio, it is the cry of life itself, the outline of an existence battered and diminished as if it had been tarred by a ruinous fog, and, Fleur thought as he listened to Claudio, with what empathy does this man grasp what I myself have trouble in expressing, but this is how it always is, Claudio replied, even for a conductor, the timbre of the music is always silent until we make it vibrate and sound out, and then all at once the music inhabits us, this is the music that inevitably guides us, Claudio promised to present his symphony at summer festivals, and Fleur thought of how his life had since taken on an order it never had before, think of the energy in Prokofiev's Third Symphony, was it even permissible to imagine an energy like that, and Fleur thought of Prokofiev's mother in St. Petersburg introducing him to the piano at so young an age, and the grand masters who taught the precocious child composition, and how Claudio knew nothing of his insular past and that he, Fleur, was no more than a street person dressed up for a special evening in a Roman concert hall, when a few months earlier he had been sleeping under bridges and listening to Wrath's ramblings in his ear, Fleur telling himself that the defrocked rogue priest, his appearance so wretched, was a madman, someone fallen by the wayside though still endowed with ineradicable oratorical and cultural gifts, an understanding of life and death he'd certainly encountered in no one else, a high dignitary of the wretched who'd permitted himself everything until he was rejected, punished, denied all privilege, stunned by the judgement and persecution of others, falling until he was no more than a tramp living beneath bridges, a nothing, and as Claudio conducted the music so that its stridences soared and its dissonances sang, Fleur thought he heard Wrath's overbearing voice grating at his temples as if it were still close in the fog around the docks, under the baleful sky of the poor and the outcast, what Wrath had called the icy caves of hell destined for those whose infamy can never be redeemed, that place from which Fleur, searching in the night for his friend Su, coughing badly, sheet music under his arm, a cigarette between battered gums, a tooth missing, following him until he disappeared into the Métro, no more than a negligible shadow of his former self, things were not always this way, Wrath intoned so close, so close to his ear, to his cheek, his acid breath escaping his barely moving lips, oh, when I prospered, he went on, Tai and me, we stayed in the finest hotels in Bangkok inhaling the perfume of white orchids and the sulphurous smell of money too, always pleasing, there were baths, pool halls, and spas and restaurants in jungle settings, you can't imagine the types that frequent these hotels, how much this population of the rich construct a paradise exclusively for themselves, how an entire industry attends to them, to their insatiable appetites, billionaires who never leave the suites that another debased population visits only to serve them, a population of slaves, isn't it the case that no empire has ever been built without slaves, Wrath said, and yet one day when Tai and I, we were indulging all these orgiastic pleasures, terrorists attacked and Tai, my Tai, wanted to join them, I'd sensed this dichotomy in him before, yes, as if he'd set himself apart from me, there were twenty young terrorists prevented from blowing up the hotel and all of them arrested, they turned out to be former employees of the hotel in a collective revolt, said Wrath, massive it was, but they didn't pull off their insurrection, at least not this time, said Tai defiantly, in defiance of me, me who'd lifted him out of mire and beggary, you'll see, one day they'll win, yes, that's what he said, and I told him that once upon a time empresses and princes stayed in the Orient, that grand hotel, a palace of nine hundred rooms, they studied the arts and sciences and now you're talking insurrection, of sacking this palace, you who could have been a mandarin servant in red livery opening doors and laying out a carpet for people like me saying, sir, you are welcome among us, but they won't always be rolling out the red carpet, Tai shot back, do you know what a boy like me earns at the Orient, not even fifty dollars a month, not even, if you want to feed your family you need to turn tricks at night, they all do it, so did I, and when so many soldiers are on the streets, armies passing through to watch over us, we go to them, we're their street recruits, back then, said Wrath, I could silence him by playing games with him as if we were partners in karate, a little thing I did with a certain apprehension, I'd say, be quiet, and he would, but always with a malevolent smile, I'd say, you have no right to talk to me that way when I've saved you and your family from the most terrible hunger and misfortune, from appalling servitude, and now here you are renting porno films in a regal hotel the way you always wished you could, all the while rolling around in my bed so indolently and lasciviously, you're mine, don't ever forget that, was that what happened or did I just chat with Tai, Wrath said, did I only listen, I don't remember, I don't know anymore, and in the concert hall where his music was being played, Fleur banished all memory of Wrath's presence, of his voice, of the cold in which he could still feel Wrath's breath upon his cheek, instead he settled his gaze on Claudio, who was dedicated so wholly to his music, Fleur still haunted by his mother's words that morning, you're doing what you love and want while Kim feels abandoned, she'd emailed, why was he reading her incoherent messages when really he should have erased them, yes, that's what he should have done right away, you've dropped everything for your music, even Kim and me, your mother, Kim wanders the streets with the baby she had by Raphaël, your friend the Mexican, the artist in his smock, he with his medallions, an out-of-work druggie, do you think it's okay for a mother and her nursling to live in his loft, Fleur, must you always create such chaos wherever you go, must you lose those you love the most, forgetting all of us though not your dogs Damien and Max, you ask me how they are doing, they eat well and Kim never leaves them, yes, thought Fleur, these were hurting words he would like to erase and wished he had never read, but at least he knew the dogs were not being mistreated and that Kim was with Raphaël, not squatting with the baby in some park by the sea, her baby, Raphaël's baby, that she carried against her chest, his mother Martha said the baby was so tiny she hardly existed, nothing more than a tiny doll between her breasts, and as for your friend Jérôme the African, he is often in police custody, locked up and released, yes, life is unfair for all your friends, wrote Fleur's mother, railing against injustice and the abuse of power as she always did, she'd wanted to adopt Kim and her child, but Raphaël told her to go back to her pub and refugees, she had her hands full there, it was against the law to hide illegals even for justice's sake, said dumbfounded Raphaël, telling Fleur's mother that he'd be responsible for his discordant family, for his children, he already had a few with other women, and this baby, this sickly little girl, would not be too much, one more among the rest of the toddlers in the loft, and to encourage him to be a better father Martha bought some of his artwork, his medallions, his necklaces, Fleur's mother, as always, was generous to a fault, admired by the illegals she protected from deportation, whom she welcomed to her pub and home, offering what shelter and sustenance was in her means and Raphaël saying to her, aren't we two of a kind, that in his home he had kids of every race and colour and that all these women and children were a privilege, that Kim would find her place in his harem, except that she often refused to talk to him, no, it was not Raphaël she'd always loved, but somebody else, that musician living way off in Europe and who, who could say, would probably never come back home to his people and to his island, yes, said the Mexican Raphaël, she loved him, loved the prodigal son his mother, Martha, had known how to punish and destroy as much as protect, and the truth of what Raphaël said hurt Fleur deeply, he'd wanted to cut all of them off but could not, for wasn't Kim's baby also a little bit his own, so sickly and spindly that Raphaël said she almost strangled herself at birth, just a little pip of a thing whose birth was a miracle, the only child of mine with white skin, said Raphaël, all the others are dark, very dark, but their mothers are always around so why not Kim, though why is she so silent, thinking of somebody so far away, yes, if only we were able to get her to speak and to start loving her child, but the very thought of Kim's erratic existence nagged at Fleur, the thought of Kim dragging her newborn everywhere and maybe the two of them napping on the Old Salt's boat abandoned in the port, where, as had happened once before, but this time in vain as the old man was no longer at the helm, no longer standing with his wrinkled face confronting the eastern winds and saying to Kim and to Fleur, look, if it isn't him, a grey heron hovered over the water, hovering above and then so close, just a slow movement of his wings bringing him so close to Kim, who, in the last strong rays of the setting sun, was holding her baby's soft round head tight to her chest almost suffocatingly, smothering her with an uncommon but desperate love, yes, the thought of this solitary mother and child tore at Fleur, and did this thought not bring him the same throbbing pain he'd experienced a few days earlier, when he'd had extracted from his mouth the miserable, cavity-ridden tooth that was the reminder of his days of hunger in the streets, of the vile food soiled by others' hands he'd eaten with Kim and the rest, food pulled from the garbage, or was it the shame of it all that hurt most, thought Fleur as he watched Claudio conducting his music, Claudio overjoyed while Fleur felt so ashamed, this in the moment of the *New Symphony* in which you can hear in the violins' playing the cries of the little girls of Hiroshima hanging tattered from the trees under a burst of orange suns in a sky as quickly darkened by the detritus of smoky eruptions, what had happened for night to come so early and for us to hear the cries of little girls, what strange night was this, or was it still daytime, would this same residue of the smoke and flames cover the little girls' bodies hanging from flowering trees stripped bare in a second, now there was only the red dust of the flowers, soon to melt like the asphalt streets and the sidewalks, no, thought Fleur as he heard this lament inside of him, the music Claudio was directing not as sad, Fleur no longer calling himself Fleur, needing to bury forever the Boy Fleur of whom, for so long, his mother Martha had been the proprietor and manipulator, making him her plaything on stage or anywhere that suited her, even in his street hideaways and the cardboard boxes he slept in at night on the beach, anywhere he went to escape her, so that much as he still loved her, how senseless that he would, he'd taken instead the name his parents and grandparents had first given him, the name on the musical bill was his resurrection, his rebirth, no longer Fleur, formerly Boy Fleur, but Andrew Adam, and this Andrew was well turned out, every bit as handsomely dressed as the conductor Claudio or any of the musicians in the orchestra, finally he was enjoying a comfortable anonymity, and perhaps he was nothing after all, no more than a man without a name, his hollow form that of a wayward and uprooted young man learning, in a new body cleansed of its ills, its blemishes, that tooth, the tooth of his street miseries, finally ripped from his mouth, a second time what it means to live, though who is really able to extricate himself from the past, isn't the past always with us, tripping us up at every step, and what is more deceptive than a person's appearance, for even Claudio, who seemed so sure of himself, so congenial and serene with his peers, perhaps he was not all he seemed, born into a house of musicians he'd not needed to face the obstacles that impeded Fleur's career, but, the junior in such a talented family, maybe his was an impossible and troubled perfectionism, a yearning to make something flawless of an art that is by nature latent and roaming, and is this striving for perfection not destructive in the artist, in a short-lived moment of trust at a café Claudio had confided that sometimes before a concert he was seized by incomprehensible fright, he would shake and tremble, I feel such pressure and intransigence around me, explained Claudio, but I can't possibly let my family down, they're all fine musicians and all I've done is inherit their passion, how can I be other than I am, so naturally is my destiny tied to theirs, and Fleur reflected that even when his influences are many the artist stands alone in judgement of himself, that's true, except that Claudio had been undermined neither by perfectionism nor the desire to please his family, he suffered no neurosis and did not need, like Fleur, to give a boost to his conducting with a little snort of cocaine, just enough to curb the fear, Claudio's ardour was not artificial, though maybe Fleur was mistaken, did not Claudio's elite milieu make anything possible, even the discreet help, secretly relied upon, of a minor substance addiction to rein in whatever were his anxieties and the fear he could neither describe nor name but that was so integral to the physical anguish of appearing on stage, to the delivery of the triumphant music of which he was merely the messenger, Claudio had a large family and as a conductor had so little time and travelled a lot, and did not Fleur see Franz and all his brood in Claudio, who, apart from that single moment of trust, of confiding in a friend as Franz used to do in another time, was no longer present, the scene to which Fleur had been witness, after leaving the coffee shop for streets animated with people intent on finding each other as evening approached, was one Claudio did not even seem to notice, he'd said, I'm late, I have to go, I'll see you tomorrow at rehearsal, Andrew, and disappeared in as little time as it had taken him to knock his coffee back in a single gulp, a moment awakening in Fleur the memory of the indignant but more so disgusted company of Wrath, for the scene playing out before his eyes belonged to another day, night would soon fall and imbue the city with the *sotto voce* activities of evening, light and the music of voices from cafés, and there they were as though before the Vatican gates and the kingdoms beyond, a mother and her two children were preparing for another night out on the streets, the mother leaning against the storefront of a shop selling taunting leather goods as she wrapped up her two-year-old in a blanket and held the smaller one, not yet a year old, tightly in her arms against her damp clothes, for even though the weather was milder now, an insipid cold rain seemed to be falling, that was the scene, one of human sacrifice offered up to predators that Wrath, beneath the bridges of the god-forsaken city where he dwelled, had told Fleur about many times, yes, that was the scene replicating itself in one European city after another, as it would again once the vagrant mother went with her sons to lie down by religious buildings where it would not be quite as painful to hold out an open hand, whoever went into a basilica could hardly be indifferent either to the child pressed against her chest or to her arm stretched out in the rain, did not indifference, the indifference of those who kneel and pray in a chapel or basilica, strike this woman as the meanest of cruelties, oh, what she would have done for them to notice her, though her children most of all, the little things were especially hard to look at, her calculating eye said it all without censure, thought Fleur, she'd smiled his way, miserably but complicitly, that or she'd disguised her rage in a smile half-realized, Fleur feeling the full force of its acerbity, and much as the scene was so lamentably concrete and real for him, Claudio had not an inkling, or had he simply moved on before seeing her, before seeing the three of them, he'd said with self-deprecation that he was meeting someone important in the musical world, that he no longer had a moment to himself and then, noticing Fleur's hollowed eyes, Andrew, you really should get some rest, Claudio surely having no idea what was the cause of his hollow look, Claudio who knew nothing of his famished days and sleep-less nights on the beaches watching over Damien and Kim, another continent, another country, though in this era of globalization, even if the community of nations was no more than a virtual one conjured by the illusion of transmitted images, spun words, and the all-powerful technology that now rules our lives, Claudio and Fleur could appear similar despite being so essentially different, for at the very least they carried the same miracle phone, the fabled device that drew human lives together but at the same time kept them at a pitiless distance, the device that let Claudio speak to his agent instantly, to look upon his face during their conversation and take in all its tics and fidgets, the tight close-up of the screen often revealing that which we refuse to acknowledge in reality, Fleur was horror-struck at the very idea of speaking to his mother, of hearing her voice and watching the tears abundantly roll down her face swollen with grief, it would have been as easy to be in touch with Kim directly, the prospect of a face-to-face conversation with her also worrying him because Kim, like the Rainbow Children, the audacious rich who came with their cell phones from Russia in winter, squatting in historic houses they would in no time leave trashed, Kim too had a cell phone, one Raphaël had stolen for her, to better protect her, he said, this way, Raphaël explained, no matter what happened he'd always be there for her, she who had a tendency to leave the loft with her baby under her arm, yes, he would always be the vigilant father he was for all the other children and their mothers, I make enough from my crafts to take care of you all, he said, but alongside his artisanal work, thought Fleur, Raphaël undoubtedly engaged in more illicit activities, like trafficking in stolen cell phones, so it pained Fleur to think of Kim and the baby hiding out in the hold of the Old Salt's boat waiting for Raphaël to call and show his face when a message would never come, even less so a cell phone conversation in which she might look upon Fleur's face as he spoke, as if she were all of a sudden able to take his face and caress it, this was her irrational longing, that maybe, by means of the cell phone Raphaël had stolen, she might finally be in touch with Fleur, it was just another rainy night, and there they were camping out in front of the leather goods store, the woman wrapping her shawl around the head of the youngest as if the street was their regular lay-by, she couldn't let her kids get a chill, the eldest had a cold already, so she told him to stand closer to Mama and keep warm, there there, she said, this picture of Wrath's portal to hell pursuing Fleur wherever he went, soon, Wrath predicted, all these madonnas, all these peddlers of children, their own children, would be clustered around the most hallowed monuments in the city, look at them all, these degraded, fallen madonnas, nothing at all like the ones sculpted and painted by the great masters often in the service of popes as Raphael was, women portrayed as the Virgin and Child and not as they are here before us, degenerate, these madonnas and children situated amid filthy walls and greasy sidewalks, not roses and flowers, their children in a state of quiet stupefaction as the one attempting to mother them was, the woman livid and furious that predators would soon come and seize the elder of the two, barely pubescent, who would soon be working for a father he'll see leaning over garbage bins on the boulevard and of whom he'll be ashamed, and the child will say, Papa, Papa, not in front of other people, can't you wait till nighttime, and on the coldest days the child will stifle his tears and humiliation in the folds of his father's coat and the rich passing will take pity on him, feel his excruciating heartache as he says, not in front of others, Papa, they're coming out of the movies and they'll see us, please not in front of them, at least wait until nighttime, said Wrath, I can hear this child's voice, and Fleur, who was himself ashamed because he could not forget what Wrath had said, again saw Kim nursing her baby in the hold of the Old Salt's boat, innocent Kim and her round-headed infant, the two of them being rocked, this mother, this child, by the rhythm of the sea's storm-tossed waves, Kim suddenly convinced she heard Paul the trumpeter marching with his band along the wharves, yes, was this not the hour of Paul's improvising, hey Kim, he yelled, what'll it be, jazz or rock, c'mon and bring your tambourine, there are men in town who'd like you to party, what can I play for you, maybe some pop music, like that icon David Bowie, will he come sing with us, the heteroclite musician putting on several performances in one, even painting his face blue and pink as though he were a common criminal, wearing the tattooed face of a gang member, except that he is accountable to no one but himself, so mercurial an artist he might as well be a statue that flies and lands where it wants, maybe he'll come and share some of his stories of the miraculous in the covered amphitheatre that's going to be built in our new concert hall by the sea, its roof, according to the plans of the slightly demented architect, in the shape of a gigantic seashell, this so that during the rainy season we'll not have to flee even the most turbulent storm but can take shelter under its spiral roof, and Paul repeated to Kim that making music is simply an act of joy, an epiphany, eternal happiness that didn't cost him a thing, and Fleur thought that perhaps Paul had learned this idea of a concert hall with a spiral roof suspended like a seashell in the air from his mother, but it was actually Franz's idea, exasperated as the composer had been of seeing effectively redundant musicians in rarefied concert halls that no one wanted to frequent anymore, halls in which the musicians who were not yet unemployed were nevertheless underpaid, Franz taught musical direction and composition to young women who'd succeed him on this elevated amphitheatre above the sea, open to the winds when the weather was good, and Fleur was thinking how they were all making music in order to fill the lacunae in the immense silence of a conspiratorial universe in which insidious chemical attacks rained down upon the heads of innocents, mute targets seen only at a remove and indirectly, these weapons remotely controlled providing a whole new reach to war and Fleur wondering if, in painting a pink flash like a wound across his face, Bowie had not been thinking of the rose-coloured blood of Pakistani children, thinking of their faces, of their lives obliterated in an instant like ants or spiders under the feet of a giant, was this not the reason musicians lost themselves in the turbulence of their compositions that, despite their beauty and translucence, corresponded to the sound of drone strikes happening in the furthest regions of the world, for nothing, thought Fleur, could be closer to the ear than these strikes' detonations, these persistent blows of a random assassin inflicted upon thousands, so close to the ear, there was no such thing as a distant region anymore, just the one world, robot weapons flying overhead, and what, wondered Fleur, would remain after such a furtive campaign of destruction by the operators of these murderous engines, yes, what would be left, he asked. I want to go play with Misha by the egret pond, said Angel to Dr. Dieudonné, who, with the help of Lena, Lucia, and Brilliant, was preventing the young boy from getting out of bed, your temperature is not high but you can't go out today, said Dieudonné emphatically, your mama says you still won't eat, what are we going to do with you, should I take you to hospital for intravenous feeding, really, what am I going to do with such a bad patient, Dieudonné repeated, but I can hear Misha scratching at the door with his paws, said Angel, and Dieudonné said, you can only go out on the veranda when your fever's down, Misha's smart, he's waiting like a good dog, and Angel said, if he wasn't eating it was because he couldn't taste anything and had no appetite even though he loved the delicious food his mother cooked, but when I nap in the afternoon and Misha is by the bed, said Angel, together we travel the galaxies, and Bryan took Angel's damp hands in his and asked if it wasn't a little cold out there in the Milky Way, aren't you warmer here with us, he said, here among the heady cornflowers and the palm trees, yes, aren't you better off with us, and Dieudonné said again that even though his temperature was slight, he needed to stay in bed, I'm off, said Angel, teasing, Misha and I'll be leaving together, he'll carry me on his back if I tell him to, yup, he's a good dog alright, said Bryan, Dieudonné amazed to see such strength in the boy, they almost had to tie him down to keep him from jumping out of bed, you're a regular little devil, said Dieudonné, how am I going to treat you, don't you understand how much I want you to be cured, so does your mom and every one of us who loves you, Angel, you must see that, but still you worry me with all these stories of galaxies on your mind, oh yes, you worry me, said Dieudonné, you're a real devil, and Lucia thought Angel might improve a little tonight, so strong-willed he was, they might all be able to have dinner out by the pond where the white egrets come, she couldn't remember whether she'd paid her month's rent at the Acacia Gardens, she must have done, she was no longer forgetting things the way she used to, and Bryan was there to remind her, saying, Lucia, it's the first of the month, don't forget now, and if she did forget she knew he would take care of such tedious day-to-day matters, that he was always here for her despite working long hours as a nurse's aide on the night shift at the hospice run by Dr. Dieudonné, who, this man as big-hearted as Brilliant, was also overworked, and Lucia wondered if Angel was getting worse or better, he did seem to have a bit more colour despite the general pallor, though Lucia was not about to mention what she'd seen, how Children's Aid had taken Jill's son away, the law was the law, said the lady, she seemed well meaning, it's hard separating children from their parents, she said, it was so upsetting she wondered if she could keep up her social assistance work much longer, yes, she'd said these things even as she declared that little Jono could no longer live with his mother, she was turning tricks to pay for her heroin and Jono was always clinging to her, even in the hotel rooms, they caught her with a john in one of them and said no, this had to stop for the good of the child, for his future well-being, the two needed to be separated until the mother was in rehab, said the social worker, nothing else could be done, but still Lucia wondered how the woman was able to sever the bonds of mother and child, it was a cleaving, a separation terrifying for them both, and Lucia recalled how much she had treasured her own son when he was small only to feel betrayed by him now, no, better to forget, he was her son no longer, just a man like any other, cold and distant toward the woman who'd put him in the world, he'd actually accused her of promiscuity one day, or had the little ingrate merely sensed, early on, how unsuited she was as a mother, had she not seen a resemblance to her own frail boy in little Jono led by the hand as his mother staggered drunk in the street, her face bruised from Rodriguez's blows that day, her pimping boyfriend free as usual while Jill somehow, somewhere, was cleaned up and rehabilitated, Lucia could still hear the shrieks of the mother and child as the social worker tore them apart, a police officer taking the child away in a dark car as the sun set and night fell and Jill screaming, he's my son, they're taking away my boy Jono, Jono, and Lucia, Night Out perched on her shoulder, had dropped her bike and run toward Jill and Jono and the officer's car, and Brilliant instinctively comforted Angel, telling him they'd bring Misha for a short visit come evening, and Dr. Dieudonné, in a rush, stroked the boy's forehead and told Angel that he had to go, there was an emergency, he would come back that evening, and Angel's mother Lena also caressed his hot forehead and told him not to panic, his fever seemed to be diminishing, and said yes, maybe he'd be able to play for a while with Misha later on, Angel seemed calmer after the medication, Brilliant was holding the boy's hands in his own and they did not feel as damp as they'd been and he said, I have to go too, I hear my phone ringing, and Lena wrapped her arms around Angel and said, do you understand, you must eat, you heard the doctor, Lucia watched Lena and Angel, this mother and child, and suddenly wondered why her own son had been taken just like Jill's, why and how did it come to pass, she wondered, remembering nothing of their time together, how she'd watched him grow, how she'd dressed him every morning for school, and she thought, I won't think on it anymore, otherwise I'll always be seeing the face of little Jono in tears, I'll always feel shaken, feel the shock of separation, but she could say nothing of this to anyone, no, not to anyone. Look at the crowd around Yinn, said Robbie to Petites Cendres, look at all the queens on the stage waiting to greet him, this press conference is for Victoire and her alone, wow it's impressive, said Robbie as Yinn signalled for him to be quiet, this followed afternoon rehearsals and the girls, Geisha, Heart Triumphant, Cobra, and Santa Fe, were in their boyish outfits, loose tank tops and bare feet, Yinn in a white vest and wrinkled shorts, all of them having leapt and danced on the stage under his direction, Yinn correcting their moves endlessly and saying, girls, if you dance like this for the audience of tonight's Saloon cabaret, no one will applaud you, and as they lingered, sweating, before getting changed for the evening's festivities, they stared at Victoire, just as Petites Cendres and Robbie were doing, Petites Cendres never again to be known as Ashley or, mockingly, as Little Ashes, and the pair of them back from their session jogging along the seashore amid the cyclists, skateboarders, and other sporty types defiantly racing in the sun as if the wide sidewalks reserved for runners, cyclists, and skateboarders were on the point of melting, yes, they stared at her with such curiosity because who was she, this Victoire whom Yinn was introducing, an unknown and mysterious man transformed into a large and rather timid woman hardly daring to speak, forget about the man, said Robbie to Petites Cendres, this was a woman standing before them, and Yinn said she's demonstrated such courage, from now on Victoire is one of us, and Victoire, who said she'd left her Doberman, Déesse, in her apartment at the Acacia Gardens, it wasn't like her not to take the dog everywhere, Victoire said how moved she was to be welcomed so warmly, she would dance one or two evenings though in the daytime, her real job, she'd been an engineer and she would be so again were she ever offered a position, but you must understand transsexuals are generally refused employment in the same way that they're not allowed to use women's public washrooms and all these complications are intended to denigrate us, said Victoire, she was not taking pity on herself, Robbie thought, and the outfit she'd chosen made a statement, she could not appear more feminine than she did in her skirt and high heels, in that t-shirt clinging tightly to her breasts, no, she was as feminine as could be, but in her house was another country she never talked about, flags on her bedroom walls, her guns, and undoubtedly military honours too, not mentioning any of it because since her discharge she was no longer a soldier and had been thrown back into civilian life, no, as she said with such remarkable candour, now she was simply a woman, orphaned and without a job and banished everywhere, even from restaurants, she said, so truly she was grateful to Yinn and the assembled, she may be unemployed but she had a place to call her own, yes, a roof over her head at the Acacia Gardens, it was often like this, she said, such outpourings of human generosity, without them where would we be, yes, she repeated, I believe in the generosity of individual people, yes, I believe society cannot evolve without it, for more than empty declarations of tolerance it is goodwill that brings society along, otherwise we're all done for, and Petites Cendres thought how incongruous it was that Victoire should speak of so rare a quality, wondering if her expressing the necessity of being kind and friendly was no more than a courtesy to her hosts at the Saloon, or was being this way how she'd survived the most injurious and violent acts of war, wars she would exit stripped of her uniform due to a pretty well national prejudice that provoked her superior officers, when they learned she was a transsexual, to discharge her, you see, she said,

I was searched and they learned very quickly I was taking hormones, though of course, she added, this other war has been going on for a long time, this is the battle against hate that a child starting school must endure, the child already metamorphosing, already different, already freighted with ambiguous sexual traits only too visible to others, with the singularity the five- or sometimes four-year-old child experiences in being himself, social scrutiny already heaping the most vile contempt upon him, that's why I plan to tour the schools, colleges, and universities of the country and through love share in the inexpressible sorrow that is the consequence of that hate, then suddenly Victoire fell silent and looked around, brushing her long brown hair back with her hand, and fascinated by Victoire's gesture Petites Cendres glanced across at Yinn standing on the cabaret stage and looking as if he was still choreographing the evening shows despite all his attention being on Victoire, she whom he was listening to so intently, and hearing all her tormented and hesitant silences, the still-raw memory of her past humiliations welling up to the surface, Yinn was struck by how much Victoire had suffered for no good reason and it enraged him, he seemed to be thinking no, this can never be allowed to happen again, and during this moment of Yinn's furious reflection, Petites Cendres contemplated his bare neck free of his black hair, what was this hairstyle that seemed to be the fashion of men secretly wanting to prolong their youth, copious locks on top of their heads but their necks monastically shaved, oh, this Yinn was not the man Petites Cendres so adored, so venerated, his elongated neck like a dancer's, though Yinn danced and sang as well as ever he was so changed now that Petites Cendres could not help but love the person he no longer was, restoring from memory Yinn's hair as it used to be, dark and undulating and tumbling to his shoulders, and the disenchanted smile Petites Cendres could discern through the cigarette smoke of bars at closing time, and here was Jason running the lights from his elevated booth and adjusting them now for the evening show, tonight's, he announced from his booth concealed beneath the rafters of the theatre, would have mauve tinges, yes, some yellow too, Jason now lowering a screen onto the stage for several minutes so that he could introduce the performance with scenes from past performances projected as though they had happened just yesterday, risqué scenes that seemed, because some of the players were no longer around, to arrive from somewhere outside of time, scenes in which Herman and Fatalité offered up their red lips for kisses, or walked naked backstage before the pageantry of the show, these unrehearsed moments Jason had filmed, Herman and Fatalité's faces repeatedly animating the screen, were so vivid, thought Petites Cendres, that you wanted to press their capricious, laughing lips to your own, did these scenes not emerge in the cabaret at the Porte du Baiser Saloon to say, look everyone, we're Herman and Fatalité and we're still here, and after seeing them again Yinn said to the assembled, we've lost Fatalité and Herman, but my belief is that nothing dies, look here, Victoire is the courageous continuation of their ideas and their bravado, welcome, Victoire, said Yinn just as Petites Cendres saw the director's latest discoveries on the screen, Cheng and a young African queen, both of them trained by Yinn to express their work with less flamboyance and more discretion, and were Petites Cendres to compare their work to Herman and Fatalité's, the two of them such uninhibited dancers, provocative girls who had known, like

Victoire, the fissure of being two selves in a single body, who'd known the same gender confusion, the same rupture of the spirit, and even if Cheng, Yinn's most recent discovery, was still young and imperfect, but whom Yinn had trained with such paralyzing rigour, Cheng, who had the same Asian eyes as Yinn's but none of their piercing magnetism, Cheng, wearing the white necklace and black robe Yinn had chosen for him as he advanced toward the screen, his eyes half closed as if he were ready for sleep, Cheng, whom Yinn called his Prince of Asia, Cheng in whom Yinn had sought to awaken ardour and pride in his race, was this Cheng not the dormant bloom in Yinn's mixed garden of flowers exuding their forbidden perfumes, and Victoire broke her silence and started to speak again, saying, what I didn't realize is that you can be a war hero as I was, someone who served, courageous, a man of valour, because you've been taught to take up arms against the enemy, how to handle weapons and a lot more besides, like being able to kill without knowing the people we're killing, to drop bombs without knowing the people we're bombing, because a soldier's duty is to act and not to question what he's doing, blast the oceans, I could have done that, die, I was decorated for my courage, only what I didn't know was that this hero was me but also someone else, someone other, and this other had aspirations every bit as heroic, only what I didn't know was that everything would be snatched away with my uniform, every honour, every glory, everything, simply because I was as you see me now, simply because of that, no more than that, because I am a woman, because I am the person I have wanted to be so profoundly from the moment I was born, when my true nature was contradicted, hijacked, this the reality I have known since I was three years old and helped myself to my sisters' dresses, to their dolls, when what I was telling my parents and they refused to hear is I'm a girl, not a boy, we're living in an era of transition and shock and everything is changing, said Victoire, and everything must change, repeated Victoire, no, yelled Robbie, we're living in a time of blindness and bigotry, of the return of the Ku Klux Klan and of criminals going unpunished, of vile anti-Semites storming synagogues and killing families during a service, of white supremacist nationalists wanting to massacre us all, Robbie said, they want to torch our houses and the bars we go to and, just like they did yesterday, they scream *Heil Hitler* as they pillage, no, I'm sorry, Victoire, nothing's changed, not for us, we're still denied our rights, and Victoire said to Robbie unflappably, no, this is the beginning of a slow revolution, and Petites Cendres looked at Robbie in astonishment, who knew he had such prescience in him, and Robbie raised his voice again saying, and when this persecution becomes a legal cabal approved by a legislature, president, and ministers, when they make it legal to kill us as they've done in Nairobi and no one in the world could be bothered to protest, is this still an era of transition and evolution, asked Robbie, calmer now, though this time Victoire said nothing, just looked at the silhouettes of Herman and Fatalité dancing frivolously on the screen, perhaps she was contemplating their deaths, much too soon for both of them, said Yinn, that's why we keep them with us on the screen, really, said Yinn, they're immortalized, but Victoire had started to speak again, her tone confessional, there are times, said Victoire, I miss my comrades-in-arms just as you do, every night I dream we're back together, guns over our shoulders, eating and sleeping together in the same tent, I know they developed a sudden and irrational hostility toward me, and that they were told to, they still have to follow the orders of their lieutenants and commanders, and I'm still waiting for just one of them to utter a word of understanding, of friendship, because before my transformation, which is not yet complete, we were indivisible in our fear, as if we were experiencing a respect for death that each of us carries inside of ourselves, something ready to explode, yes, as ready as our bombs, for it was always written in the lines of our tired faces that one of us would die and perhaps even that very day, and often it was whoever had been the last to leave the tent or the barracks that morning because he'd taken too long to put on his boots and lace them up, slow to get a jump on the day, such a mundane thing delaying him, yes, I miss my combat buddies, and all of a sudden Victoire was having trouble expressing herself, or she was stopping herself from saying anything more, and Yinn took her hand and in a commanding voice said, well, I believe in the transsexual revolution, enough of this epidemic of children's and teens' suicides, enough, said Yinn, holding Victoire's hand high like a trophy, these children, these teenagers, rather than their giving in to the suicidal impulse because they have been marginalized, excluded, and abused, let these kids join the ranks of activists standing up for their rights, yes, that would be best, said Yinn, for them to stand by Victoire's side, there would be revolution in the streets, everywhere, and an end to invisibility, which is when Robbie made himself heard again, saying, that won't happen without a cost, the cost of a lot of lives, and Petites Cendres looked at Yinn and at Victoire, at Victoire's long hair and Yinn's shaved neck, and marvelled at the transformations and new beginnings in evidence around her, when for months Angel had been content to play sick in bed, only leaving the house for his morning jog with Robbie, or to lie in his hammock on the sun-drenched veranda with his tamed pigeons and turtledoves, out of their cages and perched around him, domesticated birds Angel loved so much, and when he came to Petites Cendres' apartment with his mother for a short visit, short because Dr. Dieudonné was always worried about germs and viruses, even when Angel put on a bit of weight Dieudonné said it was too little, it was always too little, it was because Angel was not eating enough and dreaming of stars and galaxies, thought Petites Cendres suddenly, this is how it was, Yinn was more than thirty years old and had adopted a stylish haircut, the same as his husband Jason, Jason who was so slender and tanned that he seemed as dark as Robbie, the two of them almost identical now, Jason who'd lost his curves due to his spartan workouts at the gym, who'd been so lovable when he was younger and chubbier, and Yinn, who, deprived of his luxurious dark hair, suddenly resembled Jason, they could have been brothers, both with striking long necks and a heap of wavy locks on top of their heads, theirs the traits of a gorgeous and seductive set of similar twins, all this making them even closer, and as for Robbie, had his newfound militancy and impassioned speaking not made him more defiant than the gentle Puerto Rican friend who'd always been hanging around Petites Cendres? The day of parades and celebrations was approaching and, thought Petites Cendres, the queens would be seen marching through town, some would be on floats draped with orchids, like Geisha, Heart Triumphant, Santa Fe, and Cheng, the Prince of Asia with the half-shut eyes, would be standing close to Yinn, luminous in a white dress and gold belt strapped around his waist, the Queen of Queens throwing necklaces to everyone in the streets and all of them seeing only him, Yinn like a sunburst through clouds, thought Petites Cendres, yes, this would be the day, the week they called the week of acceptance, tolerance be welcome, though suddenly, as had been the case with Victoire when she'd deplored the emptiness of such words, the words no longer pleased Petites Cendres, and he told himself that tomorrow he'd go around scratching those words off the posters and write some more inviting slogan over them even if he did not know what that slogan would be, he thought of a heart in the colours of the rainbow flag that would fly across town from one ocean to the other, and of Robbie scattering flowers from a limousine with girls on its roof, and he thought of Alexandra and Léonie, whom he'd see again, skilled carpenters who, in a few months, had completed the construction of two houses at the Acacia Gardens and finally married, much to the dismay of their conventional parents up north, so much shifting and changing, thought Petites Cendres, maybe Alex and Léo would be toward the front of the procession, the maladroit Victoire marching even further to the front, uncomfortable, thought Petites Cendres, because much as she knew who she was beneath her prim skirt and blouse, she'd have preferred to present herself with more grace, the grace, thought Petites Cendres, of Yinn or Geisha, Victoire not yet able to put out of mind the soldier's battle scars that in her new incarnation she could not yet shrug off, could not Petites Cendres himself attribute several lives to Victoire though she was still only twenty-eight, Victoire of a thousand rebirths and existences, Victoire seared by war, Victoire debased by sexism and the blows of a rejection she had not anticipated but nevertheless victorious, Victoire whose glory had been diminished in the course of these blows, though what is certain, thought Petites Cendres, is that she'll be at the head of the procession and not left to face the crowd along the sidewalks on her own, no, her dog Déesse, her surest friend, will be walking by her side. And on this day Eureka came to the Acacia Gardens with aromatic flasks of shampoo for the convalescents and those who preferred not to go out, Angel waiting excitedly because Eureka not only massaged his neck and washed his hair in the tub, she also made him laugh, laugh as the soap and creams streamed over his body, Angel turning his head toward her and laughing and Eureka laughing too, so there, this tickles you eh, that's what I want to hear, said Eureka, so laugh away, she was a large, corpulent woman, and, more than a volunteer offering her services as a masseuse and hairdresser to the community, she was also, on religious occasions, a singer in the Black Ancestral Choir, she was God's envoy, or that's how Reverend Ézéchielle described her in her sermons, someone who appeased suffering on this earth because, as the reverend also said, had she not received the gift of love at birth, the gift of song so powerful that in church she made the Black Ancestral Choir tremble, and the Sunday faithful, stirred by her zealous singing, would spontaneously start to dance and sing along with her, Eureka also helped Dr. Dieudonné as a nurse at his clinic and hospital, not every day because she had so much else going on, but Angel could count on her not to forget him, knowing that under her care, gentle and intense if a little disquieting when her mauve nails burrowed into his temples, he would feel invigorated and also less hurt by his father's failure to write, not answering the boy's letters and emails, it's because your father's very far away, working in another country, Lena told her son, and when her son asked why does he not come and see me here at the Gardens, Lena understood in the words of the boy yearning for his father that what he meant to say was, why does he not come see me before it's too late, and Lena would answer that we don't think or behave in the same way as him, or she would say nothing at all, offering no explanation because a father refusing to see his son, especially when the boy's condition was so precarious, was inexplicable, so her face grew sombre but she remained silent and Angel, confronted by his mother's abrupt silence, remembered just when his father left them alone to wander in exile together, two itinerants taking to the car and a life on the road, retiring, late at night so they'd not be noticed, to motels on the outskirts of towns far from home, the neighbourhood where Angel had been expelled from school because he was thought to be contagious, they'd become no more than a nomadic family forced onto the highways of North America, like so many others tossed out onto the streets by misfortune, poverty, or the unemployment of a parent, many of them often seeming well-to-do because they had a car, but who were in fact a new kind of wandering tribe, not knowing where to stop with their children, never wanting to be noticed in their sorry exodus, broken families hiding behind the blinds and tinted car windows, the young ones inconsolable despite being sated with chocolates and candy, not even realizing why they were crying so much and their harried mothers having no time to clean their dirty faces, Angel often thought of these families, of their disparate means, and their having no idea where on the network of highways they'd end up come nightfall or dawn, they were fugitive families, some of them evading deportation, once Angel had played with a little Muslim boy in a grassy park beneath palm trees with a tiny play area for children and a swing, behind a motel it was, you could hear the roar of trucks and cars nearby, and too, there was a picnic table with benches the boy's family had drawn together for a hasty meal the mother had prepared, he was almost certainly younger than Angel, who remembered the mother handing him a sandwich and then milk that the boy spilled all over his clothes, his mother loudly scolding him, rebuking her son for playing with his food, do you hear me, I forbid you to play with your food, I forbid you, she said, loud enough that she regretted it immediately, her tirade interrupted by the boy's bursting into tears, and seeing him so unhappy and feeling herself in the wrong, she took him in her arms and said imploringly, no no no, it was a mistake, I know you couldn't sleep at all in the car last night and didn't mean to shout and look, your brothers and sisters and father and I are right here with you, come, to make you feel better we're all going to the airport together, we'll be there soon, Angel realizing that he'd been playing with a young boy whose face he would never see again, nor would he see the boy's father, who'd seemed so anxious that day, was he the one the mother was driving to the airport, she'd said to her children several times you won't be seeing Papa for several months, you must give him a hug, the eldest asked why he could not travel with him and the little one who'd been playing with Angel on the swing, still sniffling, had hugged his father, stains from the food on his clothes, and the mother, in such warm clothes on this torrid day, a shawl covering her beautiful hair, told her son playing with Angel to say goodbye to his friend and Angel, who was feeling older and protective, hugged the little boy as he bid him farewell, goodbye, the boy said, though perhaps he'd said nothing and merely extended his small arms toward him, yes, maybe he said nothing at all, thought Angel, and when Eureka was done shampooing and massaging him, well, that was the sweetest moment of the day because, wrapped up in his blue bath towel, Lena and Eureka, teasing him about his long legs all the while, would together lift him up and carry him out to the deck chair on the veranda, how indulgent and easy it was to let himself be cradled like this, Lena would say, but our Eureka can't make it every day so I suppose you're right to let yourself be spoiled today, and portly Eureka would grab Angel by the neck saying, didn't I say you'd feel better, didn't I say so, am I going to hear you laugh again, and, despite the heat, they would stay on the veranda, a warm breeze coming off the ocean and across Atlantic Boulevard, and in his blue towel, as soft and velvety a nest as Eureka's arms, Angel would pretend to nap as she sang gospel to him, aware even in the white lie of his sleep that the doves had not stopped cooing since noon all the while, and that below the veranda white egrets were flying over the pond, deep in his heart, Angel always felt the curious happiness of being alive and loved, of being loved and alive. My dear Mai, I'm writing you from the Writers' Village where you can see, all along the roads and avenues, many of them named, for these few days of festivities, after writers of every nationality, benches painted a luxurious green and authors sitting on them as they write on tablets or laptops thin as paper and resting on their knees, I'm writing you during a pit stop on Charles Dickens Street, close by is a row of authors signing their books at the special tables assigned to them, and I should tell you that the village's Auditorium of Fine Arts, schools and convents, a media centre and main library are also at our disposal, not to mention all the pubs and cafés where readings and panel discussions take place, as my friend Eddy told me at the Celtic Tavern last night, there's a whole series of events this year to commemorate the festival's tenth anniversary, though I must say your dad's feeling a little gloomy during this pastoral fantasia, especially because he always arrives late for his sessions and now the time has come again for me to sit and sign books with the others, and you, Mai, dearest Mai, you know how reluctant I can be, often thinking myself unworthy of the very title of author, in this instant, in fact, I'm wondering what I'd have done were I eleven or twelve years old and my parents in debtors' prison as was the case with poor Dickens, how would I have surmounted the terrible privation of such a childhood as he knew, I wonder whether would I have had the audacity to write my autobiography after such penury, I think that writers, my sweet, need to be born with a soul hard as stone, when actually, like the English novelist keeping me company here, they're born with a soul pervious to everything, to any vile dust; this morning I met a highly successful and celebrated author who has published several books on the scientific prolongation of lives perhaps soon to be eternal, this author maintains entirely without proof that soon we will be freed from the very idea of death and everyone supports his view because the suggestion, the completely fictitious invention through the sorcery of writing, of a body that will last forever, is so pleasing, even to me, your father who dreams of utopias, and since breakfast this morning this author has sold hundreds of copies of his book to passing readers already believing they can surpass the limits of their earthly existence, this finite term the most harrowing element of all the frightful realities this imaginative writer denies, claiming as he does that the barrier between life and whatever lies beyond can be dissolved if we wish it, you'd never believe, sweet Mai, the extraordinary impression he has made on his readers, these people who suddenly see themselves as the masters of innumerable future incarnations in an unbroken line, and yet we must ask ourselves a question this fanciful writer does not, which is that without the ineffable ephemerality of our lives leading us to the same end, at almost the same pace, how can any of us become saints, or at least creatures leading exemplary lives, this is the quandary I put to the author this morning, but he had no answer for me, he's elderly and it's surprising he doesn't share these concerns regarding the ephemeral, this writer, a fervent devotee of technological developments and a health reform advocate keen on diets and special regimens, suggested with a certain condescension that I read his works on the body immortal and the right of our bodies to be so, so that this encounter, my dear Mai, rather than reassuring me, left me perplexed at the actually solitary nature of each of our bodies and the presumption of a writer who has the effrontery to recount such lies, but this is the way with authors, rarely do they tell the truth, or they see the contours of the stories they tell differently, all of them, like this author, are inherently disposed to fabrication, these were the words Daniel wrote while sitting on the green bench, as lusciously green as the hills overlooking the town, and which prompted Mai to reply that if Daniel was in possession of an elixir for eternal life then she really hoped he'd stay with her forever or even longer, and though it was too soon for her to contemplate such longevity for herself, she approved of the author's theories despite her father insisting the man was a utopian writer and decidedly commercial, this because he was making a fortune writing things that could never be true, much less made to happen, and Daniel wrote that he took advantage of his readers' credulity, and Mai answered that writers, more than anyone else, were free to dream, but, thought Daniel, Augustino would never be so indulgent, judging by Augustino's comments that he'd been able to read in various literary magazines popping up all over the place, and wasn't that just like Augustino, he reflected, to give his sardonic remarks a voice even in his absence through irreverent articles, who knew, he might even be here among this motley bunch, Daniel had been searching him out among the young, invariably hanging out with each other and welded to their iPads, and among them a punkier lot listening to music and saying nothing much at all, but there was no sign of him, and perhaps Daniel was also afraid that were he to meet his son he'd no longer know how to talk to him, would Augustino even be his son anymore, oh, he would recognize the boy's unkempt hair, the holes in his jeans exposing the knees, but what would their encounter be like after all this time in which he, the father, had changed as much as the son, though what Daniel did know at such a remove was that his son was to be found in the words he had written, furious and intransigent as ever, and Daniel, reading Augustino's lacerating review of the featured author of the day, found himself disconcerted on the writer's behalf, someone with whom he had engaged amicably that morning and who'd even upbraided him a little, and given that this writer was already of a curmudgeonly nature, already pissed off because he was still living, just what, wondered Daniel, about a body condemned to eternal life was going to thrill him, and would not this author, crotchety despite the success of his books, tear a strip off Daniel for what his son had written about him in a magazine, might he not say, look at that, your boy Augustino is insulting me, me and my work, daring to call it all smoke and mirrors and proposing that we should dispense with writers like me, he dares, your son, he dares write this, though Daniel wondered if perhaps he was in agreement with Augustino, who'd accused the author of playing tricks with his readers, his project an illusory one perpetrated in bad faith, Augustino had denounced the self-interest of those who'd found recipes for eternal life in his manipulative work, and it was important to note, wrote Augustino, that the indefinite longevity of the body the author was propounding was amenable only to Westerners, to the white races, only they would find the idea of a long life appealing, given that today's children born into countries of famine are devastated before they are twenty, absolutely, Augustino was right to lash out at such idiocies, for sure, and then one of the Writers' Village hostesses approached Daniel opening an umbrella, it's raining, friend, haven't you noticed, it often does in these foggy autumn hills, come with me, we'll take shelter in one of these houses, they're always open to the writers, to all of them, and rest assured the weather will be fine for tonight's woodland celebration, we'll honour you all, we'll pay homage to this distinguished conference, mind you, the celebration is not reflected in the variety and diversity of the meal the villagers have whipped up, we'll be managing simply and within our means, there'll be candles and lanterns and rows of buffet tables, no, the word *celebration* is first and foremost in honour of the writing we've been sharing here with you, a celebration in which the written word is triumphant, words, we hope, of peace, oh dear, it's pouring again, quick, follow me, it's a real downpour, it happens a lot here, and Daniel rose from the bench and followed the hostess, who, beneath her huge umbrella, seemed to be wearing the same pink wool Mère was in the dream he'd had the night before, the kind woman protected him with the umbrella and let the rain fall on her pink sweater and said, come come, we must collect all the books we put out for you and the others to sign, this storm won't last long, and Daniel opened his eyes, he'd dozed off while writing to Mai, unable to resist the sweet temptation of slumber that seized him whether he was seated or standing, so much did jet lag undermine his biological clock, how surprising, he thought, to find himself alone in the rain and still sitting on his green bench as the rest ran to the nearest house for shelter, every house opening its doors to the strangers with books under their arms, they'd fled the storm and Daniel thought he heard Mère's voice, wasn't that her in the pink sweater telling him to take shelter, this voice of hers, in a reverie lasting no more than an instant, as insistent in his ear as if she were standing right beside him in this deserted space in which he was not expecting to be joined by anyone, perhaps those we've lost relish the opportunity of empty spaces, they who do not knock on doors, indifferent to barriers their bodies transparently sift through like a veil, and Mère was suddenly just a few feet from Daniel, though, despite her presence being so real, he was not sure where, you see, he felt her say, these houses that are open to you all day long, their considerate hosts so self-effacing, they're as I was when during that appalling refugee crisis I opened our doors to Jenny, Marie-Sylvie de la Toussaint, and Julio, Julio whose entire family had perished at sea, yes, thought Daniel, I remember, their names were Ramon, Oreste, and Nina, none of them knew how to swim, no they didn't, said Mère, as soon as they swallowed salt water they stopped breathing, that's what Julio told me, suddenly he'd seen a helicopter in the sky and a pilot yelling, won't be long now, Julio striving to bring them up to the Homeland Security helicopter with him but Ramon, Oreste, and Nina had stopped breathing, refugees flooded to our house in those days because we lived at that time close to the shore upon which their makeshift rafts fell apart, Mère was saying, but all Daniel could hear was the rumbling of the storm so that he too ran for the first house and subsequently was moved, as Mère said he would be, by the conduct of his hosts so unassuming they might have been invisible, tea and biscuits were served, the waxed tablecloth was red, the walls were red too, some writers were chatting among themselves and others, rocking in wooden chairs that creaked imploringly as they rocked back and forth, preparing their evening readings, and the noise of the chairs squeaking against the floor was beginning to irritate Daniel who was impatient for the rain to stop and also unaware of where or even who he was, but for the memories of his family unexpectedly surfacing, and in those days, when Mère was still about, was not the world Daniel and his family were in better, or, wondered Daniel, when Mère was offering shelter, and her daughter Mélanie doing the same at her own house in solidarity, did it have another quality, Mère who took in so many Cuban and Haitian refugees, was there not a greater sense of retribution and justice back then, was that not true of Mère's day, yes, thought Daniel, it was, though he also remembered Julio being beaten up on the beach, and that the thugs who'd assaulted Julio where he often went for walks because the young man felt it was his duty, after Mère had taken him in, to check for some other raft landing, for yet more ramshackle vessels adrift in the storm, and always he heard the cries of Oreste, Ramon, and Nina, those he'd not been able to save, as if they were still floating around him as the helicopter rumbled overhead, the thugs had screamed, we don't want you here, you Cuban and Haitian refugees, go back to sea and take all your germs and infections with you, no, you're not welcome here, they beat Julio with sticks, they pelted him with rocks, which was when Augustino asked his father, his son still so young then, why Julio's head was bandaged, why, Papa, why does his head hurt so much, and Daniel felt compelled to explain to his son that Julio had been attacked, but why, Augustino repeated, why, Papa, what was the reason, and was this not a question Augustino could be raising at this very moment, why these young children, why these mothers, these infants surrounded by barbed wire in Lebanese and Jordanian refugee camps, why these millions of families without a house or a country waiting wearily under a dismal sky for a daily ration of bread from international agencies inevitably arriving too late despite the decency of their intentions, why these young boys returning come nightfall to their refugees' tents and carrying round loaves in plastic bags slung around their necks and often, on the way back, handling the loaves, these loaves in bags around their necks, the boys' hands protecting their families' only rations, which they needed to protect if they were to survive, because although more than two hundred babies were born into the camps each month, those who died from malnutrition or respiratory infections matched and even exceeded this number, and in these camps the young boys, often risking their lives, sold food and cigarettes, sometimes cell phones, these, like an offering, held up to the night sky and just possibly facilitating contact with a parent in the country left behind, who could say, the scratchy voices and words interrupted by exploding bombs perhaps the last to be relayed by these phones as they lost their charge, a mother or father waiting through the evening, had they not been told life was pretty well normal in the camps, that the influx of three hundred Middle Eastern refugees a day, the hastily pitched tents and repugnant prefab huts, the hospitals and even schools, that all this, the degraded condition of these structures and the noxious stink of the streets, the skilful disguising of such squalor was normal, even acceptable, so that one should not to be bothered by or even think about any of this, okay, thought Daniel, there was no answer to any of Augustino's questions, neither yesterday nor today, except for a state of permanent revolt, anger, and pent-up indignation, and Daniel's peers rushed up to him asking if he would read them his presentation, the inaugural one of the evening's conference, okay then, friends and colleagues, here, it begins with the refugee camps, yes, this first image is of the global conflagration I wish to speak about tonight, but Daniel began to meander as he read, his text evoking the names of Julio, Jenny, and Marie-Sylvie de la Toussaint, those of Oreste, Ramon, and Nina, children lost at sea even as the courageous helicopter pilots shouted we're coming, we're coming, you'll all be saved, and disappearing beneath the waves, and I also remember, said Daniel, that my wife Mélanie and I taught our kids to swim early on, first in the pool and then in the ocean, this around the same time the Haitians and Cubans were arriving, and that I'd felt

Augustino's feet get away from me, he was swimming on his back but then turned over suddenly and I couldn't see him anymore, mind you I was shouting out to him, Augustino, Augustino, and this was when, reading the digressions and jumbled words of his paper, Daniel heard a flurry of applause and came to, rocking in his chair as an antique clock struck noon and several young people cheered a poet reading something he had written just that morning, he listened to the voice of the poet declaiming, this morning, he said, walking the length of Virgil Street, isn't it true that the Latin poet's name has been loaned to one of the streets of the village, rebaptized like many others, for the duration of the authors' stay, this is Virgil Street, I said to myself, and what with my being no schooled bourgeois but the son of a peasant, and not having studied at all, am I not envious of a poet who was also a philosopher and who wrote such beautiful lines, and yet they say that some days he was plagued by dark thoughts, so disturbed was he by the politics of the time, perhaps it is better to cut oneself off and write from some mystic retreat, certainly this was how the notion that souls might survive independently of bodies came to him, this idea, yes, that it is possible for the soul inhabiting a body of such a primitive sensibility as his own to survive it and live on into some other realm, could it be, for as you can see, my friends, we are talking now of a modern poet, one who, despite so many personal and political setbacks, despite his house being confiscated, knew how to sustain his peace of mind, minimal as it was, but as he listened to the poet Daniel was distracted by the presence, just feet away from him, of the author of our extended days, the author of *Esthetic Eternity*, his expression as morose as ever, coolly nibbling the salmon, chocolate, and strawberries on his plate and intruding upon Daniel's space so unpleasantly, it's noon, the man said, the hour of my perfect nutrition, and it's still raining, typical of this place, my raincoat's soaked and as for my shoes, well, I've been walking these muddy streets since morning, and you know I mustn't catch cold, it'll turn into pneumonia in no time, my wife's right, I never should have gone out, certainly shouldn't have come this far, the secret of longevity, my friend, is to stay home, not go out, yes, excursions and encounters with other people are perilously wearying, we mustn't give in, to give in is to succumb to mortality and all the miseries that precede it, you see, the body that stays home is not exhausted, it rests, nothing that happens at home will disturb the body or shock it, no, nothing at all, and as Daniel listened to the writer, full of resentments and muttering despite his resounding success with the reading public, he glanced over at the photos of other authors in silver frames, strangely he'd not noticed them, so struck was he by the deep red colour of the walls burnished by reflections from the fireplace, and suddenly he'd been struck by the appealing, affable, and open face of a poet who used to visit the festival from London each year, Eddy had said at the bar the night before that in one of the houses where you'll be offered tea and a place to rest you'll see the faces of several poets who've left us this year, this year there are several that aren't with us, and this was him, the poet with the red hair that had suddenly turned white, the guy who, Eddy said, loved to dance and party, was smiling upon Daniel serenely, he was the poet who'd spoken of *chains to eternity*, was the image that or some other metaphor, whatever, Daniel remembered him, and here he was in the company of a coterie of other poets on the reddish walls, men and women both, their charms inexhaustible and Daniel finding it hard to imagine them no longer in this world, so much were their faces still iridescent with passion, some with an ironic confidence, and one photo in particular intriguing Daniel, the radiant face of a woman he recognized as one of his own poet friends, of course, he realized, it was Suzanne, her photograph there on the fire-red wall amid the other deceased writers, his friend Suzanne with whom he had eaten by the sea so often as she read her latest poems to him, frequently laughing in the middle of a recitation in the February wind, yes, this was her, Adrien's wife Suzanne, of whom he was so fond and who seemed to be posing the question to Daniel, from the immobility of the frame, is it due to my husband occupying so much of the emotion and feeling in my life that my books were overlooked for so long, they called us the golden couple in those days, though I'm sure the brilliance was only attributed to him, to my adorable and insolent Adrien, and as we used to eat together so often, dear Daniel, might I ask what you thought of it all, I did write once there'd be no glory for us, that what we write will be invisible for far too long but then suddenly take flight in a flamboyant assertion of our emancipation, yes, at the time Adrien refused to see me for the author I was, so much was I simply the wife devoted to his writing, though how could it have been otherwise, because this is the way we women loved, making of ourselves a ridiculous gift, yes, that's what we did, keep watch over my husband, dear Daniel, because he's become infatuated with Charly, who's already been such bad news for our friend Caroline, he'd do better to finish his third volume of *Faust*, oh, how I wish I were still by his side, writing every day behind the Japanese screen, Daniel, do you remember they wrote of my poetry that it was a river of words, a carefully directed deluge, yes, that's what they said, I wore a hat and cape in those days, no one knew who I was behind that eccentric disguise or how sure I was that the river of words offered neither hope nor redemption, yes, said Daniel, I remember our meals by the sea, and I know now how much Adrien and I both miss you, dear Suzanne, to which she replied in a slightly disapproving tone, and Daniel, surely you've noticed these streets bear the names of writers like Charles Dickens, Virgil, and Oscar Wilde, but that the streets named after women writers are in more wooded areas, we even have a lonesome path named for us, the Emily Dickinson Trail, did you notice, dear Daniel, this oversight, this neglect, and Daniel awoke from this daydream in which Suzanne had spoken to him from a photograph taken in her youth, though perhaps it had not been hers but a picture of someone who looked like her, though what was certain was that Suzanne had revealed herself to him through the photograph, the sensation he'd had was of hearing her voice, her laugh, of feeling her presence in illuminating thoughts she'd kept to herself for so long, and then an author colleague reminded Daniel they were being picked up by bus at five for the celebration that would take place high up in the mountains, yes, in the mountains, as Eddy had told him, a feast for the authors but a simple one, to be held at dawn when the sky over the Scottish forest seems to be aflame, at which point five of Eddy's women friends giddily burst into the house with red walls, they'd been dancing with Eddy at the North Sea Pub all night long at a bachelorette party for Daphnée, soon to marry Peter, a guy she was crazy about, her friends said, though it was too bad about her getting married so young, still, nothing for it but to celebrate, and the friends gathered round Daniel and asked him to sign their notebooks, the books themselves cost too much, they said, so all they could do was roam the streets and byways of the village and collect as many authors' signatures as possible, it was amazing, everywhere they went there were books on tables, and in kiosks, and so many authors, oh, they said, we'll read yours when we're old, no, no time now, not when one of us is getting married, the wedding's in just a few days and besides we're all a bit drunk, they were holding beers in one hand and their notebooks already overflowing with autographs in the other, these'll be worth a lot someday, one of them said, believe me, and Daniel replied, they'll be worth no more than the writer's heart and soul, and one of Eddy's friends laughed and said, but won't they have a certain historical value, each of us will be able to say all these authors were living once, we asked them to sign our notepads and now they are immortal, forever a part of our own stories, and Daniel gazed at them thinking how like fairies they were, like pollinating bees, and besides, said Daphnée the bride-to-be, you're very funny, you have a funny face and your smile is funny because you blush a lot, odd for a man to do that, though it must be said your writing is weird too, and then they vanished in a cloud of laughter just as they'd arrived, the signatures in their notebooks so ephemeral, mused Daniel before considering again just how behind he was with his interminable book, *Strange Years*, and how despite the relentlessly slow passing of time he'd still not managed to find his son Augustino, no, not yet, he reminded himself. The yellow-and-orange parakeet had been Mabel's gift to Lucia, such a young thing, thought Lucia, a baby, we'll call the chick Orange and now, thought Lucia, alongside Misha, who visited Angel at the Acacia Gardens almost every day, it'll be the little patient's new companion, as she wheeled her bike along Atlantic Boulevard, both parakeets on her shoulder, the beak of the other bird, Night Out, rubbed against her cheeks, and Lucia, barefoot in sandals and topless beneath her coveralls, adored the sensation of the burning hot wind in her short hair, she'd long reproached herself for being so lethargic in her misery, living but not living, her existence ponderous in her empty days, so naturally she looked forward to evenings and to seeing Brilliant in all his exuberance at the downtown bars, their companionship reinforced by an overindulgence in wine and hard liquor, though since he'd been working as a nurse's aide at Dr. Dieudonné's clinic Brilliant had been partying much less, though even sober he was every bit as loving toward her, she thought how lucky she was to have a friend like Brilliant and to be able to zip around on her bike all day helping out other residents at the Gardens with their shopping and errands, how pleasing it was to be useful at last, let her dismal days be over, forever, no longer was she feeling the burden of time, to the contrary, her anxiety had lifted from her shoulders, she felt rejuvenated, relieved of all the appalling worries that had left her feeling so empty, and it was a pity Fleur was too far away to have been present during the scene of tender reconciliation Angel had witnessed that morning, that's right, of the Mexican Raphaël and Kim, Kim holding her baby at arm's length as Raphaël, his dusty hair pleated to his waist, said to the little roundheaded girl, kiss your mommy, go on and give your mom Kim a kiss, and the little one turned her head as if to say no, I won't, the baby already as stubborn as Kim, and passing the three of them in the street Lucia thought of Fleur,

Raphaël was saying, we'll teach her to give kisses, she's just like Kim, she resists, and Lucia wondered if there had not been the shadow of a smile on Kim's lips, on that face of hers still betraying her disappointment at Fleur's absence, at the suddenness of his departure, at the success overseas that the newspapers reported, no longer was she a homeless kid sleeping on the beach with her dog, the terrible jealousy etched into her face had aged her, Raphaël might be a bad seed, but he did good business on the street with his jewellery and his weaving, assuredly shadier dealings too, Raphaël, in his long tunics and his medallions, crucifix pendants on his chest, his hair dusty and pleated, his guru's splendour arrogant and excreting the odour of hashish, still, thought Lucia, you can be a bad boy and a rogue but also be a good father to your brood, the right word because really he had a surprising number of women and children in his loft, go on, he was saying, kiss your mom, come give Papa a kiss, but still the child turned her head away, bah, barked Raphaël the Mexican, you'll soon learn my angelfish, yes, you'll learn very quickly, but the child was much more interested in Orange perched on Lucia's shoulder than in giving kisses, it made no sense, why kiss these two grownups who happened to be her parents, the gestures she was being asked to make were incomprehensible, to be offered up for no more reason than to follow orders, and what about the splendid parakeet dipping its beak into Lucia's cardboard cup so that it could drink more greedily, was the little bird, inexperienced and undomesticated, not an infant just like Kim and Raphaël's little girl, her infatuation reserved for Orange the pretty parakeet alone, Orange beat its green wings, opening and closing them, and bent its yellow-and-orange head toward Lucia's fingers from the bicycle's handlebars begging for its head to be scratched, Lucia and Kim's baby marvelling at it the same way, the chick, Lucia told Raphaël, was a little apprehensive at first but can be trained easily, and she was overjoyed at the moment of harmony among them all, between Kim, Raphaël, the baby, Orange, and Night Out, not for a moment had Lucia anticipated this sudden return of calm and order after so much chaos, and though Kim remained taciturn and pensive, Raphaël talked about how they also kept two velvety rabbits for their daughter, Sabine and Boo, in the garden behind the loft, Sabine and Boo had come all the way from Arizona where they'd been found in appalling conditions, poor things, abandoned in some kind of aquarium throughout the winter cold and summer heat but now, said Raphaël, they could nibble all the grass they wanted and had their own little cabin, Kim's baby girl loved them, and we'll get a dog as well and call him Beanie, said Raphaël, who sometimes imprudently pulled wads of banknotes from his tunic, business was good, he told Lucia, Fleur needn't worry about Kim, I'm looking after her, but still, thought Lucia, even if Raphaël did tend to all his children, and even if he was such an ardent lover, still you couldn't forget he was the wrong sort, a bandit guru, and while he was instinctively attuned to Kim's despondency, he knew how much she'd been undermined by the death of the Old Salt, by his murder on the boat at the hands of two miscreant thugs he'd always generously sheltered, the Old Salt's flaw his believing in the obvious perversity of humans, Kim incessantly returning to the forgotten boat as if the Old Salt was still there waiting for her, saying, today's the day our grey heron will come see us, isn't that right, Kim, it'll be today, unless he decides to wait till tomorrow 'cause he doesn't like these northerly winds, who knows, said Raphaël, maybe Kim loved the old guy like the father she never had, she whose parents were junkies, Kim always saying that her parents would've sold their kids for a bag of coke, yes, they'd have sold all of us, maybe, said Raphaël, she loved him like a father who respected and cherished her in turn, but that's life, Raphaël said to Kim, I read in the tarot cards that soon you'll be free of your worries and free of Fleur too, that opportunistic musician who takes up way too much space in your life, can't you see that nowadays we move from one existence to the next, and that each one gets better and sweeter, our lives improving until at last we are overwhelmed by happiness, we're just not made to be miserable, that's right, it's not our natural state, and Kim's baby held her head up without hearing a thing her father had said, as if she was thinking this guy talks way too much, no, by far the most interesting thing in the whole wide world was Orange, Lucia's parakeet, its colour was that of the sun, Orange, the bird with the piercing yellow eye, yes, thought Lucia, wouldn't Fleur be comforted to know Kim had a friend and a protector in Raphaël the Mexican, would this not reassure him a little, or in the success of the new European life he'd chosen, had Fleur simply erased Kim from memory, erased her name forever, and lying in his bed with Misha, whose day it was to visit, curled up asleep on the white pillows next to him, Angel read Kitty's letter, the letter was written on paper, Kitty's mother had no computer or cell phone and it had been nearly a year since Kitty and her brothers last went to school, they were still in room 3206, at the motel where Kitty met Angel, whose mother had been living for some time in room 3207, and it was the manager cum handyman who told Kitty, you're living next to a boy who could become a friend, the man said kindly, I know you're lonely here, you walk around all day in your brother's sweater which is way too long for you, you're bored, that's what happens when children stay here with their families and can't go to school, they're bored or they get into trouble, they break windows or bounce balls off the walls in a rage, it's a sad sight, all you footloose kids, all these angry and desperate mothers, yes, it's depressing to see, how old are you, Kitty, you're maybe thirteen, yes, I'm thirteen, said Kitty, well, I'll get you some math books so you don't drop too far behind, the caretaker said, my dad was a teacher and I'll bring some round tomorrow, so Kitty wrote Angel that she was still reading and studying until they could live in a real house, it's not fair, she wrote, that moms alone with their kids are always the poorest, this itinerant life is already so disturbing that it's a shame the children of the homeless can't go to school, it means you're not even a citizen in your own country, you lose everything, even the right to learn, wrote Kitty, who said she did not understand why Angel and his mother were homeless too, why they were also wandering nights in their car, why, why was this happening when they were both well dressed and Angel had a phone and a computer, and as soon as he read Kitty's question, why are you in room 3207 and here with us in this motel, Angel lowered his eyes and said nothing, why are you all on the run, who is it you're running from, Kitty asked, my mom and my brothers and me, they're after us for the money we owe, that's why we're on the run, they cut off our electricity and our heating, here in the motel we do have electricity but no fridge so I get ice cubes from the machine in the hallway and we keep canned goods and vegetables cold in the sink, Mom says we have to eat, sometimes we have milk and cheese the caretaker gives us, but I hate living off the charity of others, boy do I ever, 'specially now I'm thirteen, it's humiliating, it's so humiliating I want to yell, but Mom says come and help me with the little one instead of complaining, all these younger brothers and sisters, it's too much for me, still, I promise you, like I told Benito the caretaker, one day I'm going to be somebody, you'll see, and now what about you, why are you so quiet, why don't you answer my questions, maybe you just don't like talking about yourself, and as Angel read this, he frowned and said to Misha, hey, look at you, you've taken all the pillows, you're taking way too much room, and when Misha snuggled up even closer to him, letting out his canine snores, Angel said, I understand, it's because you've been busy chasing egrets by the pond, you've been running after them for ages, that's why you're sleeping so much, but as for me, said Angel, as for me, he repeated, but not finishing, the voice trembling as he admonished himself for being so impatient toward Misha and hugging him in apology, what he was unable to express to either Kitty or Misha was that he was suffering a sudden weariness, this something he would admit neither to his mother nor to Dr. Dieudonné because what he wanted above all was to go out to sea with Brilliant, no, it was impossible to speak to Kitty of how he'd been shunned by his class and school because his blood was toxic, or of how, when he was little, he'd received a transfusion of contaminated blood after an accident and perhaps this stranger's blood had saved him for a while, for had his mother not said few children survived car accidents at such an early age, so he shouldn't curse this gift of blood he'd received and who knows, maybe the stranger who'd given the blood had no idea he was infected, he might have been very young, no, thought Angel, Kitty must not learn any of this, she might shun him as the students had done, and not just the students but the mothers who'd ordered their children not to hang around that boy saying, don't touch him, you could die, don't touch him, keep your distance, even my father panicked and ran away, thought Angel, my own dad, it was so shameful and humiliating, and suddenly he felt even more weary, though despite his mounting fever he was determined to go to sea with Brilliant and into Captain Jöe's boat at dusk, he had to get out of bed and bring Misha with him, hey Misha, you're coming, right, and Misha responded with snores dredged up from the deep sleep brought on by running by the pond and jumping and bounding all day, nevertheless Kitty had written Angel and her letter had brought him a curious joy, they say kids like us are the delinquents of tomorrow, she had written, but you'll see, it won't happen, I'm going to be a force for good, I'll learn things and teach math at university, Benito is teaching me algebra, I want to be a mathematician but Mom says I'm up on my high horse, just imagine, you, a math specialist, but I'm going to be one, we can't forget that we all have a right to go to school, even children in families like ours, the kids of mothers in refugee shelters, oh, I hate shelters, we were eight families in the last one and you could hear babies crying every night, I was ashamed to be there but at least we had three meals a day and, besides, I'm not quite so bored since a black family arrived from Chicago, Cristal is the oldest and thirteen like me but she's convinced her future's going to turn out bad, they're at the motel because it's not far from the prison her father's been in for several years and they can visit him, but Cristal says that with a father in prison everybody turns their back on you and how can things not turn out bad, she can't go to school any more either, still on Sundays the whole family goes to visit their dad and talks to him on a telephone through a glass panel, Cristal really loves her dad a lot, she kisses the glass every time and says, goodbye, I'll be back next Sunday, she's sad because her father's in a gang, she's afraid for him, they're up against the White Supremacy Gang and his life is in danger, Cristal says later on she'll sell drugs like her dad, she doesn't care about her future, anyway she goes to the Congregational Church with her mother Elvira every day, but she doesn't believe in the power of prayer like her mother does, no, she doesn't believe, she says praying helps people forget their misery by putting them to sleep but she'll never have faith like her parents, Cristal says, it's just a false beacon in the darkness, yes, that's what she says, and she won't let Benito bring her books because she doesn't want to read or study, sometimes she says she's done with school, they go from one shelter to the next but now they have to wait for their father's trial, he's in jail not far from here, Kitty wrote, and sometimes the two of us walk along the tracks behind the motel, I think her life is harder than mine, at least I don't have a dad in jail, my mother and brothers are always near me and we have two pretty big beds, I sleep in the narrower one with my mother and my brothers are in the larger one beside it, though my brothers are bored and spend all their time watching television, I tell myself they're going to end up really ignorant because they don't go to school, they never study, they just argue and sometimes they get into fistfights with the other kids here, but what about you, Angel, you never tell me about you and your mom, Benito said you had to leave quickly in the middle of the night because you were expected at the apartment in the Acacia Gardens where you are living now, you gave me the address the evening you left, oh, it was way more fun when you here with me though you never said much, and Angel wondered about the weariness creeping over him as he read Kitty's letter and why he had lied to her when she had been his friend for several days, at first he thought it didn't matter since he would never see her again, but now all of a sudden he missed her kindness, he who had it all, he who was overwhelmed with presents when his mother Lena came from work come nighttime, when often he was too tired to return her affection, sometimes he felt so sick, why had he not given Kitty his electronic toys and videos, why, when he would never be able to play and distract himself as he used to before, why, and yet there would always be days like today when Misha came for a visit and he was tempted to wake up the dog and run with him to the veranda where he waited every day for his mother's return, but today he felt low and without the strength to climb out of bed, so he decided he would rouse himself and Misha once Brilliant arrived, that would do it, and Daniel was thinking about the lie he'd told Vincent, Vincent, who was such a delicate child, terrible for a father to do that, maybe he'd lied because he'd wanted to spare his frail son and for him to avoid another choking episode, there are times, thought Daniel, when we have no choice but to deceive, to tell a simple white lie, where are you taking me, Papa, Vincent asked, so far from you and Mama and Samuel and his boat *Southern Light*, where are you taking me, and Daniel tried to calm him by saying, look, you've had several attacks lately and your mother and I want you to get the best possible care so I'm taking you to a holiday camp in Vermont where you'll be very happy, just you wait and see, the mountain air will improve your breathing, you can ride horseback, cycle the trails, though what Daniel did not say was that he would not be back for his son until much later in the autumn, yes, Daniel told his son, you'll be able to do all that, you who love horses so much, but father, said Vincent, I know they have dormitories for sick children there, and Daniel repeated that they have bicycles and horses, Daniel, who had consulted the doctors and nurses at this mysterious holiday camp, leaving out so much, that the youngsters there were unable to exhale, for instance, that in the dorms and tents filled with pure and purifying forest air, bronchial asthma caused the children to convulse, cries of fear lifting their chests, and yet perhaps it was, as he said, a sort of holiday camp for them all, that was the lie he told, what else could he have said without causing Vincent anguish, what else was he to do, Daniel knew the treatment would be a lengthy one lasting till autumn and that Vincent was hoping to come home after only a couple of weeks in this holiday camp his parents had chosen, that he'd really not wanted to go, he'd been forced to, in fact, but also that Vincent, who was now a pulmonologist himself, had in turn lied to his patients to keep up their morale and stave off their own insurmountable anxiety, and now when his patients suffered attacks of asphyxiation, he too said everything will be alright, everything will be fine, just relax and get some rest, and Daniel suddenly realized he had been walking for an hour and traversed the entire town, the Writers' Village, and that the rain had stopped, a few drops were still landing on his hair and eyelashes or was this just a heavy mist in the wake of the storm, unexpectedly he found himself on the edge of a wood with a small park and a clearing from which he could hear the laughter of a group of young girls at a picnic table having lunch, they were Eddy's five friends, still celebrating and gathered around Peter's fiancée Daphnée, Daphnée, who was showing off a big, shiny new ring, let's toast the bride-to-be, one of them said, these were the five in whose notepads Daniel had added his own evanescent signature when, a few hours earlier, they'd displayed pages already signed by numerous other authors, and the elation of the girls' charmingly improvised forest feast meant not one of Eddy's friends had noticed him, who knows, thought Daniel, maybe they're five workers who've escaped the confines of the factory and their boss's eye, and the veil gathered up on the bride-to-be's head was a little rumpled from her walking in the rain, the other four had tiaras, and was it the effect of the fog and mist or of the sun breaking through and hitting the hills that, in the rambunctiousness of the moment, each one of them appeared to be wearing a crown of precious stones, some blonde, some brown, all of them with long hair still glistening from the rain and, the way Mai would do, they were dressed in jean shorts and halter tops that showed off their flat stomachs bronzed by the sun, and like Mai their legs were long and slender and they were wearing ill-fitting shoes high as stilts, thought Daniel, dizzying and dangerous, all of them princesses like his daughter and as determined as her as well, and he, Daniel, was merely the father of a child who effortlessly projected, as did these five, royal airs not at all their own, how refreshing was this scene in the forest, thought Daniel, such a welcome distraction from the sombre meditation he was to deliver during the evening's conference, and with admiration, but also concern, Yinn surveyed the girls trying on their beautiful costumes for the evening show, all of them his laborious creations, Geisha needed knee-high boots made of material as light and versatile as feathers in order for her to seem more a creature of the natural world as she danced, yes, for Geisha to give the impression that she was flying she needed to go with the striped bird-like outfit that clung to her voluptuous, sexy body, this is good, he thought, be a little less indecent and a little more creative, my darlings, you don't always have to be caressing your sex, and Robbie remarked to Yinn that the provocative gestures they were making were often inspired by Yinn's own dancing and poses, that may be, said Yinn, but make them with grace, so that the provocative has elegance even when it's lascivious, be subtle, make only the suggestion of sexual desire because, my beauties, no matter how deceiving your costumes are, tonight every woman and man must lust after you and cry out we love you, we adore you, yes, you're good enough to eat, okay, and then suddenly the dictatorial Yinn dragged Victoire off to the fitting room and sat her down before a mirror, saying sorry, but this space between the dressing room and that old velvet curtain separating us from the stage is the only place where we can try things on, I can see you're preoccupied, said Yinn to Victoire, I can see your past is troubling you, so make this cabaret your home until you are back on your feet as an engineer, you have an open invitation to join us on the set, but I know nothing about the stage, said Victoire, isn't that the truth, even for a short time the stage is much too delicate a profession for a soldier, for the warrior I may be or am not anymore, and Yinn said again, that's all in the past, it's appalling that they've stripped you of all your credentials and combat medals, so then I'll be a woman engineer, answered Victoire timorously, really, I can do that, I've been asking around at employment agencies and have left them my new name and address, though I've been waiting for months already and I've heard nothing, that's the silence of discrimination, said Yinn, nothing but, now look in the mirror and tell me how you feel in these wigs, Victoire, ha, you've got great hair, and these little tricks delight our audiences even more, heavier eyelashes and you'll look like a diva, let me have some fun with your makeup for the sheer pleasure of revealing the striking woman you're going to be, a divinity from this evening forward, and Victoire said her mind was a jumble of images, not mentioning they were bloody ones and that, as always, her soldier's baggage meant she wanted to sort out the problems of the world, she thought of the pointless suffering in Burma, that if there is no harmony, just hostility, between Buddhists and Muslim fisherfolk, if Muslims cannot sell their fish or vegetables in the markets, theirs is just one more form of apartheid, and when, Victoire's mind travelling on to devastated countries elsewhere, countries in which parents weep over the gravesites of children who have perished for want of medication, these people oppressed by the junta and in misery for more than half a century, chased from their homes and villages into refugee camps where they die in the thousands, refugee camps overwhelmed by disease, countries where they burn mosques and children's prayer books, burn everything, and yet, thought Victoire, Buddhists and Muslims should get along, what was in fact so seditious was the military, soldiers seizing power and then doing what they always do, commanding and destroying, rapidly spreading a blanket of hate across a country and installing dictatorships, these thoughts left her inconsolable, when, she asked herself, when would the so-called reforms of military dictatorships be contested, could soldiers embrace compassion rather than destroying and laying waste to everything around them, could they ever be decent, and Victoire wondered what she might have done in Burma, would she have protected people or killed them, and here she was now on a stool in the fitting room of a cabaret looking at Yinn's large silhouette in the mirror as he bent over her to do her makeup and hair, so tonight she would be a female impersonator, better to have no work at all, she was thinking as she said to Yinn, you realize I have no clue about this, I'm no good as a dancer, oh, I'll teach you, Yinn replied, the main thing is to forget all the injuries you've suffered, we'll make sure you have a good time, and Yinn, thought Victoire, was pretty convincing, how enticing but very strange it was to be surrounded by the lot of them, she was still jolted by the language they used, like when Robbie yelled from backstage, hey Yinn, you made these panties so tight I've got one ball hanging out all the time, I gotta tuck it back in before the show tonight or if not... prompting laughter from all the others trying on their outfits after rehearsal, and, immobile before the mirror, Victoire felt Yinn's hands tussling a head that, metamorphosed by a wig and overbearing makeup, was no longer her own, she who was normally modest, did this flattering wig and novel array of colours not make her seem overbearing, Victoire wondering who she really was and who she would become with Yinn and company, she thought of all the guns and flags and weapons of her previous life she'd laid out so proudly in her room along with her medals and decorations, that was the secret she kept there, she could still recall the military engagements of the past and how her strength and vigour had been honoured because she'd been, in those days, such a courageous man always looking out for his buddies, Déesse was in the apartment keeping watch so that no one would enter this sanctuary in which both her past and present were sacred, where she still feared she might be attacked, not as the conquering soldier but as the woman she had become, or would be once her transformation was complete, once she was that woman of future days, the woman she so ardently longed to be so that the final battle between her two selves, the terrible vulnerability of being two people but always so alone, would end, at last the choice had been made and yet it was now this woman at the dawn of her new being, of her innocence, who was being threatened and hunted down, how could she possibly explain to Yinn that even though she felt a degree of peace in the Acacia Gardens, that place of friendship and warmth, peace in its arcade of lemon trees, peace listening each morning to the cooing of doves at her window knowing that in the Gardens she was finally free of racists and sexists, rescued from all of them in a new community so winning in its understanding and solidarity, that she still could not shake off her terror of segregation, yes, she thought, the flame of hatred burned so bright that despite her not being persecuted, still she felt this way, and then, as if he could read her mind, Yinn gripped her shoulder gently and said again, Victoire, this is just bad stuff from the past, you must live in the now, Victoire, wake up, the present is everything and the present is ours, and Victoire listened without daring to believe. Daniel followed a path of thorny roses, it was, the sign was there for him to read, the Oscar Wilde Trail, its rose hedges glistening in the rain and beginning to steel themselves against the fall and winter, not to flourish again until the spring, in the wildness of their being they were so thorny and uncultivated that touching them in cold weather brought a drop of blood and, recalling those less ornery bushes, Daniel remembered the paths of red roses in vases that had led him so often to the house of Olivier and Chuan, or was it that Chuan had transplanted the red roses into pearled vases for Mère's birthday, the floral arrangements a show of her designer's skills, or, during the nights of celebration for Mère, had the borders of the paths been lined with the flowers Chuan called angel's trumpets, they glow at night, Chuan told her, I remember them near a fountain, Daniel recalled, and Chuan said, walk a little further on and you'll arrive at the cabin where Olivier wrote his articles, you could smell the ocean from the cabin, and Daniel remembered running toward Olivier, flanked by his dogs as he opened the door for him, Olivier, said Daniel as he gasped for breath, I read the article you wrote this week and wanted to tell you how dead-on it was, and Olivier said, come in and let's talk about it some, so my young friend, you think as I do that racist hatred will never go away, that's what you've come to tell me is it, well no, I'm afraid it won't, he said regretfully, and then his attention pivoted to Jermaine and Samuel, unruly boys he told to go play somewhere else rather than so close to the cabin interrupting the silence he needed to be able to work, still, he never said Jermaine's or Chuan's name without feeling, guess I'm just a grumpy old writer, children have to amuse themselves, of course they do, why at their age I was fighting police in Birmingham, once one of them stuck his gun in my neck before he took it away, maybe noticing I was just a kid, the days of killing and lynching kids was over, I guess that's what he was thinking when he retracted the gun, who knows why he put the revolver back in its holster, Olivier said, come on in, my dear Daniel, we can talk about your book and let Samuel and Jermaine, those little rascals, run off down the beach, yes, that was when Olivier the journalist had been furiously active on political and social fronts, was he not always out and about with Chuan on his arm in those days, typically wearing a white cotton tunic and yellow shoes, she was the one who'd suggested the yellow-shoe flourish, having decided her husband had no fashion sense and needed her help with his elegant bohemian look, Olivier, shutting himself up in his cabin for hours, surrounded by piles of paper, frequently phoned his wife to tell her how much he loved her but also to ask after Jermaine's studies and how he was doing at school, he worried about how much time the boy spent on sports instead of school, this was the period of Olivier's feverish activity in the cabin, of delivering papers at university conferences and denouncing all forms of what he described as the systemic racism of universities and colleges discouraging Blacks and Hispanics from higher education, it was the high point of Olivier's eloquence and his physical stamina too, he'd been an indefatigable walker, a time now past, thought Daniel, because for many years Olivier had succumbed to serious depression and a condition that depleted his nerves and muscles, now Olivier was not going out much at all, only seeing his writer friends at an annual celebration over which he presided, still in a white suit but not walking anymore, pushed in a wheelchair by Chuan or his son Jermaine, and he who'd so enjoyed debating would speak in a barely audible voice knotted with dread, so wanting to communicate as before but not able to, though here along the rose path withering in the fall the man Daniel remembered was the friend of his youth, the man who, from his cabin by the sea, had coaxed the words Daniel had needed to write his first book, because, said Olivier, it was imperative for the diverse and dissimilar voices of every revolution to be heard, voices united in a chorus determined neither by class nor by the colour of a person's skin, and at the edge of the woods at the end of the Oscar Wilde Trail, Daniel approached a young man on a bench reading and making notes, the young man said he was a student and that the subject of his thesis, he announced with a certain pride, was the opprobrium and punishment undergone by the great novelist and playwright, see where his name is hidden now, at the end of the path and the name on the sign barely legible, why, he asked Daniel, why this disparaging of so many writers, why must they constantly face denunciation and contempt, I have the unfortunate name of Alfred, as in Lord Alfred Douglas, the most traitorious of our great Irish author's friends and the cause of his downfall, how unfortunate, their encounter, you'd think God had plotted a calamitous meeting to plumb the limits of endurance of an author far too sophisticated not to challenge the mores expected of him, not even his creator's, and so he was maltreated and unloved by the man he adored too much and his career and reputation devastated, yes, I'll say it again, what a catastrophe to be undermined this way, and Daniel, sitting next to the impassioned and loquacious young man, said yes, it was unfortunate and, as you say, a betrayal, certainly a calamitous encounter with treason, Oscar Wilde simply did not recognize the slandering and murderous traitor beneath the angel face, said Daniel in response to the young man's affecting advocacy, someone he could not help comparing to Stephen, Alfred was probably a decade younger but they were quite alike in their anticipation of disappointment in love, or was it that this Alfred resembled, as much as Wilde, Stephen's wholehearted embrace of love in all its deception and malignancy, some way away, in Charles and Frédéric's house, Stephen was in residence and writing his novel, possessed by his own Lord Alfred Douglas, a lord of the streets, a thief, a liar, and now a pusher in the town jail wearing the numbered uniform of any common jailbird, reflected Daniel as the student Alfred turned toward him, the distinguished features beneath his large, square reading glasses were those of an intellectual and he said, it seems to me that the recompense of suffering such humiliation is the work that came later, without a doubt "The Ballad of Reading Gaol" would never have been written had he not endured two years of forced labour that usually would break a man but, in Wilde's case, vindicated his writer's purpose because, the young man suggested, to write as a means of superseding such degradation is akin to a holy quest, is it not, though maybe a pointless, inexplicable one, and Daniel, who was watching the sky cloud over, murmured, not so much a quest as fate bending us to its whimsical laws, and the student said, Lord Douglas's betrayal of an artist elegant even in his challenging of conformity, foolishness, and ignorance, enrages me, yes, Alfred repeated, it's scandalous, though perhaps the real saboteur was Douglas's father, the Marquess of Queensberry, imagine the perverse application with which the Marquess sought to discredit so great a soul, dragging him through the mud, drowning his genius, now that really is unconscionable, but it's all going into my thesis, what we're talking about is important, the young man said, adding, it's going to rain again, and rising from the bench and opening his umbrella as Daniel, lost in thought, remained seated, he says I'll come and hear you at the plenary session tonight but that he was on his way to find other, more out-of-the-way authors' trails and needed to run because the storm was coming on, and then Daniel, thinking he should get back to the hotel and write for a few more hours, said, you know there'll be hundreds of us writers and poets tonight, there'll be so many of us we'll make no sense of what the other is saying no matter how special that voice may be, no, we'll not be able to, but Alfred was already gone, his footsteps sounding along the path, and suddenly Daniel heard the storm rumbling in the distance and remembered, clear as if they were standing right in front of him, the two little girls whose lives he would talk about in the evening, they seemed to be imploring him to help, suffering in silence as only animals and children can, one of them, escorted by two men, had been turned away from the new country, barred and sent back by force to the homeland where, she knew, her destiny was a black hole, an abyss of such violence she would never survive it, despair, adult despair, was engraved in the child's fearful face, it was evident in her widened eyes and pursed lips, she was innocently holding a toy to her chest, a plush pony still in its cellophane wrapper, no doubt a gift from the country that refused her entry beyond its barred immigration office, the impersonal waiting rooms, the bedless dorms and sleeping on the floor in a heap of tangled bodies, the alluring fantasy of welcome rudely interrupted by her rejection and then deportation by bus or plane to cities run by narcos where the young girl, and she knew it, would be raped or tortured or killed. The second child gripped a blood-stained shawl tightly, she was lying down and seemed to be asleep but beneath her blonde curls her eyes were half open, her school had been obliterated by bombs and the little girl had one arm raised like a broken wing, beneath her blood-stained shawl her chest and other arm were wounded, she was waiting for an ambulance, for help, there was no remonstration in her eyes and her silence was like that of an animal wounded in Palestine or wherever she was, nothing but smoking red ruins around her, and Daniel wondered who would come to rescue her, and wasn't it already too late, he thought about each of the girls with that inertia of the spirit which comes from admitting oneself to be culpable and powerless, it was as if he were waiting late into the night for Mai to come home wondering where she was and knowing nothing, sleeping out in those early days of her disturbing relationship with Manuel who, along with his dad, was peddling cocaine to kids, yes, wasn't it so, and riddled with anxiety Daniel would say nothing to Mélanie, always calmer and more confident when the children ran free, was it that she believed the link between mother and child to be steadfast while he was doubting Mai's free-spiritedness and friends, more freedom for our children brings more trials for us, thought Daniel, who would suddenly feel contrite during the wait for Mai over which he had no power or control, yes, tonight's plenary would be the occasion for talking about the two little girls, forgotten heroines of an unending flight of children trampled underfoot in our wars, by our internecine quarrels and utopian revolutionary movements, what a mess of martyred children's flesh, yes, these would be his words, a river of animal and human flesh is how Olivier might have put it, for this we shall never be pardoned, no, never, and walking the breadth of the Writers' Village back to his hotel Daniel spied authors seated at tables with their books, protected from the rain by parasols and tents, long lineups of readers and photographers in front of them, Daniel following an inconspicuous path down a lane of pine trees to bypass them, the same photographers violating the writers with their cameras as they did every year and compiling with each visit images they'd keep for a long time, intimate and lasting portraits of the authors, many of them increasingly worn down and consumed by the experimentation of their work, others secure in their success, though, as Eddy said in speaking of his London friend, the deceased poet, there was always some gap in the ranks, some writer or two or three never to be seen again, no avoiding what is the fate of each one of us and no getting used to it, it's just the way things are, sighed Eddy, still in the full vigour of his youth, the bell also tolls for poets and picks them off one by one, isn't it outrageous for poets to die just like everyone else? And Daniel's thoughts turned to young Alfred, who was wedded, in the imagination, to the heroism of Oscar Wilde, in the toil of preparing a thesis on his favourite author the student had discovered, without knowing it, love and empathy just as Stephen, in Charles's house, working every day with such assiduity and discipline at the desk at which Charles himself used to write, had become, without a doubt, Charles in his own right, though the two were also alike because of Stephen's book about Eli, the cynical hero who was no such thing but whose intriguing flaw compelled Stephen to write about him so that, like Alfred, he was unearthing feelings of love and empathy transforming his writing into something palpable and real as he worked, Eli no longer seemed locked away but there before Stephen in the room, perhaps a cell, where Charles did all his writing, and suddenly Stephen's writing in solitude was not that but, as it was for Alfred, a chance to live the experience of many, a leap into several adventures and experiences at once, an exhilarating fugue undertaken without ever having to leave his chair, while the body laboured alone the rest was carried away on a wave of the unconscious, no longer aware of its mortality nor caring to know because the fictions his mind engendered knew none of the normal boundaries, the writer writing was no longer contained by a body or a room but propelled outward, galloping astride the untamed horse of the imagination carrying him across plains of snow and leaving no trace, ah, this is how it was, thought Daniel, just as he had said to Eddy in the bar, writing was a way of choosing madness without going mad, yes, and the challenge was to master a folly that could barely be controlled, and Eddy grinned listening to Daniel's somewhat drunken exegesis, not at all surprised because he was so accustomed to authors, enlightened or simply quixotic, confiding in him. And in the fitting room of the cabaret, safe in Yinn's care, Victoire reflected on the letter she had received not long before, and then reread every day since becoming a woman, she thought of all the mothers of young soldiers suddenly confiding in her, of the young transsexuals who wanted her advice, all manner of voices rising like a chorus of prayer, so why then did Victoire still feel alone when she was not, for she consoled and reassured everyone in solidarity, as if she had discovered some maternal instinct buried deep inside and previously mute in her man's torso, but palpitating for the mother who had lost her son in Vietnam only hours before the peace agreement of 1973, a mother still crying every day despite the passing of time, I feel, the mother wrote Victoire, as though each morning the colonel's phone call comes again, in public they spoke not about dead men and women but of the reduction in the number of troops, my son being one of that number, just another of many, that morning marked the end of my life in a simple phone call, she wrote, he was twenty-three and no more than a number, a soldier without a name like all the rest, I wasn't informed whether my son had been killed or wounded, no, just that he was the victim of an enemy operation, the number of deployed troops was being reduced bit by bit, and yet bombing had started again that very same day, maybe my son wasn't careful enough, I expect not, he was always an absent-minded boy and all he thought about was coming home, and as Victoire listened to the silent tears, becoming as she did both mother and child, the son's violent end enraged her, and the irreparable heartbreak of the mother unable to move forward or back saddened her, Victoire felt like she'd been breathing in the noxious air of a marsh so oppressive that she was suffocating from her own memories because the story was also hers, this despite having escaped at last from the same deep bog, and even though she, Victoire, had finished her tour of the incessantly renewed and upgraded insurrection in one piece, victorious and decorated long after the other young soldier's demise, long after he had fallen, in 1973, his body decomposed in a tropical swamp somewhere, poor kid, Victoire figured, she had known, above all, how to survive, yes, perhaps she'd done so in anticipation of her secret transformation, that was where her courage lay, more so than in handling weapons, she had renounced, in the body that was now hers, the praise that was lavished on her, the bravery and capacity for killing they called exemplary, she'd also received a letter from Sabrina, a twenty-year-old transsexual who, in her jean shorts, went out to the shops at night because she was harassed during the day, she'd had her handbag stolen, during the day she constantly heard low muttered insults, hey girlie-boy, you wanna slap or maybe a kick in the balls, Sabrina wrote Victoire how she was worn out and degraded by it all, by guys on the sidewalk in front of taverns spitting at me and my friends for going out together, we're simply a small group of friends, but they spit on the pretty dresses we wear, they call us negresses with hard-ons beneath our skirts, we get that all the time, so we only go out at night when there's a bunch of us, believe me, Victoire, black trans are treated the worst, you white girls, how could you know, I'd like to be a model and paint my nails, and that's why they spit on us, all we're doing is going to a store and they humiliate us, they throw bottles at us, we coloured girls, we're tortured, we're disfigured, Victoire, do you remember Brandy, Brandy who was killed in California, that despicable murder started with her being shot in the genitals, and what about Diamond who was hacked to death with an axe in Philadelphia in July, they found her in pieces days later, and what did her killer say, that he'd panicked when he found out she wasn't a female hooker, so by this logic killing trannies makes sense, we need a ceremony, wrote Sabrina, yeah, a memorial to all our sisters so they won't be forgotten, a day of remembrance for the slaughtered rebels, Victoire, you'll see how few of us die old, that's not going to happen, neither to us nor to you, Victoire, we'll be raped or we'll be killed, yes, you'll see, it can't be any other way, and that's what fills me with despair, Victoire, how short our lives will be, so let's make them a lavish display of the most gorgeous of feminine rites, why not, I'm still hoping to work as a model, they say I'm kind of cute, I used to live with my grandmother, she was a very religious woman and wanted to convert me, she made my uncles beat me and torment me, I was the oldest of eight but I had to get away because they were going to kill me, my grandmother was always at church praying for me, that's how it started, my coming out, my grandmother loved me but let my uncles be cruel to me because they thought it was right to do all kinds of bad things, to satisfy their own vices, so I got into drugs and booze, but I didn't want that life, I take good care of myself because I want to be a model and it'll happen soon, real soon, I've had some invitations already, we so-called coloured girls, we got to leave all that damage behind us, yeah, we got to stop being prostitutes too, like I've done, which is all to say that out of caution I take scissors with me and only go out at night, anyone messes with me they get ripped, you have to look out for yourself, and Victoire was haunted by all the painful messages she was receiving, sure, she was thinking, you really do have to defend yourself, and Robbie came into the dressing room and saw Victoire's shoulder tattooed with a scorpion in the mirror next to Yinn, and he said to Victoire a little histrionically, as if he were already on stage, I dream of the strength of that scorpion, I'd trade that for the words ROBBIE BELONGS TO DADDY tattooed on me because it's not so easy for a predator to have his way with a scorpion, but oh, said Victoire, everything in nature is vulnerable, and Robbie said even sugar daddies are predators so keep your distance, even if they come to see us dance every single night, Victoire, and listen to me, don't be too proud to work the audience with your collection jar, you'll need to forget the man you were and endure the humility of being a mere woman, men, really, they just take without asking but women are forced to beg even when they're scared, you'll never forget your womanhood when you hold out the bucket, yup, you'll know it, said Robbie, and you'll smile at them all, and when you're up on stage singing don't be taken aback if men, women, girls, and boys forget all manner of discretion and just shove greenbacks in your bra, oh Victoire, my Victoire, you're magnificent, said Robbie admiringly, but you're proper too and it's the whirlwind of illusion that makes the audience think they can do here whatever they can't do anywhere else, and the requisite of that illusion is you, you'll know how to play the game and just how far to go, so don't let their tastelessness put you off, not even when a man's sticking a bill down your lace panties and his finger violates you, no, don't get your back up, Victoire, it's all just a game, their caressing and obsessing is a fantasy of rape, they dream of touching us all over if only to figure out what sex we are, and you'll see Know-It-All, Heart Triumphant, Geisha, and Santa Fe leaving counterfeit bills on the stage so that the audience feels a push to be generous, and afterwards big, tall Geisha blithely scoops them up with a shovel, that's when the real money starts raining down and we all go up and take a share, this is the humble begging we do, said Robbie, and I should warn you not to be proud, much less vain, but, continued Robbie, giddy with his own discourse, consummate in your modesty as you are now, the way Yinn is doing your hair, darling Victoire, we're all so happy you're with us, and Victoire told Robbie she wouldn't like people touching her all over, not that she had ever been prudish, hell no, but she did appreciate courtesy and good manners, when you've seen what I've seen, she said, civility is of the essence, and then she was silent, and Lucia asked Raphaël if Kim had found a name for her little daughter, yes, what was to be the name of the round-headed child with her eyes fixed on Orange, the parakeet, her shining eyes indicated how happy she would be to hold the bird and have it all to herself, and Raphaël said no, it will bite if you get too close, why don't we call her our Pearl Redeemed from the Sea, that or change her name every day, Pearl Redeemed from the Sea because Kim and I conceived her on the beach under a full moon, Pearl Redeemed from the Sea because she was born right by it, isn't that so, baby, he said, dangling the child in his arms, or maybe we could call her Silence, like her mother, who refuses to speak, hard-headed Kim, except that our Pearl Redeemed, she talks and she cries, at night especially, so Pearl Redeemed from the Sea will do for now and tomorrow we'll think about it some more, when she grows up she can choose her own name, I want her to be free like all my other children, I won't box her in like other parents, she's not a toy, she's our daughter born to freedom, no boots or shoes for her, why, she already has a wild side I really like, isn't that so, baby, said Raphaël, as fascinated by his restless jumping child as, in turn, she was with Orange, it's a pity, thought Lucia, that Fleur was so far away from Kim and the Mexican and seeing none of this, and Lucia remembered Merlin, the precocious parakeet Merlin, whom Mabel had taught to tell colours apart, pecking at anything red and in his raucous voice calling out red, red, and the same thing with the colour blue, though green was his favourite, for a long time he'd astonished the kids on the wharves, so trusting of Mabel that he let her rock him, and Mabel said if he'd not been killed then her parakeet would have learned to count, and Lucia promised to give Orange to Pearl, Kim's little round-headed girl Pearl Redeemed from the Sea, when its dark waters had for so long been a torment to Kim, when she'd been no more than a street kid by Fleur's side, and that she would take Mabel's cue and teach Orange the colours, red, blue, green, and who knows, maybe she'd be able to teach it numbers too, and this promise was not lost on Pearl Redeemed from the Sea, but what the child wanted most of all was to have the bird to herself, and when her father said no, not too close or Orange will bite, Pearl screamed to make sure her wishes were better understood, high, piercing screams that still grated in Lucia's ears as she cycled along, screams communicating her urgent desire to master not only the bird but the world in which she had decided she would live, this would be her turf, a world of chattering parakeets, for the baby's cries, thought Lucia, were also cries of joy, and Daniel was worried about being followed as he walked back to the hotel, who were these people walking by in quiet cohorts, hands clasped behind their backs, where could they possibly be going, perhaps they were the same mob of students he'd seen hanging from the refectory windows at breakfast that morning, only those students had been angry militants and this lot with their heads bowed seemed utterly subdued as if proceeding to some horrible punishment, surrounded on all sides by hordes of children, teenagers practically, and one of them pushed Daniel back with his rifle butt and told him, you useless intellectuals will be going up with them to the Hill of Crucifixions and, said the adolescent with a flash of resemblance to Augustino, we'll waste no time burning your books in one big sacrificial pyre, except that Daniel's son would never have been one of these terrorist thugs, no, never, crucifixion hasn't been practised since primitive times, he told the boy, and then Daniel awoke to find he was in his hotel room putting the finishing touches to his evening presentation and writing to Mai, my sweet little Mai, he wrote, in such primitive and barbarous times, my dear Mai... but the words faded and went out and he was left with only his dream, a terrible one, so awful sleep could not extinguish it, dear Mai, today I tried to find your brother Augustino among the other young writers here, alas, he wasn't with them, who knows, maybe tomorrow I'll find him, there are quite a few who haven't got here yet, some were sentenced to prison for their work but our international writers' associations or unions finally managed to free them, some were supposed to be here yesterday but we don't know if their departures were delayed or cancelled or even where they are at the moment, and that has us all worried, it's too soon to say they've been disappeared, too early, and Daniel's train of thought was interrupted when he noticed an envelope had been slipped under the door of his room, it was a message from Eddy suggesting he be in the lobby at five, buses would be waiting to take the writers to their dinner and conference on the mountain, Eddy also inviting Daniel to raise a glass in friendship at the Celtic Tavern before he departed, a toast to harmonization among peoples, that word *harmonization*, the awkward wording and naïveté of Eddy's hastily scrawled note moved Daniel, it was a spirited term but so outdated no one used it, he wondered if Eddy had registered nothing of this heinous life but then remembered the group of girls picnicking in the sunny park and their carefree laughter and decided that harmonization was perhaps the most apt word even if it was seldom uttered, was not the laughter of Eddy's five friends like the song of birds so marvellously unconcerned with the ugliness of the world, with its *disharmony*, that they were unable to be sour, a harmonization, Eddy added just as awkwardly, comparable to that shared by poets, and then Daniel reflected on his bad dreams again, malicious dreams, nightmares determining our futures, for do we not dream today that which we shall be tomorrow, these dreams, sometimes so malevolent, are they not predictions sometimes, forewarnings to an emperor and president bound unavoidably toward the hara-kiri or the assassination they'd dreamed of the night or week before, and worked so hard to avoid, their terrifying nightmares warning them of these perils, each trying to make light of his fears with unflappable good humour and a show of appetite for life, one saying, of what he'd seen in his dreams, it's so easy to kill a president from the top of a building with a telescopic rifle, they'll be done with us and there's nothing we can do, dismissing any anxiety almost with amusement, his relaxed and jovial manner noted by family, by friends, as if there was nothing unusual or worrying in it, just a will to live better, the monstrous clarity of the inimical dream dulled by the routine of days, as is so often the case with the warmth of friendship or passion in love, so that one might conclude the terrible dream had dissipated, casting just the subtlest of punishing shadows over every pleasure, over each day and hour the emperor and president continued to live, one seeking to sidestep the advent of his ineluctable suicide and the other the eye of his aggressor's weapon through routines self-consciously undertaken in a state that feels unassailable in the moment, the walk along the seashore must be taken, so too the swim and the deep breath before, or come afternoon, losing oneself in trying presidential speeches that use up the beautiful and lasting effects of the dawn, for addressing others means taking on division, though in mornings by the sea nothing was tarnished yet, and it was still possible through salubrious living to exorcise the bad dream, the nightmare, the sobering assessment of an enemy, it was still possible to forget everything of the gratuitous night-thought until later, until the hour of reckoning when a bullet hurtled toward you from the top of a building as if heaven sent, thought Daniel, who, holding Eddy's invitation in his fingers, decided that he too needed to expunge the bad dreams nagging at him with a felicitous lightness of being, as we usually do, for how else are we able to get up every day in a world replete with terrors, do we not do the opposite, rising confidently in the morning expecting the sponge of the new day to wipe away the stains of the night, and now Daniel wondered if he might again run into the young writer of erotic literature determined to remain incognito behind whatever pseudonym he'd chosen, his lighthearted nature something of a tonic in these terrible times in which writers can be locked away like common criminals, when the young author was still writing books the critics deemed too serious, he'd changed his *nom de plume* to something more racy, because the erotic trifles he was writing were also titillating and he needed to eliminate all traces of the poor, starving author he'd once been, so poor that he'd been looked down upon like some bum, it's not worth writing if you're poor and despised, he declared, nothing is more goading and depressing, imagine, Daniel, publishers arriving at the airport in taxis to fetch their bestselling first-time novelists while I'm there waiting for the bus into town in the rain, think of one of Balzac's miserable characters in dirty clothes, worn collar and suit, like them I'd become petty and mean, no more amiable than Balzac's miserable folk, no, the poverty of a serious writer was lesson one for me, lucky are the few that haven't had to learn it, so I decided that was all going to change, I'd be *admired* because of my books, I'd be rich, and bingo, once I'd decided to write in a different way, to write to entertain and for the pleasures of the senses, every door was open to me, after all, who wants to hear about the world as it is, my friend, I was misguided in being so grave, and Daniel listened, thinking this young man was in some way the antithesis of Augustino, here was an Augustino setting his own values aside and writing breezily in order to draw people in, but Daniel was not able to listen for long as their conversation was cut short by the author's agents, secretaries, and friends sweeping him off to the bar, to Eddy's Celtic Tavern, where, with the arrival of the writers at the hotel, the drinking went on late into the night, though the young author did have time to ask Daniel one thing, what would you do in my place, he said, I mean how can an author be well meaning and write fluff and still hold on to his reputation, be what he wants to be, a patron to down-and-out writers, a prince to outcast girls, money should allow you anything, shouldn't it, without corrupting you, I mean can't a person have it all, or am I simply guilty because I am rich, I who'd been so impoverished and unknown, try living from your pen as I did and you'll see, you'll be destitute in no time, just another hungry vagrant pitied by no one, and Daniel would have liked to console the prolific young man who was barely out of penury, answering, paternally, as he would have done with Augustino, are not the terrible circumstances of poverty and misery often part and parcel of being a writer, think of young Dickens, aged twelve and slaving in a factory with his parents in debtors' prison, or of the young Norwegian novelist Hamsun wracked with hunger during his lengthy, self-imposed, and penitential exile in the United States, except, the young author was quick to interrupt, I despise poverty and hunger, and besides, why should it be those who choose art over mediocrity who suffer the most, let's face it, the truth of poverty is that it's degrading, I've turned all these tribulations into a lab of unexplored projects, the young author said mysteriously before disappearing and leaving behind a quizzical Daniel for whom a second message was waiting at the hotel, this one from Stephen the recluse, alone in Charles and Frédéric's place with the book he was writing, and, just as had been the case with the young erotic novelist proclaiming, if only to spice up his writing, his ennui, Daniel no longer knew what to think of Stephen and the narrative he'd invented around his new hero Eli, in Stephen's account, though where did truth end and a novel begin, the facts were that a sexual predator was being hunted all over town, this man a perpetrator of the worst of crimes because he was aware that he was seropositive for an illness as incurable and infectious as the plague, he'd had numerous partners, male and female, but had been indifferent to the risk of contaminating the men and women now laying charges against him, victims he had seduced a year or two before but who were only now reporting they had been infected, and despite nothing being said of the man's heroin addiction, the description of this murderer by fornication, a serial charmer you could call him, the description so closely resembled Eli that Stephen was sure it was him, Stephen, who had been unaware of the dark sunglasses Eli wore in his encounters because he was never allowed to accompany him to the clandestine meetings in secret places he used for easy hookups, Stephen wrote that he was anxious for Daniel to come back, quickly, he needed his advice before Eli was freed from jail for the most recent of his misdemeanours, and he'd be free very soon, shouldn't he turn him in, Stephen asked, given his certainty was this not his duty, how much it weighed on him, wrote Stephen, that the sexual predator was Eli, it could only be him, but Daniel, reading Stephen's incriminating words, was more worried for Stephen than for Eli, for Stephen's frustration, his disappointment that Eli was not the person he expected, though most of all it was Stephen's having made Eli the focus of the novel he was writing that disturbed him, a story in which he was elevated from common thug to romantic figurehead, was Stephen not being too swept up by some vindictive impulse against the man who had so abused his trust, was he fantasizing that his hero, already so perverse and toxic, would be accused and summoned and finally tried in court, did Eli have to be punished for not loving Stephen and never being able to, for that was his real crime, was it not, Stephen transported not only by the anger he had suppressed for so long but by his vast and unbridled imagination, in the course of his book he was going to have to spell out just how dangerous a man Eli was, the man he had not feared enough, he who was rendered timid by everything, he who was afraid of germs and bacteria in particular, and yet this man whom only yesterday he had held in his arms was something he did not fear at all, and yet, in his impassioned condemnation of Eli, Stephen also wrote Daniel that Eli pretended to love but avoided any intimacy, and Daniel pointed out that already Stephen's portrait of Eli was changing, that someone as cold, narcissistic, and disdainful of other people's bodies as Eli would have infected no one, and besides, such was his heroin addiction that he was completely narcissistic, any seduction was of himself, his treachery and every calculation he made was to procure drugs, it was only his effect on the young that was deadly, for despite his slick exterior, he had long been nothing more than a tawdry little pusher, Daniel wrote this to diminish Eli's standing in Stephen's eyes, and counter the unwarranted grandeur of the monster Stephen had created in writing his book, and Daniel would have liked to reduce him to nothing at all, so upset was he that Stephen was miserable on Eli's behalf, Eli who was just one more incarcerated miscreant and merited no sympathy from Daniel. You must know, Stephen wrote, that we writers can foresee disasters a short time before they happen but, steered through the night in the low light of our premonitions we can also get it wrong, and oh, how I wish this were true of Eli, that his was still the innocent face I thought I saw when we first met and all the rest of it simply lies, and as Fleur listened to Claudio conducting his music in the Roman concert hall, he thought about what Claudio had said between rehearsals, summarily and hurriedly as always, he'd spoken with remarkable haste, in fact, though even so Claudio liked confiding in Fleur, who was so unlike him, what was it he said with that same extraordinary confidence he displayed as he conducted the orchestra, that he was profoundly religious, yes, adding that it was perfectly natural for him be so, it was family tradition, and Rome struck him as a pious city, or at least one imbued with the faith that was his, he adored the rituals and liturgy of his faith, but Fleur, who only felt rootless in an equally rootless world, listened and asked how Claudio, with such a rock-solid foundation, could possibly understand and conduct music like his own, because was not the shock of living Fleur felt in the music he composed, the sounds of his music those of a universe fraying at the edges and disintegrating, one at odds with Claudio's basic certainties, Claudio, who was always able to respond to chaos with order, or at least with the principles of Christian faith that seemed to him ineffable, inherited as they were from his parents and that he would pass on to his own children in turn, certainties allowing him always to seem so fulfilled and self-assured, free of the torment of egotistical questions such as Fleur asked, and Fleur who found it odd that in the face of the monolith of Claudio's belief, he should feel even more baffled and less certain of himself, perhaps this was the instant in which Fleur thought of the big black notes Beethoven scrawled on the pages of his manuscripts when he turned his attention to himself, did he not write the editors of his music that God was punishing him, yes, that God was abusing his child still so young, this when he started hearing the humming of his incipient deafness as though he were locked in an iron helmet, at least this is how Fleur imagined young Beethoven's intolerable suffering, his no longer being able to hear, not even his own music, and even more humiliating were his nausea and agonizing stomach pains, the raging struggle of his innards that prevented him from going out, the painful colic and assorted afflictions that would never cease, it was essential that his body not abandon him, that he summon his strength, and this was the prayer Beethoven made to a pitiless God as he begged his publishers for the money they owed him, or as he tutored children without talent, but it was an implacable God that descended upon him and stirred up his guts, a chastising God intent on inhabiting his body and breaking it down, yes, God punished his child as if he were not the creator of songs of light but a miserable wretch, a commoner disdained by the women he loved, women who, much as they praised his music, saw in him nothing but an ignoble artist far beneath their social standing, they were not about to risk their fortune and status for this unworthy-looking man with a churlish expression begging them for a quiet space he might compose in, an apartment in the châteaux they didn't know what do with, like any unhappy lover he persisted, persisted despite the mortifying refusals repeatedly made for the sake of the husband, the children, or simply on account of the respect due women of their class, the door was closed to him, and perhaps the travails of the unrequited lover are what can be heard in Beethoven's Violin Sonata No. 4 in A Minor, Opus 23, that Clara had performed so well in concert, the violin's plaintive voice seeking reconciliation as much as pity, then broadening out and appropriating deft notes written for the piano in a swaying movement of anger and indignation, yes, what splendour and fury there was in the violin's lament, here a little subdued, thought Fleur, this the point where the musician must be asking Josephine or one of the other women, why do you not love me, don't you see who I am, who I'll become, need Beethoven really remind himself that none of them was about to live with a man whose companion was pain, colic, an abscess in the jaw or an infected and nearly amputated finger, no, given the grim company of bodily Pain who would become his everyday muse, no woman was about to stand by his side and surely he knew this, thought Fleur as he listened to the song of the violin, it was definitely this sonata that Clara had interpreted so marvellously in concert, and it would have been him at the piano, and where did Beethoven learn, as the astonishing modern composer John Tavener did with the early onset of a cardiac condition, to live with that which tormented him, that if Pain, if Sickness was his muse, then he needed to find inspiration in his arduous duel with himself, of course Tavener claimed to have the Passion of God inside him, a force alien to Beethoven, who repudiated all religious sentiment even as he was writing a mass for a prince to file away neglected in a drawer somewhere so that subsequently it was necessary for these masses, these requiems for his secret Pain, to be sold before they could make their way to us, and their journey would be punishing and humiliating, to what end, hope, to what end, ambition, to what end did God abuse his child, Tavener, by contrast, Tavener, who was a church organist for some fifteen years and claimed to have the Passion of God inside him, Tavener would become God's pianist, pounding the keys until drops of blood appeared at his fingertips, playing his music to the point of manic exhaustion, was this Passion of God something Claudio also felt, Fleur wondered, had the music become for Claudio, conducting one of Fleur's symphonies in all his fervour, as it had for Tavener, more of a prayer than the furious lamentation Fleur had conceived in the streets, in his foul dens, Tavener had also plumbed the depths of the soul, writing, out of the desolation and sorrow he shared with others for a princess lost, his loveliest song of bereavement for a national day of mourning, a poem of William Blake's, "The Lamb," already encapsulating the painful sacrifice of a life, not just in a rain of crystal notes but in the slashing wind and rain and cold, Tavener had written for the masses as much as for the solitary man, alone in the shadows of a Greek chapel lit only by votive candles, a long-haired, dark-skinned vagabond and an aesthete disturbed by the irregular beating of his own heart, this was

Tavener, he who said the voice of a soprano, the voice of a cello, was his cosmic consolation. And what exactly would such a thing be like, wondered Fleur, could it even exist, but as to his music, the *Celtic Requiem*, Tavener, chest so weighed down by crucifixes and his poor health that he likened it to being on the cross, Tavener's music, like Fleur's, either delighted in his ills or was their consummation, a cacophonous requiem of colliding sounds, of footballers, of people yelling, but having also, as so often in his work, the peal of gongs and bells in the silences, Tavener had done well by the materialism he professed to despise but, when the failing heart tolls its own bell, why not have beautiful cars for the race, the race into death's waiting arms, why not taste all life's pleasures before that last gong sounds and then tumbles onto you with its full weight, yes, why not, the music of both of them was tuned to discordant and rebellious hearts, thought Fleur, and it was this art of imperfect music that Claudio, a wise man, seemed to understand in his direction of the symphony, this even though it must have been incomprehensible to him, so foreign to his nature, Fleur was anarchy's child and Claudio raised according to the scriptures of the religion he thought just and enlightened, leaning on it like a rock, did he not go to Mass each Sunday with his wife and children, and had he not said to Fleur, oh my dear friend, it's not simply loyalty to a long-held tradition, way back when I was a soloist for a children's choir in Rome, and then an altar boy, those sharp and ancient smells of chapels, the perfumes, incense, roses, and candle smoke always troubled me, made me think of the faithful kneeling there, I still wonder if any of them had their prayers answered, yes, it's the humility of poor people's supplications that troubles me, I don't share their obeisance and, as concerts are all I think about, I never will, but ah, thought Fleur, Claudio's guileless absorption in music stopped him from contemplating Wrath and any of the wraiths resembling him, phantoms who'd traded in priestly pomp for habits of the street, lurking in the shadows of the genuflecting men and women so as to get closer to the unsuspecting choirboy unaware of anyone stalking him, glancing at him, a shadow in the shadows mingling among the supplicants whose heads are bent in prayer, Wrath's litany of exploits on the banks of the Seine and under its bridges came back to Fleur, yes, had Wrath not delighted in telling him how familiar he was with the cities of Europe and Asia too, how he'd loved Rome especially, and even though he'd taken a good deal of time off from his duties to sojourn there, neither Wrath nor any like him had ever crossed paths with little Claudio, the young soloist of the children's choir who also served as altar boy, the easiest prey, said Wrath, less corpulent and noticeable in those days, though Fleur had no way of knowing whether Wrath's libidinous stories were true, were told in good faith, the dotard, a cynical old man, surely cracked, and Su's indistinct silhouette evaporated with the skein of cigarette smoke sliding from his lips, Su the young musician friend Fleur would see no more, or, thought Fleur, if he did, he'd see shivering on a bench in the Métro, laid out from an overdose, better to put them all out of mind, Jérôme the African, Kim, the baby, all of them, and now the voices of the choir in his symphony swelled, yes, it was like listening to the waves of the ocean, all in a single surge, the call of the flute was like the sun giving way to night, the flute-voice overrode everything, its solitary sound like a siren, yes, there'd been huge black notes full as dark moons, thought Fleur,

Beethoven's musical characters filling the manuscript pages and the ink hardly having the time to dry, still damp and refusing to be effaced beneath the tide of black notes, for the work was never finished, notes abounded in the workbooks Beethoven carried with him everywhere, on the country walks he took outside Vienna, yes, he needed to find succour in some pastoral scene rather than in the city that disdained him, to flee Vienna, yes, Fleur should forget all about them, Jérôme the African and his drumming in the night, Raphaël and Kim, Kim and her baby, all of them, even Max and Damien, the dogs that had warmed them during their cold nights on the beach, Fleur could remember how they smelled after running through the waves and shaking themselves off, only the two dogs sensing the night cop's footsteps, ears standing alert, Damien and Max so brave and watchful, how could he forget them, Fleur wondered, and Daniel accepted Eddy's invitation to meet at the Celtic Tavern even though it was nearly time for the writers to gather in the lobby of the hotel, so many that some were already outside and out front on the sidewalks, the lot of them waiting for the buses that would take them up the mountain to the evening session, the sky was suddenly pinker, streaked with motionless grey clouds, the sky being what Daniel saw from his barstool, its pinks and grey reflected like stained glass on the first autumn frost of the windows above the gentle fire burning in the fireplace that Eddy had lit as if with sleight of hand, Daniel, laptop under his arm, found Eddy who steered him to a quiet corner at the end of the bar where, he said, Daniel could write without being disturbed, Eddy knew writers were always behind in their labours, and did Daniel not have the preoccupied look of a writer dissatisfied with himself, Daniel admitted he was late, and that even the screed he had written was neither completed nor sufficiently convincing, he told Eddy it was impossible to list all the writers who'd been oppressed and persecuted simply for having an opinion, there were too many, too many men and women, journalists and poets and novelists, still being imprisoned, tortured, and killed, one Nigerian writer had been hanged, but Eddy, who was rinsing glasses at the other end of the bar, was not listening, though as if he'd suddenly intuited what Daniel was thinking he came over and said, you may have noticed many of us are wearing black or white, so will a lot of the writers going to what I humbly call our village's celebration for the tenth anniversary of the Festival of Literatures tonight, yes, a lot of them will be dressed like this in memory of the writers we've lost in the past year, many of them friends and colleagues, and also in the name of writers we believe may have been disappeared, said Daniel, this his way of enquiring whether or not the writers expected from Burma, Iran, Turkey, and Vietnam, hours overdue, had arrived, where are they, Daniel asked, but Eddy was busy with a client and seemed not to be listening but then reminded himself of Daniel's preoccupation and, intent on soothing him, said, a few minutes later, but Daniel, don't worry, they still might get here tonight or tomorrow, sometimes it takes a while to get here from Iran or Turkey or Vietnam because they're held up at the border, you know how it is these days, every country is suspicious of strangers, even more so if they've been imprisoned for their work and besides, isn't every writer a stranger in their own land, to be a writer is a singular undertaking, isn't it? Listening to writers, Eddy said, has made me think about all this, the writers I meet right here in the bar, some forced into exile and thus without a home or homeland, and Daniel said, you're right, it's a strange profession indeed, reproaching himself for knowing nothing of exile nor imprisonment despite the audacious claims of his book *Strange Years*, it's easy to feel guilty for being a free writer when so many others are not, thought Daniel, and in the moment it seemed to him that his kids were still sitting on his lap as he wrote, that he was stroking them in their nest as they played with his manuscripts and coloured in the books he was reading, and though of course he did lose patience at being invaded sometimes, he could not write without them, without their laughter and rough-and-tumble, but oh my, that was long ago, he thought with melancholy, even Rudie was no longer as cuddly and affectionate, like the rest he'd grown up too fast, all he could think about now was flying planes through his parents' apartment, the rest of his talents and tendencies electronic, already, thought Daniel, yes, already, and how do you sit a boy on your lap who knows so much and talks like an old soul, this disappointment not one he was about to share with Eddy, who was in the process of pouring a third rum for someone, now doesn't that look good, said Eddy to the reddened face in front of him, one more and I'll forget all my woes, said the customer, you're lucky, the man said, to be so young and able to seduce women, oh well, not all of them, said Eddy, just a few at a time, and overhearing this Daniel thought back to the girls he'd met that afternoon drinking champagne in the park, he thought he heard their laughter bright and clear as Mai's, their garden party had been for Daphnée, soon to be married, and Daniel wondered if it was a mark of senility to constantly wish to be surrounded by joy, by a gaiety now so rare it fuelled great bursts of creativity in him, or was such happiness quotidian and everyone's due but drawn upon only parsimoniously, Eddy's good mood was pleasing to Daniel and as he listened he felt his own lift, promptly telling himself the writers they'd been expecting for several days would be here tonight or tomorrow, he'd been wrong to imagine the worst, he banished the thought of Augustino, missing in his own way from his father's heart, and took comfort in the thought they would be reunited soon, if not, well, that would kill him, the prospect of not seeing his son again was unimaginable, so he would go on living and working, busy as an ant, a mole burrowing into the secrets of the soul, but, thought Daniel, an awkward swimmer in a sea of memories, he'd not be disingenuously morose, he was, despite himself, a lighthearted man wedded to all that shone brightly, he was not one for the dark of night, and Eddy's portly client at the bar said, ah, but my wife, Eddy, you don't know her, she'll give me an earful, she'll tell me again that I'm no more than a drunk, okay, one last glass, my friend, that'll give me strength, my farm's right nearby and I can walk there easily, go on, my friend, just pour in a little more, all these layabouts who think writing books is work have it easier than us farmers, and I wonder what for, eh Eddy, I mean they caper off into the forest for their supper and that's a waste of our money, isn't it, all that pomp and circumstance for people we don't even know, Eddy, you tell me they've come from all over and speak all kinds of languages, but isn't it a little spendthrift for our little village to welcome them like this when we can barely look after ourselves, not at all, exclaimed Eddy wholeheartedly, it's a sublime luxury to have them and besides, they deserve it, and Eddy's customer said, well, me, I don't get it at all, my wife is always telling me how dumb I am, and sometimes she's right, and then, expressing his skepticism again, he said, but hey, all these folks in our cafés and pubs with their panels and discussions that never end, what on earth can they be talking about, eh, and for so long, lounging around in our restaurants with their books in hand, really, what on earth do they find to talk about, I just don't get it, he repeated, anyway, it's time to go home, I guess, and just as Eddy's drunk guest staggered toward the door, a group of writers wandered in asking where their buses had got to, they'd been waiting for ages, shouldn't be long, Eddy reassured them, offering drinks all around, let's raise a glass, welcome to the town, and Eddy, affably as ever, said, we named the Writers' Village in honour of you all, but then Daniel, stepping back a little from those standing at the bar, noticed in the newly relaxed atmosphere that the militants of the morning, the students with their placards, were preventing the buses from pulling up, he could hear their enraged chants of protest, some of them clinging to the hotel windows again and shouting, what about us, the generation of tomorrow, what about us, yet curiously neither Eddy nor the writers at the bar appeared to notice them, and Daniel, searching for her face from the window, mused that Mai could so easily have been among them, and he thought of Suzanne as well, Suzanne who'd come to him that day in the house with the red walls and said, it always upset me when journalists and literary critics visited the house, they always came for Adrien, of course, to sit with Adrien and not me, never a word about whether or not I had written something, oh no, never, after all I was only the wife, oh, my dear Daniel, that's when I decided to leave them to it and to have lunch by the sea with you instead, and during these escapades I found a dear friend in you, you who always asked of me, Suzanne dear, is your book finished, can I read it soon, was this tone not the confiding one she adopted in their outings together by the sea, but perhaps the Suzanne on the wall, photographed when she was still so alive and celebrated for her work, that face now taking its place among those of the other writers who'd died in the past year, perhaps it was not her, and if it was not, thought Daniel, then it must be that her spirit had not quit the world and was speaking to him through the face of some other woman writer whose legacy had been equally bountiful and every bit as much in danger of being unacknowledged and misunderstood as the husband's literary reputation continued to blaze, and either her star had been extinguished by the light of some flamboyant Adrien unintentionally, or it had been put out by his desire to be the only poet in their union, and Daniel thought how, writing discreetly, so discreetly and deferentially in his shadow, Suzanne could only disappear or cease to be, and Suzanne's eyes, silent and serious, seemed to settle on him once again, her mouth creasing ever so slightly in laughter, she who loved laughing so much, hands folded beneath her chin as she said to Daniel, we women slip away quietly but our consciousness remains, we, the women, I, Suzanne, can tell you, but suddenly her words were neither spoken nor mouthed, carried away by the fog, thought Daniel, like voices in a dream. And as Yinn's fingers worked her hair in the dressing room of the Porte du Baiser Saloon, Victoire thought of all the mail coming in every day she could not possibly answer, more with each passing day, though she remembered Mick, who'd written to tell her how much he'd admired her "Sexual Revolution through Tolerance" speech at Trinity College, Mick, who proclaimed that his was one of the very best looks and that he danced like the legendary prince of rock whose dress he imitated, right down to the white socks in patent leather shoes, that was Mick and Victoire had not forgotten him, Mick had been the only one not to boo her, the young lad who mimicked the moon-walker with the impossibly light step, a legend cut short, thought Victoire, Mick had neither laughed nor whistled like the other college kids, but stood up during the class and shouted, bravo Victoire, bravo, don't listen to any of them but don't speak of tolerance either, Victoire, we need to get beyond this word that reeks of the worst kinds of prejudice, this as a clamour of angry, raucous protest rose from the audience and stunned Victoire, and Mick yelled again, bravo Victoire, you and me, we'll fight this sexual revolution together, you better believe it, you're not alone, and Victoire watched as the boy rushed toward her with a bouquet of hibiscus, and again she heard bravo Victoire and found herself looking upon the advancing boy with red lips and waist-length hair, Mick, that was his name, and now Mick had written Victoire to say his parents, his novel-ist mother and historian father, had thrown him out, such cultivated and respectable folks, wrote Mick, they'd put him out on the street with just enough money for him to live somewhere else, to disappear, as they would have had his sister Tammy also do, someone else they didn't want to see here anymore, only his sister was too anemic to follow and, her parents deciding, was now in psychiatric care, and so, Mick wrote, at first he found himself homeless in New York, and then later, hopping off a night bus in Atlanta, another big and disorienting city, he'd met Luke, a Franciscan, who had founded Homes for All in several cities, shelters wel-coming those whom no one else wanted, transsexual teens, young sex workers, and especially youth disowned by their families, expelled for having come out to their often well-to-do parents, yes, Mick wrote, these children of privilege, with their cars and credit cards, who had everything taken away because of their sexual orientation, were pariahs wandering the streets that an epidemic society so shamefully keeps out of sight, and this altruistic man, Luke the Franciscan, had the decency to establish Homes for All dedicated to children banished from their Catholic families on religious grounds, it was impossible to justify, said Luke the Franciscan, he had asked his superiors, even the Pope, to put an end to the scandal, but remained the only one who wanted to exercise any kind of preventative justice on behalf of the ousted teens, Luke had written his superiors asking how the parents' abandon was conscionable in this day and age, how can we, we Christians, let this go on, who will save the children from the heroin they'll turn to in their despair, because it will take no time for them to give themselves up to the drugs street dealers will push on them, and weren't they everywhere, these pushers, and what was Mick up to now, he wanted to create with Luke more Homes for All, often in old garages renovated by volunteers, still it was cold outside and there were not enough beds, Mick wrote, and bravo to you, Victoire, you're brave and I know you're with us in this fight, oh, I know it, if the army has denied you your rights and reviles you for being a woman when once you were an invincible soldier, acclaimed and decorated and now stripped of these honours, is it because diabolical acts are always perpetrated and spread due to some religious principle, but among us you'll have every honour, because you are our liberator, you are the pure love that frees us, you are freeing these last slaves of the shackles of taboo, because who are these banished and disregarded children left hungry and cold and to promiscuity by their parents, who are they but our last slaves branded by the irons of their masters, invisible because they are a subordinate race, whether yellow, white, or black, they're invisible, we do not see them, if only you knew the pitiful state they're in when Luke takes them in, if only people were aware, and it hurt Victoire to read Mick's words, that beds, mattresses, those so disparagingly called *queer* were bereft of everything, he would talk to Yinn tonight, beds, mattresses, we're all in this together, we've got to help them, of course we do, absolutely, though what Victoire felt most of all was her impotence, how feeble her position was because the harm had already been done, because these children were already on the streets of New York, of Atlanta, of teeming cities everywhere, Chicago, Boston, it was too late for them, there was no road back to the beautiful homes their parents had deprived them of, in many cases while they were still in school, they'd been brilliant students too, many of them, presidents of clubs, headed for careers in law or medicine like their parents, when all at once the unerring path of their destiny was moved, you'll be taught discipline and structured thought at the best Catholic schools, their parents had said to these girls and boys suddenly excommunicated and itinerant, younger and hungrier than ever, undercut, Mick wrote Victoire, by conspiring and repugnant voices, one a cardinal and another a bishop screaming from the pulpit that he would rather close the schools and orphanages in his diocese than hire any of these deviant homosexuals, here was religious homophobia in full voice, wrote Mick, and the voice was heard again in Harlem after a young homeless person was killed, saying, why not kill them all, they're nothing to us, but now here came Luke the Franciscan with his Homes for All, Luke, who knew it was necessary for the homes to be safe spaces, for in the regular shelters populated by alcoholics and the mentally ill, children were peed on in the dormitories, they risked being raped or even murdered, so yes, they needed beds and mattresses, wrote Mick to Victoire, it was a privilege to be able to sleep in one of the shelters with so many kids around, their number always growing, every large city was exploding with them, down-and-out runaways, and wasn't this a real scandal, said Franciscan Luke as he denounced the crimes, indifference, and cruelty of his church, we Christians are to blame for this irreparable segregation that is much harder for the girls, in regular shelters and women's centres they get no meals and no showers, so they either peddle drugs or work as hookers and live in the streets, or, if they do use the women's shelters then they're so afraid that they sleep with a knife under their pillow, and yes, in Luke's Homes for All, despite his good relations with volunteers and donors, they were still short of beds and mattresses, truly it was an epidemic, this disavowing of queer children no one but the few social workers in Luke's circle wanted to see, so much needs to be done, some of them are only sixteen or seventeen, but I'm not giving up, wrote Mick, because I know more Homes for All will be established and soon we will have beds and mattresses, and Victoire, I know you understand the scale of the problem because you know what it's like to be set apart and shut out, and Victoire thought, yes, she needed to perform with the others onstage tonight, all these outlandish friends of Yinn's, and despite being unemployed, who knew if she would ever be allowed to work as an engineer again, that yes, she would support Mick and Luke the Franciscan however she was able, she'd not forget her fight in a revolution that was also her own even if, from time to time, she lost faith in any positive aspect to this revolution, for what was the nature of this revolution amid all the others breaking out these days in so many parts of the world, was it a revolution undertaken simply to exist, for people to acquire, without force, the right to be themselves, or, wondered Victoire, could a revolution ever really occur without force, could it ever be non-violent, and Victoire was concerned about Mick, such a frail boy, who knows why his hateful parents had sacrificed him on the altar of their aspiration, perhaps because they were wealthy writers who regretted having brought children into the world at all, that you could reject your own children was something Victoire just could not understand, her own parents still loved her and would go on loving her when her transformation was complete, yes, thought Victoire, tonight, as she and Yinn proclaimed their campaign against hate and prejudice, she would be thinking about them all, and Petites Cendres contemplated Yinn's bare neck yet again, repeating to himself over and over, how can it be, the man I adored had a lush abundance of wavy hair falling over his shoulders, when did Yinn decide on this cut the young kids of the day were getting, had he not betrayed Petites Cendres, was he not less attractive, he wondered, though Petites Cendres still loved him, of course, if in a more qualified way, the flame of passion devoured him less, though perhaps true love was like this, one was no longer entirely consumed, the fire in the grate cooled a little, yes, maybe that was it, he thought, as he noticed a young black man wearing a pink hat coming toward him on a skateboard, hey, Petites Cendres, do you want to jog with me around the square this morning, Petites Cendres, where are you going, by the Wall of the Dead, no no, don't go there, we've lost another seven since the New Year, come, let's have a little fun, Petites Cendres, don't go looking over there, follow me, and Petites Cendres gestured to the skateboarder whose smile flashed in the morning sun that he would not, as if he'd said goodbye to his lost youth, yes, that's what he felt, though not painfully, so sensual was the skateboarder's glide past him, so sweet the sea air, and declining the skateboarder's invitation, he ran along beside the memorial as a procession of men and women carrying armloads of flowers on this day of commemoration, when seven new names would be inscribed on black granite and brass plaques in the cemetery in full bloom that was such an airy place next to the sea, seven names of residents who'd chosen not to leave their families, families supported by the caring attention of Dr. Dieudonné, his nurses and nurses' aides, tended to until the end as if they had been Dr. Dieudonné's long-term patients at the Acacia Gardens, the parents, brothers, and sisters were all there to honour those whose lives had been extended by medicine, though was this an extension of life or simply life, as one of the sick asked his sister, how is it possible to live with the thought that the cup is empty, or if it is half full, knowing it might be emptied in an instant by a heart attack, by worn-out veins, or the constancy of a depression that in the end corrodes nerves subjected to far too much radiation, and then came the moment when it was true, thought Petites Cendres, when indeed the cup was drained, and kneeling before the plaques on which the names had been inscribed Petites Cendres listened to Reverend Stone yet again claim, as he had done before with

Fatalité and Herman, that all these children had a Father called God who was waiting for them in His kingdom, and what a kingdom it was, there were iguanas there, and all the wonders of the animal world so familiar to the island, iguanas, snakes, and birds, he said, white herons and pink flamingos everywhere, these women and men had struggled so, waged the struggle that is life, my friends, and now let us pray to the music of Elton John played here by our friends on the guitar, let us pray for God to open his kingdom to Yan, José, Irvan, Elisabeth, Rachel, Pink, and Tony, oh, helping our brothers and sisters to survive is not enough because, more than surviving, we must *live*, in joy and serenity, my friends, and let us pray that we do not mistreat iguanas there as we do here on this island, that there we shall care for birds that are so often neglected, O Father of these, your humblest creatures, welcome into your bounty those for whom, ineffably and without presumption, we lay red roses upon this stone, this granite, and Petites Cendres listened to the litany of names Reverend Stone pronounced one by one, Yan, José, Irvan, and the names of the women, Elisabeth, Rachel, and didn't it seem as if these last two names, Elisabeth and Rachel, shimmered in the air, who were they and why had Petites Cendres never met them even in Dr. Dieudonné's company, why, among all the other women equally affected, had the suffering of these two been so secret, who had put Elisabeth and Rachel aside when Dr. Dieudonné might actually have visited them as well, these two suddenly appearing in their innocence like Angel, Angel often concealed with his mother behind a screen of lemon and orange trees in the tropical foliage, Angel who hardly left the house any more, Yan, José, Irvan, Elisabeth, Rachel, let us pray for them all, my friends, said

Reverend Stone out on the seaside jetty, and what made Petites Cendres think of Timo in that moment, what made him wonder, then, where the coke smuggler might be holed up, or had he already been stood against a brick wall and shot in some Mexican dump, hadn't the Mexican coast guard, out on a routine patrol, seized his boat *The Majestic* with nine hundred kilograms of high-end cocaine aboard, the boat on its way to Puerto Rico and two suspects arrested, but neither by the name of Timo, no, no one by that name, Petites Cendres remembered as the last of the waves scattered with red roses heaved beneath the sun, and who were Pink and Tony, their families also here today to mourn them, Pink, Tony, Rachel, Elisabeth, headed alone or together to the depths of the ocean, leaving only red petals to be gradually dispersed by the rough water, and with his hair scattered to the wind, Reverend Stone imbued the words of his sermon with a sudden infusion of hope, saying, my friends, our county, so often behind the times in its debates and its laws, at last allows you to marry, oh, this is a historic day, my friends, young or old, marry now, Reverend Ézéchielle of the Community Church and I will have the greatest pleasure in performing your marriages, no requirements, for it's so much sweeter celebrating a collective wedding than blessing the dead, life must bring forth life and happiness, and we have progressive lawyers here to help you with the licences, and all Reverend Ézéchielle and I ask is that we stand together in the spirituality and dignity of our various churches and religions, for did not He Who Sees All say *love one another*, certainly He did not say *be wary of one another, sling mud and cultivate hatred, spite, bigotry, defamation*, no, He said the only precious thing is the gift of love, inestimable in value and not to be coveted but kept alive and as fresh as water from a fountain, as the grain of the earth, yes, and as Reverend Stone came to terms with the sadness overwhelming him as he spoke, Petites Cendres thought about Yinn in his velvets so short on his slender frame during the winter holidays, Yinn so delectable and shivery beneath the red ribbons of his G-string as he strolled along the sidewalk outside the Porte du Baiser Saloon in the January cold, Yinn walking the streets in a bikini or white robe adorned with gold sequins during the dances on cabaret nights, yes indeed, cried out Reverend Stone, his voice hoarse against the wind, yes indeed, there are honest judges who stand up for liberty, but there are other pernicious ones who go about their business with murderous intent, so think, think, my friends, that what is offered to you here today may be taken away tomorrow, defend your rights relentlessly, at midnight Reverend Ézéchielle and I shall bless your unions, but while you are here, heady with the joy of your marriages performed here by the sea beneath an effervescent moon complicit in your emancipation, in your happiness, you'll also hear the infamous voices that condemn you, already I hear such a voice, that of an eminent prelate who proclaims himself Archbishop of the Tropical Dioceses, shamelessly declaring to all the media he is able to command that anywhere he has power and influence, he will call for your excommunication and condemnation, this man, oh, such a venerable dignitary, is truly diabolical, and he will try by any means he can to rescind your rights and to damn you, so marry and pay no heed, do not be as you were before under the heel of such tormentors of the conscience, persecuted and martyred, no, raise your heads up and unite, my brothers, sisters, and friends, for it is a terrible day when I see the names of those we mourn added to the rolls: Yan, Pink, Elisabeth, Rachel, though by this time Petites Cendres was no longer listening, but running further afield, telling himself Yinn was somewhere close by, protecting him from harm, and wondering where, beneath the wave of red roses, were they headed at last, Yan, Pink, Elisabeth, Rachel, Tony, José, Irvan, to what night or oblivion, where were they all going, asked Petites Cendres as he told himself the wind would eventually dry his tears. Yes, thought Daniel, the revelation having come to him as he sat in his armchair by the fire, chilled through and through because the alarm of his nightmare exceeded anything in his constantly changing and unpredictable reality, he'd learned in his dream that not one of the writers they were expecting would arrive tonight or tomorrow, no, the Chinese, Vietnamese, Nigerian, and Iranian writers, all of them listed in the festival program and travelling together out of precaution, not one of them would arrive, their plane had been shot down over the coast of Ireland and none of them would be seen again, not tonight, not tomorrow, their books no longer read but censored and burned, they'd been the victims of a systematically fought war on intelligence and culture, massacred in mid-flight, at first, following the plane's disappearance, came suspicions, then the thunder and lightning of the abominable dream came to pass, the plane in which they'd assembled for their protection had been shot down, taken out by the weapon of some terrorist, this term inadequately describing the grotesque and pervasive tentacles of such an endeavour, this slow extermination of individuals and, who was to say, perhaps whole peoples and nations, the ideal of the pursuit being the destruction of all those coexisting intelligently and in peace, no, none of the invited writers were going to show, thought Daniel, this enemy craved the triumph of grinding free spirit down and eliminating it from the universe, for at the core of such fanatical teachings was an exaltation of nihilism by religions run riot, it didn't matter whether the crucifixions took place on hilltops or in the sky, by executing men and women at a distance, none had a chance of survival, the invading enemy's one true god was death, the murder of victims made possible by their own denial of death, here was the face of a vengeful medievalism, crucifying and flagellating with great cries of glory, yet were not these new Middle Ages even more fragmented and formless than the original, more ferocious in their militancy, more deleterious, Daniel's nightmare had been so graphic in its depiction that he'd seen bodies strewn along the path of the crash on the Irish coast, smoking clothes covering shredded limbs in seaports, fields, and pastures, a funereal rain sending shivers through his bones when suddenly he heard a voice on his phone, it was Mai's voice murmuring, Papa, Papa, we planned this call, don't you remember, maybe you forgot that I wanted to talk to you about my time in China with Mama, and about my photos in the exhibition, Papa, wasn't this the time of day when I always wanted to see you, wasn't this our special time together every day, but Daniel was immersed in the acrimony of his dream and did not answer his daughter's call, haunted by the thought of all those writers lost at sea, all those whose works had been extinguished with their lives, yes, he was terrified his dream might be true, and then he felt Eddy's hand on his shoulder, Daniel, your friends are waiting in the last bus, your friends are waiting and there's only one seat left and it's for you, really Daniel, I'm sorry to disturb you like this, especially when you're writing, but they're getting impatient, you understand, and Daniel shook Eddy's hand saying, thank you Eddy, thank you, and Eddy suggested Daniel would marvel at the stunning autumn colours of the fields and forests, as it was not yet night Daniel would be able to see red sky over the treetops and all of that would make the drive up the mountain shorter, yes, said Eddy, because it was not yet night, and Daniel noticed the outfit Eddy had on, the black tie and white jacket he was wearing; everybody seemed to be in black tie except for Daniel, who, yellow shoes aside, had dressed in white in Olivier's memory, the memory of his friend like a beacon of light shining a path toward the speech he was about to make, Daniel, who, when he spoke at universities, was typically a stumbling orator who hesitated even to read from his own work, really he was no more than an awkward pretender when compared with his assertive intellectual friends, and he wondered why it was that after all the agitation his disturbing dream had brought on, he was mollified by a vision of Mère pointing the way down a sandy trail in a dream that settled his turbulent emotions in an instant, here, she said, behold the blue expanse of an ocean calm and smooth as can be, Daniel, said Mère, the image of this ocean stretching to infinity intimidated me yesterday, I looked and was afraid I'd disappear beneath its soothing, mesmerizing waves, but today this vision of a calm sea is my own and now I feel perfectly good walking this far, you see, Daniel, I don't need to use a walking stick anymore, here we're rid of all that, there's only the air, neither too hot nor too cold, and the water, nothing, Mère told Daniel, that might upset us ever again, oh, how we are able to rest on these ocean beaches, sighed Mère, who suddenly fell silent for a moment, will you, my dear child, tell Mélanie

I'm just fine, I don't want her sobbing during the night at the thought of me anymore, sweet Mélanie, who always feels so needlessly worried on my behalf, do tell her I'm fine, dear child, and Daniel was sure, when he woke, that he had heard these hushed words spoken in a void or a corridor empty of people, the visiting spirits had reverted to their anonymity and away from the forms they take on for us at night, some human simulation designed to take us by the hand as we, relieved of our daily burdens, lie by ourselves in our beds, in this easing of ordinary principles the body hastens alone into the shadowland, thought Daniel, bonding with whomever it chooses, and the vision of an ocean suddenly at rest that Mère had presented to Daniel, this sea damping down the anger and rage in his soul, did not this becalmed ocean beyond the rippling sands that he'd perceived in his dream also exist outside of any dreaming, was it not the same ocean old Isaac sought out from the tower of his house on his island, the Island No One Owns, the vision of a similar expanse of blue stretching out and melding into the sky as if there was no horizon, all of which made Isaac, who would soon be one hundred and expected neither a dialogue with the supernatural nor any divine reward from the experience of his promontory, happy and tirelessly serene, who knows what he was expecting there, so alone, in his khaki shorts and safari hat, the pinnacle of his wooden house was his watchtower of delight, the acme of his tranquil conviction that life was indeed worth living, for his house, tower, and island were all the product of his own hands, he had been the creator of wonders known only to him, perhaps he was the last guardian of the wildlife he nurtured around him, all of it perishing elsewhere, the last saviour of the deer and foxes, the assiduous protector of fawns and eagles, the saviour, in particular, of the Florida panther, Isaac was surrounded by all these creatures and by eagles flying overhead, and Isaac, thought Daniel, Isaac who no longer descended from his tower except to meet the people who arrived on Sundays, descending to welcome his friends pulling up in golf carts, what with the roads on the island being barely cleared, at these times Isaac was unexpectedly effusive and, though his friends thought him miserly, his generosity was extravagant, Isaac bringing his chef in from town to prepare sumptuous feasts on his primordial island, for what would he not do for friends, Daniel reflected, outings on yachts, fabulous wines, even the gift to his poet friends of a place to leave their ashes here in the grasses or under the dunes, or there in the ocean where those of Jean-Mathieu were, under the peaceful blue reach of its stunning tumult of waves, in that ocean of silence Isaac contemplated from his tower in the early hours of the dawn, when, but for the singing birds, all things slept, yes, there in the quiet ocean were the ashes of Jean-Mathieu, he whose loss had pained old Isaac so very much, his dear friend Jean-Mathieu so much younger than he was, the hurt comparable only to that which would strike Caroline, she who would be overwhelmed by the confusion of her loss, never to recover, it was only now, at the top of his tower, that Isaac could say, at last, Jean-Mathieu is near, no more of his peregrinations in Italy, which was quite far enough to have had to retrieve his body, did Jean-Mathieu not know he was too weak to travel, the flu, a cold in a damp rooming house, and it would be over for him, and just what was he looking for over there, museums, paintings, would he close his eyes when he contemplated one of Paolo Veronese's paintings, his dreamland was there, oh, how ridiculous, I should never have let him go off like that and, as for Caroline, well, why on earth did she not accompany him, they always travelled together, Italy in winter, why die simply to contemplate an allegorical tableau, I should have kept him from going, yes, and all I have now is his red scarf, that's it, Jean-Mathieu was a poet and a sailor, am I too prosaic a man to understand him, sleep my friend, sleep, let the ocean watch over you, these were the thoughts Daniel attributed to Isaac as he imagined him high in his tower standing in his khakis before the immutable ocean, this image of a calm sea one that often returned to Daniel during his disputes with Augustino at the family table, how incongruous it seemed that Augustino was no longer the young lad whose manners his father criticized, the way he dressed too, how can you come to dinner like that, how do you dare, it was not that Augustino was a man with whom his father, also a man, did not discuss everything acrimoniously, but how it had all happened so quickly that they were no longer the friends they had been before, how was it Augustino forgot that only yesterday, only a few years ago, Daniel could carry his son on his shoulders and play with him, oh, why did it have to be like this, thought Daniel, why, like that moment of the dawn when the ocean is still, had the bond of father and son lasted really so short a time, why did it have to be this way, and Orange dropped her head to Angel's hand, cautiously gripping his fingers with her talons, sometimes stepping up to his shoulder, wanting to feast with her crackling beak on the salad she was crazy about, Lena, Angel's mother, had made it especially for her, greens hanging like clover from the bird's beak as its eyes shifted rapidly from side to side, and Angel thought, Lucia's lending me Orange because she knows I'm sad and, if we don't go to sea with Brilliant tonight, that I'll be worse, yes, thought Angel, Mama can't stop saying Papa isn't coming to see me, and soon astronauts and cosmonauts will depart in their spaceship for other galaxies and Mama and I must also leave so that we can attend the rocket launch, Papa is saying again he won't come see me, but the joy of this day will conclude, should Brilliant and Lucia and Lena not forgo it, with a promenade by the sea, though they won't if the wind's too strong, the joy of it was that Lucia had loaned Orange to him and to Misha, and that she was flying all around the room and into the sun-filled kitchen and gently placing her orange and yellow head, more orange than it was yellow, in Angel's welcoming open hand, is it true you also like plantain, asked Angel, and organic plants, and is it true you're a really good singer, that you are well fed and happy, there, there, answered Orange, and caressing the bird's green wings Angel said, but what you like most is flying outside when the weather's warmer, isn't it, yes, the joy of this day that would be over too soon, thought Angel, was that he'd written to Kitty, because if his father so resolutely refused to see his son, well, Kitty might, and nowadays he was writing Kitty, who was at the motel pretty well permanently, I have gifts for you, Kitty, the electronic tablets I'll not be needing anymore because my mother and I are off to see the launch of the astronauts and cosmonauts, we'll be leaving very soon, and, somewhat more sensibly than Angel, Kitty wrote back to say, but you're not a cosmonaut, you're not an astronaut, and it won't be you who's going up in a rocket, and besides, I'd never want you to do that, because if the rocket launched and burst into flames I'd never see you again, I wouldn't be able to write you anymore, and I need to write to you every day because it's no fun here, my mom doesn't like the way we're living and my little brothers are crybabies, but Benito the caretaker is still teaching me mathematics and I'm going to be a mathematician, you'll see, my parents will be so proud of me, and then Angel thought a little more rationally too, maybe my dad isn't coming to see me, he reasoned, because he's afraid he'll catch something from me, and if he did come then he'd argue with my mother about me or for some other reason, and without a doubt they'd be at it again after the rocket's departure for unknown galaxies, so maybe yes, they've always quarrelled because of me, and if the rocket's fuselage breaks up what will become of me, wondered Angel as he held Misha close, look, Misha, Orange our parakeet is talking, don't you know, it can talk, it can sing, there there, replied Orange, yes, I can sing, and I can peck away at that whole salad, and I won't ever hurt you even when my talons grip your fingers tightly, how I love to perch on your hand, Angel, even if they amounted to no more than the ordinary chatter of birds, these were the mellifluous words Angel was sure he heard the parrot speak, Orange either whistling or whispering them right into Angel's ear, through his hair smelling of Eureka's excessively perfumed lotions, Eureka the caregiver who still rocked Angel on the veranda despite his legs seeming too long for that now, they're way too thin, she said, this boy, she grumbled, he must be fed, and contemplating the planets and galaxies, there were also planetoids and asteroids and so many satellites to consider, Angel wondered why they were all so close and how the planets managed not to collide, after all they were no more than stars wandering aimlessly, and if they have no light, why do they shine so when we look at them in the night sky, and as Angel was daydreaming all this he scratched Orange's tiny head and Misha paced heavily around the room, for was this not the time of day when Brilliant came to take the dog out, it was all very well that Misha had been assigned this charming and capricious sick kid but the time had come after all these hours of the dog being so patient, of his putting up with Angel's moments of irritability and the brief bad moods his fever brought on, the time had come to have fun, yes, to run outside, to be out on the beach with Brilliant and land his big paws on the gangplank of Captain Joe's boat, keeping watch over a child like Angel was sometimes too demanding for a dog like Misha who loved nothing better than to play outdoors, and besides, there were way too many birds fluttering around in the room, Petites Cendres' doves, Mabel's parrot Jerry, and now Orange commanded all the attention of his boy master and this was all too much for an unruly dog that loved greenery, swimming in the sea, and ponds where white egrets and pigeons gathered, he needed to splash and to splatter all these birds, yes, to really have fun, to run through the water and snort and sniff his way through the jasmine, all Misha could smell in Angel's room was medicine, even when Lena opened the windows to the blue sky or, because Drs. Dieudonné and Lorraine spent all their days at the house and Angel, brave as he was, often crying, did not close them even when it rained, and if Angel cried into his bed sheets, as he did into Misha's fur when he held the dog a little too snugly, most of all it was because his father did not come to visit him, he'd not seen him for several years, and then Angel would stop crying and laugh a lot, anything could set him off, and he'd say to Misha, you're a funny one, you're a big-toothed wolf but you don't scare me, now stop running after those egrets and pigeons in the pond, Mama won't like that, and when it rains, no coming into the kitchen with your paws covered in wet sand, I love you, Misha, yes, with great displays of joy and exclamation he would tell Misha that he adored him, and it was especially while, toward evening and feeling a little better, Misha was waiting for Brilliant to take him for a walk by the sea, that Angel loved Misha, and Misha waited for Brilliant impatiently, where had he got to and why was he always late, and Angel said the sunset over the sea is going to be spectacular tonight, mustn't miss it. Papa, wrote Samuel, you told me the representation of darkness in art should never exceed a work's capacity for light, I'm still reworking my choreography as we begin our tour, you can see in the video of *China, Slow Movement*, that the outline still has imperfections, and what you must know, dear father, is how much I hate the darkness, same as you, I'm not like Augustino who plumbs the depths and revels in them, but still, in this piece the darkness must make itself felt more than the light, you're shocked, you say, by the sight of these young dancers, kids walking to school with gas masks, but not so far in the future I see Rudie among them, and that's why in this tableau, this *mise en scène*, they're deprived of the light, even daylight, and what little there is will be hazy and carbon-saturated, air that has been tainted by fire, for it's only possible to express the terror this absence of light creates with a sooty murkiness laced with garbage and filth, this is not a tableau I can alter or sanitize because it's my son I keep seeing in it even if he knows nothing of this rapacious smoke, it's him I see surrounded by birds mired in oil slicks, yes, I see your grandson Rudie throughout this painful and punishing choreography that will hurt us again when we're forced to dance it tonight and tomorrow, and just how do you think all the little children like Rudie, lovingly nurtured by parents who lavish a thousand cares upon them, how will they manage to defend themselves this day or the next, or should we, their parents and grandparents, not be the ones defending them, the children, against the carpets of oil on our oceans or the armies of ferocious children weaned on the villainy and lawlessness of their tribes, children accustomed to the most vengeful crimes because they've not been educated by their parents or well raised, these are quite the opposite, children whose parents were killed by some rival gang wielding machetes, progeny of murderous acts who are also sick with hunger, and just how, Samuel asked his father so far away, am I to explain all this to Rudie later on, and when Daniel realized he had no answer to give, he said in his email that some of the images in Samuel's choreography were sublime, that of course art can evoke what troubles us, that there are times all of us must live the unnameable, not knowing, even as adults, how to react or take action, it was Augustino who'd said to his father that no time has been more obfuscating than ours, not even the dark age of the Inquisition, and now Daniel found himself countering Samuel's ideas as, the day before, he had done Augustino's premonitions and dour observations, all your opinions strike me as so extreme, Daniel wrote Samuel, why are my children like this, he wondered, your mother's a moderate woman and as for me, well, aren't I the same, yet Daniel knew how unconvinced Samuel was by his circumspection and restraint, his son was having none of it and thrust right back at him saying, you, Papa, you conceal your aggression but it's there, otherwise you wouldn't be writing the books that you do, haven't your critics called your incitements to violence, even your analyses of violence, scandalous, isn't that what they wrote, and Daniel closed his laptop on Samuel's words, still preoccupied with the images his son's choreography conjured, all he could envision was the sight of his grandson going to school each morning with a gas mask on but no, thought Daniel, the dance of *China, Slow Movement*, was happening not in his gaze but somewhere else, he left Eddy's bar and the hotel in a hurry, knowing he would be taken to task for being late, especially by the author of *Esthetic Eternity*, who would say in a disgruntled tone, why make us hang around all this time, you know there's a hot meal waiting for us up there, and Daniel replied, I thought you were on a strict diet, no no, said the author, not tonight, the cold around here has stirred my appetite, my wife warned me not to travel so far, journeys like this are always so disorienting, and Daniel mused how much more disturbed and aggrieved the author would have been had he read Augustino's thoughts about him, likely saying, I could sue that son of yours, oh, I could, believe me, and before Daniel was able to join the others in the coach, a young woman ran up to him with an armful of books and held his most recent, the one with the purple cover, out to him, she wanted Daniel to sign it before he got away, this one's abrasive and it helped me so much, she said, out of breath because she was running after him and speaking as she did so, it's abrasive, asked Daniel, really, and he stopped before his young reader and saw how moved she was and her emotion unexpectedly settled him, would you come and speak on our campus, the young woman asked, it's kind of remote, yeah, really remote, but you have a lot of fans there and you'd get a great reception, that must be appealing, and still short of breath she went on to describe her homeland and how the Atlantic Ocean bordered it to the east and south, icebergs along much of its coast, even the fog in winter is icy, she said, we eat herring and smoked cod and the cold is unrelenting, but my, the country is beautiful in summer, surrounded by mountains that we can finally see, really, believe me, you have a lot of readers where I'm from, why are you smiling like that, this invitation's for real, and Daniel looked at his book with the mauve cover, this emblem of his writing life, the key to his pride that the woman was waving in front of him like a fanion, oh sir, please, may I have your autograph, she begged, I'll be able to tell my friends in Terra Nova where I live that I actually met you, and, with a certain affection for the young woman, Daniel did sign it, her adulation reminding him that he still had readers even if his work was published sporadically, the writing coming slowly despite his impatience for it to be underway, getting up every morning as he recited the day's first sentence in his head, words he would have dreamed during the night, and suddenly it occurred to him that his isolation was not as complete as he thought, he had readers on distant and frozen islands that were almost glacial and surrounded by the powerful waves of the Atlantic, circumstances that would be completely unknown to Augustino, whose readers were so close that he was able to see them every day on campus or at internet cafés, his readers responding so viscerally to his scathing *Letter to Young People Without a Future* and answering, in effect, that yes, the children of the middle class who found themselves unemployed, who were weary of being laid off, they too had little to look forward to, standing by Augustino's worldview and no longer daring to hope, but his readers were many and they were various and the response of others was to debunk the author, lambasting Augustino's deep-seated despondency and the arrogance of his false prophecies, for they had made it where he had failed, their endgame to be rich and attaining as much in the careers in which they prospered, pharmaceuticals or information technology, these men and women pursuing remunerative though often unscrupulous futures, and for whom the development of medications for future generations was just a game, wrote to Augustino that their cancerous clients were guinea pigs bound to die anyway, ethics were not theirs to worry about for science is amoral and always would be, or, computers their business, they'd write that they were tomorrow's designers, the keepers of universal memory, gods of a world as changeable as it was all-powerful, and in such a domain who needs a soul, Augustino's shortcoming, his readers wrote, was that he actually had one, or at least this was how Daniel imagined his son's frequently vexed dialogue with his readers, for the thing was Augustino's books were so successful that he who was so tight with his friendship, or who did not lend himself to it easily, had close and fast readers popping up all over the place ready for a duel, ready for the thrust and parry of a debate, this totally unlike Daniel, who often felt he was writing for some abstract readership and ruminating from afar, or only for himself, and here suddenly he'd discovered a young student in whom he'd awakened a passion for reading, who would have thought that they were reading him in Terra Nova, well well, he thought, in Terra Nova, how reassuring, and in the same instant his humility grounded him, yes, he recalled a dream in which he'd seen Charles, Charles the metaphysical poet so admired by his peers, Charles bedecked with prizes, Charles, and how had this come to pass, appearing in his dream in a kimono somewhat the worse for wear, Charles, who had become, in the dream, a lowly streetsweeper, was this the fate eternity holds in store for all of us, Daniel thought, a humiliating diminution of self-regard that even a great poet must endure, Charles was no longer the aristocrat of thinkers nor the poet he once was, and Daniel wondered if, in this dream in which Charles's incarnation looked upon Daniel with such disillusionment and resignation, Charles even remembered the man he once was, for no, this certainly was not him, his fine intelligence, the abundant beauty of his being, even his slender form lacked the dignity it had, a body broken and defeated by streetsweeping, a body humiliated, this was not Charles's body, this was not the body of the young man that, despite the passage of time, Frédéric had so guarded and cared for, or was this one of Daniel's many noxious dreams inferring the proud poet would be punished for being just that, that Charles would be humbled this way, broom in hand and the spirit crushed, no, surely it had to be otherwise, some redeeming angel would take him by the sleeve of his worn kimono and gather him under its powerful wing and then deposit him where he was meant to be, in the celestial empire with his kin, Dante, Virgil, and Goethe, poets to whom he'd always paid tribute in his own work, or did Daniel's vision express some more sensual disappointment with Frédéric, as if in the dreams Charles was telling Daniel, I waited all night for Frédéric in this old kimono even though he never stops buying me new ones, and it's eight o'clock in the morning and he's still not home, Daniel, is that what you'd call love, to neglect the companion of your days, your one and only, to go to sleazy clubs and listen to jazz all night, Daniel, my dear friend, would you say he still loves me as he used to, is that what you believe, my dear Daniel, yes, that's how it was, thought Daniel, above all Charles's dream was an expression of sorrow, of his regret that Frédéric was spending his nights outside the house and without him, still, even as in the company of his musician friends the rhythm of jazz stoked a sweet fever in Frédéric that moistened his lips and brow, Charles would have said, oh no, there's nothing our union is not strong enough to fix, it's nothing, meaningless, am I not the one who wrote about all this, about the envelopment of our two lives in a rain of salt when all around us everything was still so green, when I wrote about the two of us in our youth, and just then Daniel was distracted by a message written in red paint on the coach windows that he read in the dying light of day saying, *writers, leave your rooms, join us on the barricades*, and as the wind rustled, dropping golden leaves onto the metallic carapace of the bus, did not these words again lead him to worry the evening might not turn out as perfectly as he wanted, *tonight, maverick writers, join us at the barricades or we will hunt you down*, it was the same message Daniel had received on his computer during the day, one he'd deleted like so many others, it halted him for a moment before he rushed onto the coach so that beneath the vault of the trees he might breathe in the scent of pine cones, a sharp perfume, a pungent smell that evoked the woody trails he'd walked in the afternoon and the villagers who'd welcomed him into their houses, and as he stepped onto the bus the driver shut the door behind him and grumbled, you know, sir, this is the last bus, the others are already on their way to the mountain, we've been waiting a whole hour, what on earth were you doing, there's only one seat left, come on, let's get going before night catches up with us, it seems to have slipped your mind that the road is rough in the high stretches, you'll see alright and the bumpy ride won't be my fault, it's the road, not that the altitude is much to speak of, but there are freshwater lakes and ponds amid the forests, and the climb makes the journey seem longer than it is, though you'll not make out anything at all once night falls, so let's be on our way, and Daniel listened dutifully to the guide and told himself he would stray no more, that there was nothing for him to do but settle into the cocoon of the coach with his silent colleagues and finish planning his presentation, he'd gather in all his strands of thought in a dark corner of the bus and enjoy the scent of the pine cones, and the memory of the red-walled cottage where he had rested for a few hours before in the rocker creaking against the wooden floorboards came back to him, as did the rows of framed photographs of deceased writers on the walls among which he'd noticed, or was it no more than his reminiscing, memories accumulating as they do, Suzanne's sombre face, at least it looked like her, though was it her or someone else with a voice like hers who looked like her, and now suddenly she was sharing the coach seat with him, saying yes, that really was me you saw this afternoon, I left this world on a fine July day, but don't you find that the fluid state of our consciousness seeps into all things, so is this your friend Suzanne, but is it really me, our splendid awareness drifts and drifts and is never lost, I was never fond of politics, no, my energy was directed to the resolution of humanitarian conflicts, although I always wrote deprecatingly, born as I was in a South African mining village divided by apartheid, the imperative of condemning the system inflicted politics upon me, it was a necessity and a means, and the object of my writing would become the calling out of racist lies, of the cruelty and opportunism of Whites, you remember, Daniel, my books would end up being banned in my own country, did I not write again and again that racial division is a country's agony, the apartheid regime ended in 1994 and still the riots go on, and what do people become in their wake, how do they live, I remember houses wrecked, men and women too, my short stories and essays were also banned and do you think this is right, my friend, do you, I left this world behind on a fine July morning and there was a clear blue sky and fewer riots on that day, remember, I wrote all that I did weighing my words carefully, and Daniel thought he could hear them just as the face of a writer, was it Suzanne's or somebody else's, a woman and an activist sharing her concerns, appeared and then vanished like a flame, a votive flame, and Daniel relaxed into his seat and slipped closer to sleep, but someone was coming down the aisle, a large bearded man who sat down beside him, he was friendly and congenial and asked Daniel if he looked familiar, come on, don't you remember me, look at my ponytail and black beret, we're old friends from way back, no, said Daniel, no, I don't know you, annoyed that Suzanne was no longer with him, sure, the man said, time diminishes all of us, but have I changed so much, old friend, that you no longer know who I am, we were together that year we both won an artist's fellowship, a writer's grant that afforded you and me a residency at a monastery in Madrid, ah yes, now you remember, I can see it in your face, even in these shadows, yes, it's me, it's your old friend Rodrigo, the poet from Brazil, you know that even though my poems are only slightly anarchistic my books are banned there now, I mean, really, aren't all poets entitled to a touch of anarchy, amigo, tell me, have I aged so much in so few years that you no longer recognize me? What about Mark and Carmen, that groundbreaking revolutionary pair, far more anarchistic than I ever was, yes, amigo, I need to talk to you about them, I must, but Daniel stared at this Rodrigo, not at all like the joyous, exuberant, pearl-toothed, and smiling creature he remembered, was it really him, Daniel wondered as he looked at what had become of the once flowing ponytail, grey hair now spilling out from beneath the black beret, his beard also grizzled and accentuating the yellowed teeth of his once radiant smile, I'm living in exile on a shoestring, said this Rodrigo, do you mind if I sit next to you, I have no coat and it's so cold in this bus, I see you're dressed up for the evening, amigo, I won't be able to attend, I only have this frayed shirt and sloppy pants and there's no way they'll let me in, and these woods are cold on nights like this, it gets really cold at night, please can I just sit next to you, and so the nightmare went on until Daniel decided to hand Rodrigo his coat, whereupon the man seemed to become Augustino, the child Daniel had carried on his shoulders across the lake, a gleaming lake in the gigantic forests of Scotland, when suddenly Augustino slipped slowly from his father's shoulders, slowly sliding until he lay in the water, his small body curled from the fall, and Daniel cried out, Augustino, Augustino, before his nightmare was chased away by the ring of his cell phone and Mai's childlike voice joyfully exclaiming, ah Papa, you're there at last, hi Papa, hi, and Angel, who was holding Orange in his open hand because, he reasoned, even if its stomach was pleasantly filled and it did not want to move, it needed to feel free to fly whenever it wished, Angel thinking that Lena had received an envelope from his father about which she'd said nothing, instead wiping away a tear and retreating to her room, has Papa finally written, Angel asked, tell me, mother, did he write something for us, mother, anything, but Lena was silent and shut herself away and Angel thought no, he's not written, he's just sent a cheque for Mama, had he not said a long time ago that he would send a cheque to cover funeral expenses, for that and for Angel to undergo every possible treatment, let's go out on the veranda, said Angel to Orange, delicately placing the bird on his shoulder, baby that it was, you couldn't teach it any old thing just yet, and given his own frailty Angel was sometimes impatient, just the few steps he took toward the veranda exhausted him and the thought of the letter his mother had received made him want to cry, but once the warm and humid air struck his face, everything appeared different to him, was he already floating amid the galaxies, despite his weakness and Orange pecking at his cheeks, and his heart was supercharged with an unsettling ecstasy, the colours outdoors were no longer the same, he'd have been unable to describe them even were he to draw them with pencils of every colour, an aura of luminous clarity was emanating from everything, so powerful and radiant that Angel closed his eyes, so enticing and enveloping was this iridescence that immediately he felt better, he could hear the flight of egrets and pigeons over the pond, and across Atlantic Boulevard the sea was glistening beneath an overpowering sun, this sun so penetrating and incredibly hot that it flowed like fire through his veins, and suddenly Orange went wild and started flying around Angel as if calling for help, the nervous beating of its green wings rousing Angel from his body's near fainting so that he managed to put himself into the deck chair and rest until the colours of the pond and the sea across Atlantic Boulevard regained their natural hues at this hour and the song and chatter of the birds became less piercing, an unsettling elation seized his chest and he thought of Kitty wearing her brother's oversized sweater and how he would see her again soon, he would give her so many presents that she would stay with him forever alongside Misha and Orange, and she would say to Angel, I'd rather live with you and your mother than go back to the motel with Mama and my squabbling brothers, everyone would welcome her at the Acacia Gardens, Dr. Dieudonné and Dr. Lorraine, and all the people convalescing in the neighbouring apartments would be cured, there'd be a party, Lena would make a huge cake and Angel would declare to everyone he'd seen the light of the galaxies and that it was an astonishing light, the supernatural terrifies all of us a little, he would say, insisting that he'd not been frightened at all because he was too grown up to be scared, so his mother told him, and he was too grown up for crying too, and Angel noticed that despite all the natural and familiar colours returning, among the plants on the veranda there was an effervescent halo around the petals of the yellow hibiscus, two blooms with their flamboyant centres having blossomed during the night, how mysterious it was that the silky yellow-petalled flowers had been far from opening as recently as the day before, and that they had come into flower as Angel slept in and nursed a fever, and Angel thought of the children being born at that moment, might they not live on Mars one day, though how would they ever return from their time there, perhaps once they'd been dispatched to the sands of the distant planet, to the serenity of its red and blue deserts, for they certainly would be serene and peaceful, they'd simply decide to live on Mars and not come back at all, no, why bother, they'd say, to what end, earthlings only destroy the marvels of the world so we'll never return, besides which Earth is too populated and polluted, there's no place for us, for the children mothers were bringing into the world today had the advantage of understanding, from birth, that they'd been conceived to live somewhere else, that aged eighteen they would leave and never come back, they'd be children of the Martian race, the hearts in their chests would be small or perhaps, thought Angel, they'd have none at all, and suddenly he saw Brilliant running Misha past the pond, we just got back from the dog beach he yelled, no shimmering halo around the hibiscus anymore as if they'd been struck by sunbeams from the sea, no, the colours surrounding them were as fresh as those of a painting though like the normal ones Angel saw every day, and later Mama would tell him to forget about that envelope from Papa, there was no letter in it, not a word, neither for Lena nor Angel, just a cheque to help with the exorbitant drugs that Angel depended on, that's all Lena would say today and perhaps even tomorrow, but as for Kitty, she wrote Angel to say yes, she was fed up with the motel, fed up with wandering around with her brothers' tennis balls when there was really no place to play tennis or to kick a ball around, only the motel's asphalt parking lot, and even though she was studying mathematics with Benito, she'd had enough of not being at school, she'd written that her friend Cristal still went to visit her father in prison every Sunday, that luckily for her Kitty did not have a father in jail, and Angel thought about Kitty being with him soon, perking up at the idea and smiling at Misha and Brilliant from the veranda where the two flowers with their resplendent centres had bloomed, now wasn't that a miracle,

Angel mused, that the two flowers had the time to blossom while he was asleep, yes, wasn't it, and Daniel spoke to Mai on his cell phone, seeing her face on the tiny screen as if by a miracle, because that was how it was with this shiny device, despite the minimal space it took up in its case inside his jacket pocket or slipped like a handkerchief into his shirt, it had this power, and one that never left anyone who possessed such a device to themselves, through it the incessant movement of the entire universe and its inhabitants infiltrated his pores night and day, and what a relief it was that our children, despite the chaos of images inflicted upon us, are always at hand, though is it a blessing or a curse that the very possibility of solitude, like a petrified root, has been extirpated from human experience and now, instead, we live in contemplation of a piece of mirrored glass refracting every sound we make, people tied to their telephones as if these were their homes and they had no other, and listening to Mai, seeing the piercings in her ears again, Daniel thought back to the teenager who'd asked so many questions of him, why are we born, why were so many of us born, go ask your mother had been his reply, yes, it was up to Mélanie, wife and mother, to answer all of Mai's questions, Daniel not wanting to admit that what bothered him most of all about her hanging out with Manuel and his father in this, the secretive season of her life, was that no doubt she was having sex, and was she not doing so too soon, and how upsetting it was that Mai, along with other impressionable teens captivated by the allure of wealth, was visiting two such rakish men, Manuel and his father, at their beach house, oh, what a sailboat they had, parties that went on all night, and Manuel's father had his own plane, of course, the kids having no idea this affluence was built on the perils of the drug trade, or were they only pretending not to know, this seductive but fraudulent prosperity inciting them to lose their way, thought Daniel, and was it not during this period of her lingering with Manuel and his father that she was always coming home after midnight, anguished hours in which Mère suffered so, alone in the guest house where she'd listen to music and see almost no one, just the occasional friend, or perhaps Mélanie or Mai for a fleeting kiss, often past midnight because the old lady could no longer tell day from night, and in the garden where he would wait for his daughter under the pink laurel trees Daniel could hear music through Mère's half-open window and the sound of her voice as she said to her granddaughter, your father's been waiting in the garden for hours, where have you been, child, pour me some water from that jug, would you, please, I'm thirsty and Marie-Sylvie's not here this late to help me, which is when Mai's voice would harden, Esther, dear sweet Grandmama, why don't you kick that Marie-Sylvie out, have you forgotten she slapped me, don't you remember, Grandmama, she's a nasty woman, Marie-Sylvie de la Toussaint slapped me because I wanted to see you and hug you, she slapped me and called me a bad girl, I still have the mark on my cheek, just get rid of her, won't you, besides, I know she's been stealing, she took Mama's jewels, dear sweet Grandmama Esther, and now Daniel could hear Mère saying, you mustn't speak ill of Marie-Sylvie, she and her brother were persecuted in Haiti, Mai, did I not tell you before, you who have everything, that you mustn't judge these poor people whom we've welcomed into our house because they have nothing, no, you mustn't judge them, you've never lacked for love, Mai, but Marie-Sylvie and her brother, those two have known nothing but ill fortune, poor things, you mustn't be judging them, well then, said Mai, raising her voice, why be born at all if we're going to end up so miserable later on, why, why did they come into the world, why, just so Marie-Sylvie de la Toussaint could slap me, it's so unfair, I didn't deserve it, she was hitting out at her own life through me, and Mai's angry words were lost in Mère's music and then silence, because Mai, after appeasing her grandmother with gentler words, had left Grandmama, and Daniel listened to the quiet of the garden, and then to Mai's steps as she ran to the house, the moonlight briefly illuminating the roller skates she held in her hand, he'd been able to make out the movement of her legs beneath her white shorts and thought how grown up and less accessible his daughter already was, yes, in this worrying and irksome time when Mai was out every night, when she was growing up too fast, she was asking her father all sorts of questions she really should have trusted her mother to answer, why are girls always responsible for everything, she would ask Daniel when they were on the swings or out by the pool, when suddenly he was struck by her grace and confidence even if she was as stubborn as always, that same lock of hair falling over her face, Papa, the burden and responsibility of procreation falls upon us, girls and women, so what if we decided one day that it's no longer right to bring new beings into the world, because in ten or twenty years they'll be the exploited ones, and if they go hungry, or if they are ordered to kill people or to invade other countries, then won't their lives be trying and desperate beyond understanding, and yes, Papa, I know this is the sort of dire future Augustino imagines for himself, and I mean I might bring a girl into the world who actually behaves heroically rather than one more desperate child ready to commit the worst of sadistic acts in order to survive, hey Papa, really, if I had a daughter, I know she'd be fantastic, and if I had a son I'd want him to a good person like Vincent is, for him to be a medical researcher like Vincent and contribute to humanity's progress, regress, but as I said, isn't it a little scary, Papa, that the responsibility of producing another living being, regardless of knowing how that life will turn out, rests entirely on our shoulders, on us girls, on us women, and that all of us are so alone when we make this, the biggest and most important decision of our lives, and Daniel listened to Mai suddenly chatting like a grown-up, feeling that he could have been in Mélanie's or Mère's company, though he was taken aback that at no point did Mai use the word *love* or *desire*, that her language was so cerebral and dispassionate, she was thinking about love's most unnerving consequences in the way they are conceived, if not articulated, by young people of her age, who, painfully reticent, often won't discuss the future at all, with good reason she was worried about marching with her children into a culture of violence and learning just how much that culture already permeated her universe, and Daniel, was he not a laughable father figure for keeping all those violent video games out of the house while the world was awash in conflagrations of such terrifyingly violent means, a soldiery hell at everyone's door and Mai well aware that in cities ravaged by war, men in black hoods were teaching children to kill one another in what amounted to little more than a murderous game played under suspect flags as houses burned beneath a sky black with smoke, would tomorrow be called a crime, today's crimes already past counting, their apotheosis a scene of nuclear devastation in which Mai would have to bring up her children, surely this was the question Mai did not dare put to her father, so impotent did it make her feel, she who adored little children and who would have liked to have some later on forced to abandon the dream of some young, coddled infant at her chest because she was thinking of child soldiers in whose heads the idea of war had been imprinted from the cradle, and trying to imagine the maddening hunger these children would know so painfully early, Mai thought about the mothers who had borne these children, what had they felt giving birth at twelve and having been forced to do so, delivering the flesh of their flesh in tanks at the grim behest of young men who would make butchers of these creatures, executioners, ritual assassins with an automaton's lack of feeling, their love of life long since washed away by the taste of blood, the one vague reply Daniel did give Mai was that we procreate with the aim of making our progeny happy though sometimes this does not happen with even the most loving parents, yes, what else did he have to say, that the goal of life is happiness, a harmonious existence, look at little Rudie, was he not a happy child, sure, a little capricious as all kids who are overindulged by their parents are, but Rudolph was adorable, extremely good-natured and inventive, I also dreamed my children would change the world, said Daniel, and, each in their own way, that's what children do, even you, Mai, but Mai was avoiding his gaze, she would have sobbed right there in front of her father out of sheer exasperation but managed not to, shutting down, dark and frowning. And in the dressing room backstage, where all the girls were crammed up against each other, Victoire watched as Yinn dressed slowly and fastidiously, Robbie running up to Yinn with his favourite cocktail, no drinks till after five, said Robbie, his wig slipping forward and falling over his brown eyebrows, and Victoire could see that soon the night-madness of the late shows would kick in and wondered how Yinn, looking so chaste in his new outfit of a white robe and a wig pleated with white rose petals, allowed himself to be in physical contact with so many members of the audience, the thought was repugnant to Victoire, who no longer had Déesse by her side, her dog keeping watch over the apartment in the Acacia Gardens, for it was safer that way, surely, even in the bliss of the Acacia Gardens it was necessary to be wary of intruders, of those Victoire had for some time now called *enemies*, had she not received death threats like the one on her computer that said, *we'll get you, Victoire, there are two of us and we have knives and we'll be waiting for you at night*, how can Yinn put up with strangers caressing his body, with hugs and kisses from people he doesn't know, look sweetie, said Robbie, if somebody wants to congratulate you for your performance, if one of your admirers wants to stuff money down your corsage, don't run away, when the night's over we share it all, really, you just have to accept that people will touch you, it's not rape, no need to be a prude, they don't know who you are and they have no clue about your past, the miracle of our shows is that our lives begin again every night, which is when Yinn intervened on Victoire's behalf and, placing a protective hand on Victoire's shoulder, said in that deep, manly voice of his, the same voice that onstage carried a melody or song to such a high pitch, listen, you think that fighting for your rights is futile, and you say that when you make speeches to students in all those hidebound cities you fear for your life but, believe me, because of your struggle thousands of transsexuals will soon be accepted into the army, it's already happening in a lot of countries, and you'll see, Victoire, you're not the lone fighter you think you are, soon enough you'll be teaching the most rigid sectors of society not only basic tolerance but respect, so I'm telling you, Victoire, don't be afraid, don't be intimidated by threats and bald-faced blackmail, oh my Victoire, you'll make love work for everybody, the young are listening to you, and Victoire thought that word *love*, the way Yinn said it, the way the word escaped his freshly painted scarlet lips, was it not more an expression of hope than reality, as if in Yinn's wishful thinking he'd recited the stanza of a poem in which the word *love* was the very fundament of peace, of an end to intolerance, of the resurrection of humankind that, with all its hate and aggression, was in torment, how shameful, thought Victoire, that she should have been afraid, and suddenly she was struck by the sight of Yinn's cheeks beneath the makeup, where he'd be kissed tonight, struck by the roundness of his cheeks and the baby-face folds that appeared when he laughed, thinking it was there that the vulnerability of his face resided, his humility such that were an admirer able to kiss him, the shock of it might injure or disfigure him, that it would be the sort of insult and injury Victoire had endured so many times, and yet, come close to kiss him on the cheek is exactly what Victoire did, so softly and unexpectedly that Yinn blushed under his pale foundation, Yinn, said Victoire, don't let those strangers get too close, no, don't let them, except that she had not actually spoken the words at all, and sitting back down in front of the dressing room mirror, she decided that her kiss on Yinn's cheek was the first indication of her rallying to the Yinn revolution, might it be true that they were brothers, could that happen, she wondered, convincing herself that she would be safe by his side, yes, safe, and then Victoire thought of Mick with Luke the Franciscan setting up Homes for All where the androgynous teens of New York, Atlanta, and disparate parts of the world would come to find shelter at night, there'd be a league of such homes everywhere, safe havens, and Victoire thought of all those writing her every day, so many of them, from every social class and walk of life, people seeking as she was the feminine part of themselves buried under false appearances, and just as was the case with Victoire, often their closest acquaintances, their families, their wives and children felt sullied by them, all these relations entrenched in a seemingly unassailable family fortress, unwavering in their view of what must and must not be, believing families are bastions, ancestral structures assuring the permanence of nations, they cannot be disturbed without the whole collapsing, yes, those like Victoire who identify with a gender that is not their own defile everything, that's what's said, though bringing scandal or moral shock to those around them was never the intention, for even the athlete, the actor about to metamorphose into the woman he has carried in the depths of his being, a transformation in all its splendour and perfection so unquestionably genuine even before the plastic surgery has begun, only hints at his desire for a feminine countenance discreetly, how do you tell a daughter or wife that the man you see in front of you is actually a woman, in transition, will you still love me as much, I who was always a good father and husband, will you still love me when my metamorphosis is complete, really, will you understand me, and occasionally one or another of the children of this man would notice clues of feminine yearning they'd find offensive, their athletic father of yesterday secretly wearing women's clothes or making frequent visits to the beauty parlour, some pernicious detail here and there caught by the eye of the man's son or daughter or wife, the nails unexpectedly painted red, how can this husband, this father, retain his family's love during the difficult time of his crossover when those who are closest to him leap to judgement, when his wife's fidelity and the affection of his children expire with the shell of the body entombing his divided self, Victoire would say in the speeches she made that you need to be resounding in your acclamation of the truth, leave nothing out because you'll suffer the same condemnation as it is, you'll be told that God made us as we are, as a man or woman and to change gender is simply impossible, is the greatest sin, a crime against the self, and Victoire would end her speech saying, here I am freed from the person I am not, here I am delivered to the world a second time, reborn as it were, why do you not believe me, you'll see more and more of us reaching out to claim the body that should have been ours at birth, yes, you'll see. And Victoire considered the courage of certain iconic personalities, actors, artists, activists, even soldiers, whose situations were not excoriated by their families but understood, these families having grasped for some time, gradually but well before radical surgery had altered the voice, that whether their father or brother was a man or woman, they still had the same interior identity and deserved to be loved as simply and constantly as before, and Victoire, who had never been a father, Déesse her only companion, preached that families were only truly united when a father, brother, or sister, liberating themselves from the shell of a body that had incarcerated them for so long, broke free of the habit of silence and declared themselves the person he or she wanted to be, and when Victoire proclaimed as much, hoping, who knows, that perhaps one day she would find the same happiness for herself, of a family united, her hair appeared to grow longer, her figure more slender, after so many fights, thought Victoire, the transsexual community she belonged to was confidently burgeoning, was this what living free meant, that her emancipated body was no longer suppressed by the one imposed on her at birth, yes, said Yinn, by all means be thunderous in your upholding of the truth, do you hear me, Victoire, make no concessions, make none at all, said Yinn, and Petites Cendres decided the kiss Victoire had placed on Yinn's cheek was a gesture of hope and of her openness to the future, for even if sectarian people were sinking to such appalling and barbaric depths, other men and women and children were progressing beyond that, and militant Victoire was the figurehead of that movement, of this transformation of future days, yes, thought Petites Cendres, we have to believe, and then, as he was contemplating just how beautiful Yinn was in tonight's new attire, Petites Cendres remembered the nightmare he'd had in which, just a few hours before, he'd been jogging along a country road and recognized neither the tropical vegetation nor the smells, feeling scared as he ran along a pitch-black and unpleasant road that he might crash into one of the species of hideous and leafless trees that he did not recognize, the route was parched and terrifying and he wondered why he was running it by himself, no Robbie by his side, and, heart pounding, for Petites Cendres had been jogging for a long time, he asked, where was Robbie, thinking that to find his way again perhaps he needed to utter a prayer as his mother used to do on their way to the Baptist church, this despite his seemingly pious mother having been a spiteful woman who spurned him, how did that prayer go again, he wondered, reciting in its place words quite unlike any his malicious mother would have spoken, My Lord, you who are great, why do you wear down little people like me, you who have the gift of all light, why do you extinguish us one by one, do you not feel a little shame, God, O God of All Light, have you no shame, these words contravening everything his oh-so-devout-and-pious mother taught him, and as he ran he screamed the words at the dark sky though he knew no one was listening, and then suddenly he heard someone whistling a birdsong, whose was this shrill and far-off call, and running closer to the source of it despite the shadowy route and the fields lost in the black, Petites Cendres could make out that Yinn was the one whistling, he was sitting on the steps of a cabin and wearing boys' clothes, rumpled white shorts, his bare feet in sandals, and hadn't heard Petites Cendres running and gasping and out of breath, he didn't seem to have noticed him at all, he was whistling his poignant melody as if only for himself, and Petites Cendres thought as he listened to the stirring, enchanting tune that now he would find his way again, that the dawn would appear soon, and when he woke up in his hammock under a blazing sun, Robbie standing nearby and saying you should open the parakeets' cages so they can fly to the pond, c'mon, Petites Cendres, it's time for our jog along the shore, what are you doing in that hammock so late, and don't forget Dr. Dieudonné is coming this afternoon, c'mon Petites Cendres, we better get going while the air's still fresh and before the crowds are running along Atlantic Boulevard, and Petites Cendres thought about how the bad dream had vanished or, at least, that it would soon be forgotten now that he was with friends, though a murky, sticky trace of it remained, and Robbie said to Yinn, your dress isn't hooked up and your shoulders are too exposed, let me dress you, Yinn, but Yinn was already walking across the stage and the video was playing on the screen above it despite Jason, up in the hidden booth, having cut the sound, the film of Herman and Fatalité singing and dancing continued to roll as Yinn lifted his eyes toward their silent but still insolent and mischievous faces, Petites Cendres understanding in that moment the meaning of his troubling dream, that Yinn's whistling like a bird was his calling to the dead, Fatalité and Herman both gone so young, why, that evening when Jason had filmed the show, Herman was singing "I've Never Felt So Good," not yet knowing anything of the raging cancer that would kill him in a few months, and as for Fatalité, beneath the silliness of her feathers was she not also celebrating her last days, like Herman she'd be rocking the Saloon till the end, and Petites Cendres replayed in his mind the vigil that followed Herman's last performance, they'd been in the house his mother had rented, so he'd tire less quickly, just steps away from the Saloon, and Herman was lying on what looked like a child's bed, Herman neither responding to Yinn's embrace nor to his yelling get up, are you stoned or what, Herman, get up, until finally Yinn's mother had to pull him off the body, saying, Yinn, it's over, he stopped breathing minutes ago, Petites Cendres noticed the respirator positioned by the child's bed to no avail, thinking no, there's nothing more we can do, and all the weeping queens were there, saying to Yinn over and over, is it true he's not breathing anymore, he isn't stoned this time, is he, and Yinn looked totally shaken for a moment and then said to the girls, come on, soon it'll be time for the late show, come, you know just as I do that Herman will always be with us, yes, you better believe it, he always will be, and as Yinn continued to prepare for the evening, never quite done because Robbie was so persistent, following Yinn as he went toward the screen and the figures of Fatalité and Herman that upset him so, Petites Cendres realized it was true, that Herman and Fatalité were right there alongside them, that this was the meaning of the dream and the birdsong, of Yinn sitting all alone on the steps of a country cabin and waiting, who knows, for voices from the heavens, for the voices of Herman and Fatalité that would in time surely answer him and say, hey Yinn, we're still here and so much wiser than before, oh, we were so right to be as we were, oh Yinn, if only you knew how much we miss our mad days, our crazy happiness and drunken nights, now we can live only through you, Yinn, through your memories, and was this why Yinn had drawn wings around the heads of the portraits of Fatalité and Herman painted on the cabaret walls, Fatalité and Herman, the Angels of the Saloon, wasn't this the truth of it, for despite the overdose Fatalité administered, in this way ending the slow degradation of Herman's messy decline, on the wall were two angels who would be remembered and venerated forever, explained Yinn, adding angels' white wings to the pictures of their impertinent heads just in case. Yes, thought Daniel in the cocoon of the bus making its way up mauve hills in the grandiose landscape, the jerky coughing of the engine convincing him that either the bus was antique or the driver the one needing a tune-up, Daniel still had time to mull over his presentation, would it be a stark recounting of two young girls of similar destiny, one Israeli, the other Palestinian, each seriously injured by grenade explosions, and how was he to know, maybe in the instant Daniel conjured up their faces both were already dead, a bloody hole in their throat or chest and their big, open eyes staring at him unrelentingly, at him, Daniel, the man who would describe their suffering tonight because the generals and colonels presiding over the war machine never see any of it, they never have the chance, weaponry operating at such a speed that they are acquainted with nothing but their own edicts and perhaps the incomprehensible satisfaction of a mission accomplished, and yet, and yet, just maybe they sense it, and a voice interrupted Daniel's train of thought saying, but Giovanni Boccaccio's father was a cultured man who indulged the young boy, he was never hungry like others of his generation, no, the young Giovanni was even allowed to read Dante in his free time, it's that, well, you see, the father recognized the son's exceptional gifts, ah yes, the son who worked at numerous trades, failing at every one of them but all the while maintaining his independence and earning a living, though without the help of his father what would have become of him, in Naples he served in a bank as a merchant's apprentice, work he hated, and then Giovanni's father got him into university, that was in Naples too, but another failure for the poet who wanted only to write, nothing more, for that was his true calling, the thing is his passion for poetry was ineradicable, and remember that Naples was one of the most prosperous cities in Europe at the time, Boccaccio would meet all sorts of scholars and writers there, all this came to pass along with all sorts of erotic adventures that took place in a court, in 1341, of astonishing elegance, what with the king being a singular patron of the arts who personally crowned poets with laurel wreaths, oh, to be able to write with such facility in Latin or Greek, to be able to recount pagan stories passed down through the centuries with such joy, and to write them so nimbly, though what would suddenly surprise these young people amusing themselves so, young lovers brimming with good health, was the plague, the Black Death as it was called, the plague, tumours and boils bursting out on previously fit and pleasure-seeking bodies, under armpits and down their sides, the fetid breath of the plague made itself felt everywhere, the Black Death afflicting entire families, tearing brother from brother, contagious mothers from their children, and in the face of such a virulent contagion churches were closed, people fled far from their houses and the dying would be abandoned to their agony in the streets, the whole town a rotting pile, no prayers offered for the dead, the young poet would live through this horror, in the midst of it all he would survive as if protected by an impenetrable fog of words, and Daniel could not help but eavesdrop on the writers' conversations because his colleagues were talking so much, one monologue often overlapping with another, all of which gave Daniel the sensation of being quite at home on the bus, a place where, despite losing the thread once in a while, the conversations had a ring of familiarity, and then another voice rose above the others and invoked the work of a writer who'd lived in Budapest, his was a paean to lost lands, to writers' entire canons erased by insurrection, a homily to the stories of men and women now annihilated and lost forever, to the erasure of entire cultures, and occasionally a more judicious voice made itself heard, that of a young writer remarking that whether the year was 1911 or 1341, everybody was talking too much about the past, do you really think we care, we young up-and-coming writers thrive in virtual libraries, our books, we write them on the air, our thoughts and memories are literally in clouds, we are the literary stars of tomorrow and all you can talk about are yesterday's miseries, the plague, the Black Death, and Daniel heard himself say, though no one was listening, but look, the Black Death is happening right here and now, it's what killed my two young girls, the little girls I'll be telling you about in my talk tonight, yes, the Black Death exists, of course it does, and we must never stop denouncing it, for who are we, my friends, but the harbingers of denunciation and revolution, who indeed, why, if my son Augustino were here, would he not say the same, that we are the cantors of a fury too long contained, even asphyxiated, by a hypocritical society that reduces its poets to positions of inertia and impotence, paying them so little heed they end up dying, and Daniel thought, did not Eddy tell me this morning that in the forests to which we are making our pilgrimage tonight, there's a derelict chapel in the ruins of a castle dedicated to poet-suicides and there we might pay tribute to their souls and unrequited desires in perpetual song, and isn't it the case that literature's martyrs, hyperanimated spirits that they were, tend to be forgotten, though, from the cavern of their suicides they may still light our way in these dark times left us, in their tormented premonitions they saw dictatorships that would deprive poets, artists, and writers of their energy and integrity, the dead anticipated everything, these the words Daniel was rehearsing in preparation for the evening when suddenly the coach driver announced over the PA system of the bus, seemingly suspended between two hills, that they would be stopping for a moment, after which everyone stepped out and breathed in the cool forest air, here, said the driver, behold our coniferous forest, a country of peat and briars and thousands of lochs, yes, thousands, and at the high altitude we'll eventually reach you'll see grassy pastures with sheep, goats, and deer, you'll see just a bit of the magnificent landscape we so want to preserve, but are we able to, can we, and just then Daniel saw a person in rags humbly bowing before the driver, it was his friend Rodrigo, the poet from Brazil, the pale shadow of the former Rodrigo had followed him here, I had to walk, he said, I've had to walk since dawn because none of the buses would take me, mister driver, please let me join my friends in your coach, I must attend the closing speech of tonight's program, my reasons are very personal, I need to tell everyone about my two sons, my two sons imprisoned and tortured in Venezuela, they're innocent, truly they are, Rodrigo implored, all they did was attend a student demonstration, won't you let me on the bus, and the driver who'd been so effusive in his descriptions of nature suddenly became cantankerous, saying, you can't get on this coach, not without a proper invitation for the presentation tonight, do you have one, the chauffeur demanded, every author must, do you have one, he asked again with an aggressive, inquisitorial air, no, said Rodrigo the poet, since I've been in exile none of the writers' committees have known where I am, and Daniel approached the driver and called out, actually the letter for Rodrigo came to me, it was sent to my island care of me, and out of the pocket of his white jacket he pulled a letter, here, said Daniel, here's Rodrigo's letter of invitation, but the driver said, that won't do, no, my friend, of course I want to believe the invitation went to your house, but we can't leave him at the writers' conference tonight because he's dressed so wretchedly, the shirt he has on hardly suffices in this autumn weather, and look at his bare feet in those nasty shoes, tonight's is a formal affair, a black or dinner jacket and trousers, nothing less, I'm very sorry about your friend but those are the rules, he said, and Daniel bellowed that he had two suits and would lend one to Rodrigo, that's enough, the driver answered, hurry up, get back on the bus, and as Daniel remonstrated with him, Rodrigo the Brazilian poet retreated as meekly as he had arrived and the driver, congenial once more, said, you see, your friend has gone back into the woods like a ghost, like a ghost, he repeated, our woods are full of them, these are our forests and woods, the driver went on, look, the birch and oak stretches far to the west and north, but Daniel was wondering where Rodrigo, here just a moment ago, had gone, please take your seat in the coach, said the driver, the other buses have arrived already and we don't want to be late for the opening ceremonies, and one of the African-American writers Daniel had greeted at the hotel in the morning took his arm and said come, follow me, and his stature, his stern nature, reminded Daniel of Olivier, and he remembered the writer's name was Paul, he was the poet Paul of Harlem, a lawyer who'd defended young black offenders there and the subject of his talk was resistance against force, he declared that it was something of a theological treatise on resilience, really, on resisting police decimating our youth, our people are religious, said Paul, they're killed at church, and know that churches are the only refuge our children think of as safe, and when that sanctuary is lost, where can they go, in the streets they'll just get killed, a bullet through the heart and it's over, though for the police officer who kills one of these kids, it's nothing, just a demonstration of hubris, nothing more, the policeman will go home to his family at night and think no more of it, follow me, said Paul, one of my people has been lynched in the woods, his neck is cut, and he's bleeding out on the grass, Daniel, come, help me free him of his rope, let's do that, you and me, then we'll wash him in the lake so that his body is rinsed clean of all that has defiled him, come, Daniel, and Daniel thought of Olivier being pushed in his wheelchair by his wife Chuan or their son Jermaine, Olivier now relegated to fighting from his grim wheelchair while Paul, with the same outrage the militant Olivier had demonstrated in his writing and social activism a decade earlier, was able to bravely pursue his own defiant agenda, Olivier who could now do no more than attend Paul's conferences and lectures when his wife or son pushed him in the wheelchair, a nervous ailment responsible for his condition and paralyzing him a little more each day, could it be true, thought Daniel, that Paul, with a comparable intransigence and a strength of conviction rendered all the more powerful by his youthful impetuosity, had taken up Olivier's mantle? Olivier had seen churches, the temples of Birmingham, razed, the children inside singing and dancing even as the doors were closed on them and one voice, the voice of the Ku Klux Klan, had yelled, let them all burn, and Paul, as Olivier had done before him, asked Daniel if there would ever be a day of redemption for such crimes, they're no more than teenagers, Paul said to Daniel, even swinging on the end of a rope they only seem to be sleeping, but follow me, you'll see, they've all come together in the forest here, and Daniel walked beside Paul who was still telling his story of kids burned alive in the churches, but Daniel saw no one, and Paul said to him, wasn't this the place where they were incinerated or did it happen farther on, beneath the birches, no, said Daniel, it happened in Birmingham, my friend

Olivier, who was working as a reporter at the time, saw it happen, and in the forest, but for Paul's lacerating words tearing at his soul, Daniel heard only silence, you're a writer and an idealist, said Paul, you're of a generation of writers that believes in progress, you believe in it, and I'm not saying you're wrong, what progress we have has come to pass because of you, it exists and grows due to your own persistent efforts, pathetic as this progress is when it comes to race, though Daniel, what I'd argue is there's been no progress at all, that nothing has changed for over a century, I'm thirty and I just don't believe in progress anymore, yes, this is how it is, the young author said to Daniel, and after taking a few steps along the perimeter of a thicket of pine, the two of them stepped back into the coach and Paul settled into his seat and said in the same beleaguered and disappointed tone, this is what I'll be talking about tonight, yes, whether at home or spilling over our borders, war and conflict are our great concerns, our major preoccupations and hellish ones, Paul said, deciding to sit alone by a window as Daniel, in a suddenly oppressive silence, returned to his seat at the back of the bus. It was appropriate for Lucia to be pleased with what she'd bought at the market, plenty of fruit and vegetables for Lena and Angel and a few of the other Acacia Gardens tenants, Night Out perched on her shoulder, she was riding her bike slowly so that the bird would not feel the bumps in the road, the folds and rifts in the disintegrating asphalt and cement unlikely to be repaired for some time, surely it was too hot to be working on the roads, though soon the rains would come and it would be cooler, and everywhere men in yellow hard hats would be wielding their pickaxes and obnoxiously catcalling, good morning little lady with the blue coveralls and birdie, so where are you off to on that bike, why not stick to the sidewalks so that out here on Atlantic Boulevard we can work in peace, yeah, why don't you, and then one of the men would say to another, she's a bit cracked 'cause she never listens to what I say, must have snuck out of the hospice or a loony bin, still, said another guy, we all love her, don't we, 'cause she makes us laugh and it's nice to see her, and she's been coming round so long, another would say, that or the workers would say nothing at all and it would be Lucia who'd be doing herself down, and Brilliant would have to say to her, respect yourself, my dear Lucia, you must have some self-respect, lots of it, and among the flowers she was carrying in her basket were birds of paradise for Angel, their large corollas bursting out of the pink cellophane and spreading in the sun and one, taller than the rest, touching her face every now and then as the bike bounced along, it was late afternoon and the hour of heavy traffic, when bird trainers and snake charmers on their tricycles threaded their way through the riot of noisy cars and headed toward the docks, and Lucia could hear Old Bill grumbling to his parrot, you better put on a good show and do what I tell you, not like yesterday, or you won't live past forty-five, which is plenty for a common old parrot given that we don't get to live so long, yup, us, the unfortunate folk who take pity on you, and what do I get for all your cute antics, nothing, pennies, that's all, not even enough for dinner, your sunflower seeds cost me too much, and Old Bill's parrot Emy Senior was always grouchy too, thought Lucia, Old Bill cared little for his birds and dogs and was known to have left one of his dogs out in the sun to die of thirst in the street, charges had been brought against him and, ever since, he'd put shades on the dog that had replaced the unfortunate first one all day long, but he was being watched, thought Lucia, the Society for the Protection of Cruelty to Animals was looking to catch him out, and Lucia hoped he'd never be in a position to abuse any of his animals again, though evidently Old Bill's parrot Emy Senior was still being maltreated, out of its cage when it should have been in it, cars brushing past Old Bill's tricycle and Emy Senior tossed back and forth along the metal perch he'd welded to the handlebars, the parrot balancing itself indignantly, the magnificent Australian bird gripping the bar tightly with its claws for fear of being knocked off it by a car, how offensive it was to have to listen to the sour and acrimonious discourse of its master who, Lucia knew, was always a little drunk by this time of day, poor Emy Senior's red beak had already been broken in a life of several owners every bit as nasty as Old Bill, it had needed to undergo intensive care at the Sanctuary for Birds and ever since that time utterly mistrustful of the humans exploiting it for their commercial gain, Emy Senior had dreamed of the paradise that the bird sanctuary was and hoped maybe to go back there someday, after all it had worked enough parading around for fearsome Old Bill, hadn't it, Lucia felt the suffering of the parrot teetering on the metal bar in its humiliating dance to the unconscionable music of its master's hectoring, it was as if she herself were the splendidly plumed bird of many colours, red and green and brown and a scintillating yellow, was it her relationship with Night Out, she wondered, that connected her to the vulnerability of all birds on earth, to the existence of animals relentlessly coveted and hurt, nothing offended her more than to hear Old Bill's vilification of the parrot and she screamed at him, stop it, you ignorant old man, you drunken sadist, her words were lost in the hot, dusty air but still she yelled that she would call the city's SPCA, but Old Bill just pedalled laboriously on to the quays where his bird would entertain children and tourists while he insulted it, no, parrot, you don't deserve to live past forty-five, that's plenty old enough, and Emy Senior would repeat, plenty, yeah, that's plenty you old ape, and when she came to Atlantic Boulevard Lucia remembered, how could she forget, there was to be a party tonight with a cake for Angel, who'd been waiting for his friend Kitty, yes, Kitty had promised to visit with her mother and brothers because finally the shelter for families in need had found them a home, sure, it might be some distance from Angel and Lena's place, but the two would be able to see one another and Angel would have a friend his own age close by, was not life a perpetual fount of miracles, thought Lucia, Night Out, you are my miracle, she said to the parrot perched on her shoulder, just as Kitty will be Angel's at a time when life is not much fun for him, poor kid, now he's coughing and complaining of a pain in his chest, Drs. Dieudonné and Lorraine come to see him every day, he's responding better to his meds and he's able to go to the sea with Brilliant and watch the sun set over the waves, though he can only do so on days with no wind or storms to make his coughing worse, Dr. Dieudonné says it's not pneumonia, just a bad cold, and we're not to worry, and that Misha's still doing his patient a lot of good, yes, Misha is another of Angel's miracles, one day there'll be a definitive cure, for it really is true that life is a fount of miracles, that's what Brilliant likes to say, and what a pity he's working nights in Emergency and has no time to write his novel, a novel born of his anger, yes, even if, thought Lucia, and it's truly a pity, he's no longer the young Brilliant of fishermen's bars and taverns he used to be, but he's still the Brilliant I love like a son and who's saved my life more than once, it's as if we were partnered in affliction and reborn, the two of us together because fate cannot be explained and my deplorable sisters never did succeed in locking me away in some sanatorium, that's our victory, Brilliant's and mine, that had I been subjected to such funereal incarceration I'd have ended up deaf and blind, I'd have no memories of the past or present and memory is what causes me to think about them so often, of Jonathan and his stoned mother Jill, of Rodriguez the bicycle and car thief, where are they now, I've never seen them again, is Jonathan still separated from his mother and, if so, how long has he been so, Lucia thinking, whenever I see some haggard mother alone with her child in the streets, I say, look it's her, look, there's little Jonathan, only I don't stop anymore because I'm expected at the Acacia Gardens, they're waiting for me with their groceries, maybe I should see if the two of them are at the Shelter and if the other, that scoundrel Rodriguez, is in prison, yes, that's what I should be doing, how useless I've been all these years that my sisters have been hounding me and saying, you're nothing, just a tramp, you're nobody, can't even bring up your own son, and I'd say to myself yes, it's true, I'm nothing, and now, look at me, I have nothing, ruined and dispossessed by my sisters who blamed me for everything, who told me I was a terrible mother and wife even as they stole my shop from me, stole my jewels and dresses, selling all of it for their own gain, one day you'll be homeless and sleeping on the sidewalk, that's what they'd say, if only they found themselves homeless, then they'd tell me how *they* suffer, they'd tell me what it feels like to have other people trample over you, about the indignities and humiliations of living on the streets, let them not be spared the miseries they've inflicted on others, says Brilliant, he tells me I must forget them, though has he forgotten his mother who had him beaten by a black servant saying, hit him, hit him hard, his mother the mayor, the fanatic, can he, can Brilliant actually forget, because isn't that also the point of memories, for even though I've often mislaid them myself, none of the terrible pain inflicted on us should ever be forgotten, and as Lucia was thinking this, Dorothea was in the kitchen ironing Adrien's Sunday suit, the fan overhead monotonously humming, and Adrien asked, my dear Dorothea, how should I begin my speech, you know I've not given one for ages, such a palaver they are, well, said Dorothea, I'd start by saying thank you for this Poet of the Year Award, no, I can't say that, said Adrien, sitting behind the Japanese screen where he kept his writing desk just as Suzanne had done, the desk behind the screen where she had written for so long was actually hers, everything in place just as she'd left it, as if, thought Adrien, she might appear with her journals and notebooks again at any moment, even the framed photograph of Charles she so loved, that over time had taken on a verdigris hue beneath the glass, darkish green, so that with its shadows and mysterious glints of light and its scholarly setting it resembled a painting, that of a library where Charles sat in a white sofa chair reading by the light of a porcelain lamp, the ascetic Charles lit by nothing more than an ephemeral glimmer and the white of his clothes glowing in the evocative stillness Caroline had captured quite intentionally, Caroline wanting to emphasize the look of concentration as the poet read, Charles's face, the eyelids almost closed, fixed in that glorious moment in which the poet is in the full bloom of his youth and at the height of his powers seeming as if he will remain that way forever, and he gazed at this portrait of Charles, because given Caroline's skill that's what it was, a portrait more than a mere photograph, as if the fingers of a painter had fashioned Charles's features into the soulful aspect she'd captured, and was it not in contemplating Charles's seemingly timeless spiritual features, suddenly, that Suzanne discovered just how content writing made her, or perhaps the solace that Charles's meditative face, like the close company of a friend, brought to her writer's solitude, was this not Charles's gift, thought Adrien, he who was always there for Suzanne when he was off at some foreign conference, when he was so far away and likely too infatuated with himself as poet to bother thinking of Suzanne writing at home, too autocratic, too self-absorbed, he'd forgotten her, repenting too late, and now here he was about to succumb to the despondency of his regrets when Dorothea came into his office, or rather Suzanne's, with the freshly laundered clothes he was to go out in, you're not to forget your cane or umbrella, said Dorothea, now come on, said Adrien, tell me who steps up to the podium to receive an award holding a cane, honestly, Dorothea, no cane, but then he thought better of it, for in truth he was well advised to do so, after all he'd need to climb all those steps in the university auditorium, and for the trip over there, said Dorothea, your white hat and trousers and the navy-blue blazer will do, I'll pack your bag, I don't like seeing you go off with that woman who calls herself your chauffeur, just what do you see in her, Monsieur Adrien, I'd like to know, she's a coloured lady like me, she's from Jamaica and I'm from the Bahamas so what's the difference, asked Dorothea, okay, she's definitely not ugly but I was also beautiful once, yes, back in the Bahamas, I was beautiful too, so exactly what, Mr. Adrien, do you think her qualities are, she never goes to church, she's out every night, and Adrien said all Charly does is take me to the airport in her chauffeur's black limousine, his voice trembling because Dorothea's interrogation was troubling him, and what I see in her, my dear Dorothea, is that she still possesses what I do not, she's young, my dear Dorothea, do you understand that, now please let's talk no more about it, and Dorothea stifled a laugh, why yes, she said, youth, of course, youth, maybe this lovely young woman can cast spells too, that's what they say, and that she takes drugs, they say that as well, and Adrien answered that jealousy and envy are the worst of vices, his thoughts already drifting on to other matters such as the modern version of Faust he was writing but could not finish, old Faust had broken out of the confines of his sixteenth-century German legend to haunt Adrien, who'd not have hesitated for a moment to sell his own soul to the devil in order to live again his gallant youth and all the heady sensual pleasures he'd known in it, so whether the object of his affection were Suzanne or Charly, what harm could there be in loving, oh, he thought, aren't I more like old Isaac with each passing day, and he examined the wrinkles of his stomach because he was naked under the shirt he was putting on, or in truth, that Dorothea was dressing him in as she castigated him, Mr. Adrien, she said, really now, a man of your age should not be thinking about any of that, and Adrien decided he and Dorothea had become a little too intimate, you'd think she was my partner, he thought, since I taught her to read and write she's not stopped reprimanding me, so how are your Bible studies coming along, he asked as she pulled up his trousers, white trousers, nicely cut, cane or no cane he needed to impress the auditorium, there, said Dorothea, now you look like a distinguished gentleman, and as for the cane, perhaps you can hide it a little under your blazer, hah, when they present you with flowers, even at this distance I'll be so proud and happy for you, Mr. Adrien, the year's poet laureate, oh my, how happy I'll be, now if only you'd stop seeing that lady who claims to be your chauffeur, they say her clientele consists entirely of old men, and rich old men at that, said Dorothea, ah, but I'm not rich, said Adrien cuttingly, Dorothea, you know well that I have only my professor's pension from the girls' college, it's not much, and I'm not an old man either, my god, you really do get on my nerves, an old man is someone in his last days, bedridden, an invalid, is that really how you see me, he asked, do you see me as decrepit, no, said Dorothea, you still strike me as virile and attractive and alluring, and, as regards the men I've known, when I was in my youth and just a lowly servant in the Bahamas, she started, but then stopped short, yes yes, I know, Adrien cut in, you already told me, now what time is that ceremony, he asked, a little more anxiously now, I'll finish my acceptance speech in the airplane, besides, it'll be very short, and Dorothea said, it's an evening do, you'll have the afternoon to rest, and Adrien exclaimed, rest, oh no, I'll be with the kids, so let your children dote on you for a change, said Dorothea, they should be good for something when their parents get old, she declared sententiously, but I'm not old, Adrien reminded her, it's true our children should indulge us rather than simply cause trouble, frankly mine wear me out, and I have to say living with you, dear Dorothea, really does make me the happiest of men, we live very well together, and Dorothea pretended not to hear and said, I'll pack your bag and went off to do so in his room, Adrien noting her heavy, tilted walk and wondering if maybe she, as he was, was also a little deaf, and thought, oh dear, Dorothea and me, here we are like any old couple with all our faults and failings and, on top of it all, I'll need a wheelchair at the airport, whatever, Charly can see to that, how considerate but also misunderstood Charly is, how preposterous it was that Dorothea should have compared herself in her younger Bahamian days to Charly, Dorothea, who for the longest time had not been able to read or write, Charly, dear Charly, and still motionless at the desk behind the Japanese screen Adrien thought of Charly, his dear Charly, wondering if this was how dreamers craving unknown pleasures ended up selling their souls, was this how it happened, and Fleur remembered how young a child he'd been when his love of music was born, it had come to him in New Orleans, the city where his parents had taken him before his mother fawned on him so possessively, Martha, who had watched her son grow up in astonishment, the day would come when her love would become rapacious and stifling, they were all there in New Orleans, Martha, his father, and his grandfather, a farmer from Georgia who was possibly the first to divine the boy's musical gift, and as Fleur listened to Claudio directing his *New Symphony* he thought that any soul can be a vehicle of the transcendent, yes, anybody's, it had been his grandfather who'd said they should visit the town of Louis Armstrong to listen to jazz orchestras and bluesmen, in those few days Fleur had revelled in the delight of constantly hearing wild and untamed music in the old city, he could see the little boy now, the long hair his mother had freshly brushed and the chubby child he was, dressed in the floral clothes she'd made for him, it didn't matter if the playing was restrained or uproarious, he'd jived to the sound of local musicians and bands improvising in the streets, guitars, a piano, or the violin, he felt able to play any of them and that he might lead the processions of musicians at black funerals too, the music and dancing was like a fever for him, he'd run amid the adult players and clapped his hands to the beat, and then he'd been put in front of the piano and played a few of the riffs he'd heard, and it didn't matter whether the tone of the music was doleful or funereal, still he managed to wrest more heartache out of it, the musicians applauded his virtuosity and lifted him above their heads, his parents kissed him, and he remembered his mother stroking the unkempt hair falling across his brow, yes, he remembered it all, his baptism in music, and my, was it a glorious moment, feverish and fierce, for he would never be free of music, it was in New Orleans that he first felt the fervour of being carried away by music reverberating in him so much that he couldn't resist, he was possessed by it, under its spell, as if the music was his breath, the breath of life itself, and he remembered a fiddle player going at it in the rain, a gaunt old black man whose gnarled hands looked as if they'd been ravaged by his years of playing the violin, Fleur tossing a few coins into the hat he'd placed on the sidewalk next to his feet and the musician saying, take it from me, young man, don't you ever be a second fiddle, only first, you get what I'm saying, I'm a black man so I always came last and now here I am playing in the street, listen up, this is Mozart, are you listening, young man, but all Fleur heard was screeching and grating, the old man no longer able to play his instrument supplely, hang on, the old man said, bewildered, I'm pretty sure that was Mozart, oh, now I remember, these are the notes, where did they get to, must be the rain, this downpour, yeah, don't forget, my talented young friend, you've got to come first, be first in everything, shoot for the stars or else it's not true music, just a bunch of meaningless sounds like you're hearing from my violin, so good night, young man, Garçon Fleur, that's what your parents call you, don't come see me again, I'm just too miserable playing in the rain, no, don't come no more, it kills me that I have to do this, don't be last, always be first, that didn't happen for me, good night young man, good night, yes, it was Mozart I used to play and now listen to this, this nothing at all, just the gloomy wailing of a violin, and with that Fleur ran off in the rain, and from then on his parents could not prevent him chasing his destiny, his dreams, and finally one day his mother Martha smoothed his long, wet hair with her hand and said, go to sleep now but first come here, Garçon Fleur, you know that I've booked you a gig with a Cajun group, come, honey, it's true, it'll happen in the spring, and Fleur thought hard and concluded that it must have been before he'd met Clara, a concert violinist, yes, it was before, and what would become of the fat black notes in Beethoven's manuscripts, what would become of them, for God would abuse this child of His to the very end, and what Claudio did not reckon with, thought Fleur, was just how rash and vindictive was the grotesque jealousy his absent God maintained toward the creatures He'd given life, He was jealous of their talents, of their magnificence, yes, thought Fleur, Beethoven's gourmandish mistake had been to request a glass of wine of the country from which he'd ordered a whole case, this while he'd been thinking he still had a little time, but he'd succumbed to his agonies, so why should he not wet his lips in some chilled punch, which he did, immediately throwing all of it up though nevertheless appreciating the delight of it, how could he not vomit when his liver and stomach were ruined, what choice did he have if he was to enjoy himself fully and not defer to his dying moments but to rise above the vomiting, how could he not, thought Fleur, the last moments of his life ebbing away, ebbing away implacably, and the end coming on the day when Beethoven was awarded the endowment that, at long last, would afford him the chance to work with the Vienna Philharmonic, money that came in time for a new work but was alas too late, a thousand florins good only for funeral costs, that's how his destiny played out, God would maltreat His child to the very end, Wrath offering up this toxic exegesis, of course, acrimonious words murmured in Fleur's ear under the bridges of the Seine, and it had also been Wrath, inclined only to vituperative words and ideas, who spoke of the absent God's envy of His most accomplished creatures, of how He denigrated their creative powers, punishing them horribly, trying them to the point of breaking their will, though was it necessary, even Wrath wondered, to crush and humiliate someone already broken and on his deathbed, for suddenly the old man chilled to the bone in his ragged coat appeared to pity anyone who faced such a ghastly death with no prospect of relief, and Fleur, who'd been listening to Claudio conduct his *New Symphony* all the while, imagined again the commanding black notes of Beethoven's manuscripts, and during the low beating of the drums and their interruption by the voice of a soprano lamenting the imminent death of the young girls of Hiroshima, Fleur turned to face the auditorium and noticed some of the audience had left, fleeing the crematory smoke of his music, though no, maybe not, just one person and that's all, Claudio had managed to keep his patrons in the hall, and Fleur thought, or at least some part of him did, that perhaps under Claudio's direction all would go well with the music that had kept him alive to this day. And Daniel, snug in the coach now making its way through the woods, thought of Mai's smile and it worried him that, as with any such moment of serenity, her smile disappeared and died, when some shadow fell, it had happened after Mai said to her father, Papa, tell me, will the wonders of the world you and Mama talk of so much always be around, will they still exist when I'm grown up, true, this was a long time ago, when the two of them used to travel with their children a lot, when they'd been trying to implant in their children conventional pleasures of the discovery of the arts, the sort of knowledge, thought Daniel, that would serve them well in the future, albeit cultural baggage Augustino would have taken no time to mock, trampling on his father's endeavour with rage because, according to Augustino, the right to know, the right to learning, would always be a privilege of the few, fair to say that Augustino, unlike his siblings, had always been hostile to his parents' instruction and experience, and that despite his young age he'd always been an old soul, and could one not also think of this old soul as arid and forbidding, or that his was the atavistic memory of someone who'd suffered a plethora of wounds that would never heal, why, asked Augustino, do we never speak of your great-uncle Samuel, shot in Poland in that grim winter, why don't we, and Daniel would reply, because there is nothing to be done about it, what's past is past, during the time of the pogroms none of us was yet born, our awareness of the most egregious acts of evil only comes with the consciousness of our being alive, or so he thought,

Augustino transformed so suddenly at age fifteen, perhaps that consciousness had preceded his actual being, whereas with Mai, every spark of awareness was spontaneous and attached to the present, whether she were contemplating a drought in California or an earthquake in Haiti, that smile of hers was troubled, Daniel able to read deep worry in her delicate face and bright eyes, and of course she wept a lot and often, adamant her parents not console her in her grief because she was certain that her own parents would not be dragged down with the unfortunate rest by lands and fields furrowed by drought in countries already devastated and beyond redemption, they would not be among the millions of innocent victims, though she was also aware that one day, in the vortex of a universe inexorably rent apart by the exhaustion of its resources, that she might find herself among their number, and Daniel heard the driver say, here in these woods you see, bathed in the colours of the setting sun, rare species of ferns grow, but also mushrooms and lichens and thistles and rhododendrons and campanula and what we call Scotch pine, with its sweet-smelling cones, I don't know if you'll have the opportunity to visit the west coast during your stay, so rich in the ocean flotsam that rides in with the tide, I don't know if, the driver continued, just as a clamour of voices could be heard and the coach was stopped and then suddenly rocked by a mob of men and women trying to climb on top of it, please disembark, the driver said to the writers, take a few minutes if you like and examine the woods, and it looked to Daniel like the emergency exits had been forced open and the crowd was packed more densely around them and so, when he alighted, he breathed the mountain air with relief, after their slow climb and the drive's many perturbations, whether occurrences or simply visions they'd been all too real, they must be getting closer to the site of the conference, and now here were women, men, and children advancing toward him from the forest as if through barbed wire, or that's how it appeared, because the trees of the forest were covered in silver frost and the trees and bushes were tortured coils around them, had the driver not described, a few minutes earlier, how the force of the ocean winds twisted the trees and bushes this way in the autumn, and a young man holding up a placard with the faces of several of his peers said, we are from the town of Ayotzinapa, a few hours from Mexico City, it's a poor town, so impoverished, and then another young man appeared behind him with a placard showing different faces, all of them young and poor, and the man said they were the children of the working destitute and that in the town where they were born, a miserable town infiltrated by extraordinarily violent gangs and drug traffickers, no yellow marigolds would be strewn over their bodies because their ashes had been scattered in the San Juan River by their killers, drug lords and murdering politicians in hiding because they know there'll be no mercy when we come and besiege them in their villas and palaces, they murdered our brothers and set them on fire, students from small towns who in their sweet revolution against corruption barricaded roads and raised red flags in honour of Che, we called them the Rebels of Ayotzinapa, these the poorest and most secluded of people assassinated for writing graffiti on university walls, they were taken in trucks to be slaughtered in forests like this one, look at their faces, and when Daniel did it felt to him that the face of each of the dead students was falling right on top of him, as if the placards were death shrouds flapping in the breeze, and his terrified thoughts turned to Mai and his other children, imagining they could be among them as the young man said, solemnly, that schoolteachers, professors from the colleges of Oaxaca and Michoacán, entire delegations of students, were here for this Long March proceeding silently and in unison, we raise our candles to the students and carry bouquets of white chrysanthemums against our chests in their honour, the corrupt and lying police insist they'll all be found alive but we know better, their cut-up bodies, it's so terribly sad, lie in the San Juan River, no *zempasuchil* will cover them, oh misery, that they were killed for a bit of graffiti on a wall, oh, our brothers, almost fifty of them were martyred, abducted and trucked away before midnight, oh misery, misery, said the young man, and if the boy's brown skin had been any lighter, would he not have looked like Augustino, was he not there, a part of this band of youth, was Daniel not about to be informed, as happened with the murdered students' parents, that a truck had disappeared into the forest during the night and, ever since, no one had any idea where his son Augustino was, no one had a clue as to his whereabouts, because he'd been on the rebels' Long March and graffiti signed with the name Augustino had been seen on the walls, and Daniel opened his eyes and gazed upon the gilded countryside spooling out beside him, the road becoming rougher as they ascended, these are conifer forests, the driver said, mountain birch and pines, soon we'll be at the top and from up there you'll be able to see the coast if night has not fallen, yes, let's hope the sun has not set yet, and Daniel remembered his daughter saying, often, Papa, there's nothing that cannot be solved by two brains looking for a solution, no problem is insoluble, Papa, co-operative minds have found a solution for energy and light in the solar power plants of California's Mojave Desert, so that today and in the future a superabundance of energy will illuminate and bring heat or, at torrid times of year, cool air, to several towns and soon, Papa, the whole world will benefit from this desert energy, not just a third of humanity but the entire universe will benefit, Papa, and then suddenly, as often happened after Mai articulated her hopes for the future so exuberantly, she seemed to doubt all she'd said, and although the doubt suspended on her half-open lips was mute, Daniel could not forget how uncertainty would darken his daughter's features as if, in thinking what she had, she'd suddenly matured and in that instant withdrawn into the confines of an abruptly diminished future, and Daniel believed she was right, it was true, nothing was insoluble, there was always some brilliant solution, the trick was to discover it, of course, so why had he not reassured her that she was not misguided, what failing held him back, his recalcitrance reinforcing her doubts instead of championing her hopes, fathers were so often cowards, such as Daniel himself had been when he'd refrained from telling Vincent about his serious pulmonary illness, still, by not doing so he'd saved a son who was virtually a doctor now, tending to others and with hardly the time to think of himself, perhaps there was such a thing as benign, even altruistic cowardice, the role of the father, thought Daniel, was so complex, and then he remembered that Stephen, did he not love him like a son, had sent him a second message in which his resolve was impressive, for no longer was Stephen's frailty the thing others found appealing, a quality, thought Daniel, that only led to attachments made in bad faith, Stephen had visited Eli in prison, one annexed to a farm in which young offenders were able to work with veterinarians caring for maltreated animals and to learn a profession, all of which interested Eli, who, indifferent to his own rehabilitation and equally disdainful of animals he'd rather abuse than heal, was already an inveterate criminal in the making and happily so, during Stephen's visit Eli had, without compunction, handed Stephen an envelope and, with his usual insolence, ordered him to deliver it to a friend whose address he'd provide, Stephen asked what was inside but understood right away what the mission entailed, you know perfectly well, laughed Eli, no less at ease in his prison uniform than in the elegant clothes he used to wear cruising for clients in hotels by the seaside, you know perfectly well, Stephen, I'm an open book to you, the hero of your novel, you know me better than anyone, so you know what's under the stamps on the envelope too, it's a technique I learned here where all the prison mail is checked and there's no other way to get anything through, under the stamps and on the return envelope there are tabs of what you hate, of cocaine, of course, as well as another illegal substance, I'll let you figure out which, but my, I can see by your disgusted expression that you're shocked, said Eli when Stephen protested that he would not perform the criminal task, exclaiming how upset he was that Eli was always such a grifter, that he'd not changed one bit, even in a penal institution where, in their work on the farm or in the several hours of the day they had to themselves, inmates were given a second chance, and Eli suddenly became menacing, saying, if you refuse to do this you'll regret it, I'll always be able to find you even if you go back to New York, but, Stephen wrote Daniel, after he pushed away the envelope Eli had agitatedly extended his way, he realized, just as novelists described, that in the face of such brutishness there are limits to love, though more so how exasperating his illusions about Eli had been, any passion he'd felt had given way to his fear of seeing Eli show up at Charles's house again, and now Stephen was conceding just how aghast he was at the folly of the senses that had taken hold of him from the very first time he'd met Eli, back when he'd felt the attraction of the cold blue gaze of a man who, stymied now, had turned to hate because Stephen had refused to do him a pernicious favour, he was over his love now, the bond that had engrossed his imagination for too long was broken, this was how Stephen put it, the revelation of his finite love likely putting an end to his novel as well, he'd rip it up and destroy it, except that no, when he got home, Stephen went right on with the rest of it and included the day's new developments in a narrative suffused with chagrin, disappointment, as well as the recounting of the end of his relationship with Eli, the envelope, and the stamps concealing stationery laced with toxic substances, Stephen wrote for several consecutive hours, grappling intimately with the subject of his fallen hero, of Eli finally defeated by the force of his contrariness, and how at last Stephen felt liberated from his desire for Eli, oh, what a blessing it would be not to see him again, though it struck Stephen that, despite the boundaries that had brought his love to a close, the beast of his desire still roamed Charles and Frédéric's house, he remembered how when Eli returned home at dawn he used to climb in through the window, Stephen had loved the ferocious beast in Eli, but now the time had come to stop licking the wounds inflicted on him by the carnivorous creature, wounds bitten deep into his soul more than flesh, he wrote, Stephen allowing the reality of Eli's having disappointed him so thoroughly to metamorphose, in his book, into scenes in which Eli took on the wild majesty of the most voracious of animals, Eli, who'd devoured Stephen the way a lion does a doe, for as extreme as the hurt of Stephen's love for Eli had been, the novel was a thing apart, and tears ran down Stephen's cheeks at the desk where the ascetic Charles had written so profusely and Frédéric, working close to him, sketched and painted at his easel, Frédéric, who was perpetually unsettled and always on the point of leaving, and as the night drew on Stephen wrote and wrote, thinking, who knows, the story he was writing might reach far beyond the crux of the moment in which love dies, yes, thought Stephen, who knew where these words were leading, perhaps it was better not to know, oh, what a blessing it would be to never see this man again, he who had threatened Stephen saying, you'll regret this, really you will. Yes, Fleur thought, that had been the moment of his birth in music, in New Orleans, when his mother booked him to play with a Cajun band and suddenly seized hold of him as if he'd been her quarry, of course, improvise at the piano as you like, naturally you can, she'd said, and Fleur bolted through the streets in his effort to get away from Martha, neither his father nor his grandfather there to defend him against her edicts, her possessive frenzy, and in stealing away from his mother he'd met a reclusive jazz musician they called the Indonesian playing solo cello in a smoky billiard hall, trumpeters playing in the surrounding streets that echoed diverting and disillusioned song, as if the entire city was music to be exhausted with the dawn, with the first red glow in the sky, okay kid, said the Indonesian as he took a break from his cello, you'll be a part of our group, he smoked so heavily that his fingers had yellowed, they don't let kids into billiard halls so what are you doing here, boy, he said, I'm listening to you play, said Fleur, and as Claudio conducted his *New Symphony* in the Roman concert hall, Fleur wondered if this man who smoked so much, drinking, at the same time, a rum cocktail with marinated fruit, if this drunk and drug-addled musician might not be Su or a musician so much like Su that the two were suddenly indistinguishable, would it be him Fleur would later see by Wrath's side, down at the docks that were Wrath's antechamber to hell, begging for a first and last cigarette, wasn't it him, the musician from the smoky billiard hall in which a few Chinese teenagers the Indonesian appeared to know well had snuck into the common room for minors, immediately heading to the green baize of the pool table and knocking a few balls around, wearing caps and eyeing Fleur suspiciously, have a taste, said the Indonesian, go on, have a taste of these fruits soaked in rum, not the rum, only the fruit, and delighting in the rum-soaked sliced fruit, an apple, an orange, Fleur became a little tipsy, succumbing to a floating drunkenness of the kind he'd known when, in the company of Kim and Jérôme the African, he'd play his flute on the street, a death wish, thought Fleur, born in him in some faraway place at the same time as his passion for music, how had he survived it all, how, for although these days he was always sober, had the urge to drink not been instilled in him after watching the Indonesian, after taking in his ambivalent smile, his fingers tarred from smoking too much, and what had Fleur been doing in this smoke-clouded billiard hall anyway, listening but not really listening to the undulating riffs of a cellist who seemed more of a drunk than a musician, Fleur realized at the time that he'd always be evasive, just as he was being with the Indonesian when he'd imbibed of the delectable fruits in the man's rum glass despite himself, that from then on his urge to the improper, to be disobedient to his mother and the status quo that held him down, would be as irrepressible as his passion for music, yes, that's how it will be, thought Fleur, and if on the one hand Fleur had been afraid of getting drunk on the rum-soaked fruit the cellist was offering him, he'd also had the sensation that he would no longer be so affected by his mother, kind and proud of her son as he knew her to be, and now as the memory of a prior existence, combined with the fading taste of a drink he ought never to have had, filtered through to him, the smell of his wet dogs when it rained on the beach and how all of them had been so alone, Kim, the dogs, Brilliant spreading his blankets on the sand, alone and with no one to look out for them like strays of an invisible herd, though they had the stars and the sea to themselves, and as, invisibly, they were being watched, no, thought Fleur, given this clandestine surveillance, they had never been truly alone. And inside the black limo taking him to the airport, Adrien reproached himself for refusing Charly's invitation to sit beside her up front, the six seats of the limousine being empty and, Adrien aside, Charly having no clients headed to the airport that day, come sit beside me, Adrien, I've got no one flying out till tonight and you'll be more comfortable, come, dear friend, but he'd declined, worried that Charly's invitation was not sufficiently genuine, that she'd not actually spoken the words *dear friend*, so Charly sped to the airport as if she had urgent things to do after his departure, and Adrien, who did not want to saddle her with all his baggage, briefcase, cane, and the hat he'd put back on his head was, from the moment he sat down in the limo, already slightly out of breath and didn't want Charly picking up on it though actually, he thought, maybe he had agreed to this Poet of the Year business simply for his excursion with Charly to the airport, she'd be there for the trip out and then back home and he'd feel her close to him in all her inscrutability, still having no idea whether she'd ever read his books or looked at anything beside magazines, like that time when Caroline, with the concentration and detachment typical of her as an artist, photographed Charly, Caroline seeing her simply as a model and not yet as the devil-child who would shatter her life, and Adrien, who had been visiting Caroline to give her a copy of his latest collection of poems, saw Charly slathered in sunscreen and cavorting by the pool and had a premonition that one day this girl would turn his head irreversibly, yes, she would, his writings about Faust perhaps the reason that not without pleasure was he engaging with the devil, or at least the exquisite she-devil that was Charly, whereas Caroline, absorbed in her work, saw nothing at all, the fact of the matter was that the devil, or Faust selling his soul to him, was Adrien's writer's obsession and not Caroline's, absorbed as she was by thoughts of the poet Jean-Mathieu, her lover, that night they would dine together on a terrace by the sea and beforehand discuss Jane Austen, and, united in affection but also by working on a book together, they embraced, it was the time of utter perfection for Caroline before everything fell apart, thought Adrien as the limousine drove along Atlantic Boulevard and along the long avenues of palm trees by the beach, the joggers and skateboarders were out in force, and Adrien would have sold his soul once again, why not, to be able to take flight with all of them, to run or to glide, and, thinking some more of Caroline, he thought about how one should always be wary of things that seemed too good to be true, was it not the case, Adrien reasoned, that Caroline and Jean-Mathieu were too happy together, that theirs was a perfection too much for any human to bear, concluding as well that Charly was driving too fast and they'd arrive at the airport early, what a bore, he'd be dragging all this stuff, his cane, his briefcase and, Dorothea having imposed her will again, he'd be put in a wheelchair, in case you're delayed or you have to walk too much, Monsieur Adrien, said Dorthea, yes, the wheelchair had been forced on him even though he was no invalid, just very old, Dorothea humouring and flattering him a little for being so accomplished and receiving the award, such kudos for you and for me as well, she said, for she too felt honoured, and all the more so because Mr. Adrien had been her own professor of literature, what progress she had made, now she could read and write all on her own, she'd started with the gospels and after that there'd been no stopping her, read the poets, suggested Adrien, but she preferred religious texts, and thoughts of the speech he was to make distracted Adrien and he missed what Charly said, remembering, as he was, Dorothea telling him that one had to be polite and gracious and this is what he'd do, he'd be loyal to a tried and tested formula of thanks, ladies and gentlemen, dear colleagues, no, that's not going to work, I thank you dear friends for coming out in such inclement weather, no, not that either, oh come, I'll find a way, how about, venerable Dean, dear students, my dear friends, no no, avoid the familiar, haven't people always considered me, both as a poet and a man, to be distant, and what with Charles, in his mysticism, being the incendiary poet of the day, was my diffidence not a foil when Charles wrote so penetratingly despite the difficulties his poetic constructions presented to his readers, did his view of humanity's destiny not invigorate us, whereas I was always a little disdainful of mankind, but what can I do, that's just the way I am, and I have to admit Dorothea may end up making a true man of me, or at least true enough to have some sympathy for her condition, poor Dorothea, illiterate like the rest of her family, is there any tribulation more unfair than that, and we are the ones who allowed it to happen, we Whites, hang on, *venerable* suggests a ripe old age, must avoid that too, oh really, what can I possibly say, they'll have defied the cold and rain or snow of New York to come to the auditorium, my children will be there too, in the very first row, alongside the man Suzanne preferred, that inattentive mathematician, he whose mind was always elsewhere, yes, my fine children, they'll all be able to observe just how bored I can be by official functions, they'll catch me yawning or trying not to, and as the car reached the turnoff to the airport where pelicans fly out over the sea, their heavy wings beating in a regular and harmonious motion, Adrien saw himself carrying Suzanne down from the second floor in her wedding dress, and it seemed to him that they had repeated the scene for their laughing children, the family reunited for Christmas holidays on the island, oh, they'd been laughing so, the children's congenial faces at the foot of the stairs indulging their parents, yes, thought Adrien, in truth no happiness can be too complete, he could still feel her bride's veil brushing his face, Suzanne trembling in his hands as he carried her, and then Charly's voice broke the silence of the limo in which Adrien had come to relax as if in a deck chair beside an ocean that was finally calm, announcing, as if issuing an order, we're at the airport, Adrien, please don't exhaust yourself, I'll take care of the suitcase and tell the stewardess you asked for a wheelchair, don't get out of the car yet, Adrien, that's it for our trip today. And Petites Cendres was thinking that the queens would soon be on the stage of the cabaret, Jason was in the lighting booth incessantly adjusting his settings, from violet to white and then all of a sudden red, and Petites Cendres had time to contemplate just how beautiful his hands looked with their long, slender nails painted scarlet, he thought of his parents, the progenitors of his sexy hands and voluminous hair, and how he was unable to thank them because he'd not seen them for so long, his parents who'd repudiated him for the shame and dishonour he'd heaped upon them, Petites Cendres figured he had no right to hate, though perhaps he could pity them as they'd never really understood the son who always loved them, maybe he should actually be grateful for a rejection that spared him the specifics of their misery, an ignominious misery Petites Cendres felt every time he ran into his father, he who did not recognize him or pretended not to do so as he pushed his cluttered cart along Bahama Street, the old man teetering on emaciated legs with his socks rolled down to his ankles and the tennis shoes he'd worn out through years of pacing the streets selling Bibles and playing his violin so badly, the junk in his cart included a heap of tins and boxes, a plastic garden chair, and, at the summit of it all, his violin and Bible, this was the misery of God's travelling salesman that Petites Cendres had been spared, ah, what a blessing it had been to be turfed out by his parents and abandoned so, and yet Petites Cendres was also convulsed with pity for his father walking on those skimpy legs and pushing his cart, poor man, poor *father*, he thought, God's travelling salesman sunk to such depths after dumping me, thought Petites Cendres, and Daniel heard the driver say, we've reached the venue, ladies and gentlemen, my apologies for the rough ride on the way up, our country roads are, I'm afraid, very demanding, please don't rush, esteemed writers, I've not opened the doors yet, I'm asking you to stay in your seats, said the driver, because, like Daniel, he could see the writers were rushing the exit, either to see the mountain still glowing in the sun or because they had taken to arguing as they'd been doing at a roundtable earlier that afternoon, Daniel reminded of the man who'd been so unpleasant that morning, the critic who'd taken a scalpel to Proust, bedridden and seriously ill, and described him as an unproductive hypochondriac, the man was a kind of literary pathologist who imagined he had the licence to do or say anything, thought Daniel as he recalled, as well, the person at the table sitting next to Proust's detractor, a passionate admirer of the writer who reacted as if he'd been Proust himself shot through the chest with a dart, and the critic, who from a distance looked quite like Adrien, though only from a distance, for the man was downright mean and Adrien, though often heavy-handed, bore no ill will but for the perverse jealousy of Augustino he could not rein in, the critic then attacking a group of female writers at the same afternoon roundtable and putting his misapprehension and contempt of intellectuals on full display as he set about insulting them, one of the women repeated a comment made earlier in the morning and declared that if Aristotle, Plato, or Sophocles had had the misfortune to be born a woman, they'd never have written what they did, for however encyclopedic their knowledge, women writers and philosophers were weeded out, sure, they might actually have written something but, what with the silencing and dismissal of their gifts, in effect they'd have been subjugated and censured from birth, backed step by step into that mass grave of stillborn creators in which, since the dawn of antiquity, the genius and creative spirit of so many extraordinary women's minds have been condemned to lie in grievous torpor, men dominating through their monopoly of the spoken and written word, not to mention divine revelation, and, said another of the women, in a civilization in which knowledge is autocratic and shared only with other men, is not society itself a male undertaking in which it is possible to police and "civilize" and leave only the slavish, servile roles to women, obstructing their minds' work and ignoring them, which is when the acerbic critic got all worked up over his breakfast and railed against one of the women writers saying, go ahead, break free, emancipate yourselves, but let men be, soon enough we'll need a foundation for men to be protected against the lot of you, from you and your demands and your outdated feminist revolution, enough, enough, he yelled, and now the bus driver was becoming irritable and said, okay, ladies and gentlemen, that'll do, take it easy, we're at the entrance of the mountain forest and your reception committee is waiting for you, please have your invitation in hand and please, stop jostling, I'm opening the door now, look at this countryside in all its autumnal splendour, red and gold, gold and yellow, and do you see the flags of all the invited nations over the entryway arch, impressive, isn't it, that so many of you came, ladies and gentlemen, but Daniel had been counting the flags bordering the approach to the reception committee and by his reckoning some were missing, and he thought of writers from repressive regimes who had yet to arrive and beside him, in a calmer state, the poet from Harlem was heading toward a delegation familiar to him, ah, they came, said Paul, they're here, despite being forbidden to participate on pain of imprisonment, they're here, he repeated, what a pity he had so many cases before the courts and he had to leave before dawn, police killings in Harlem were on the rise, he told Daniel, look, said Paul, they've arrived, two of the writers from Niger are here, the rest are sure to arrive tonight, and who was still there urging Daniel to intervene with the reception committee on his behalf, who, under the trees at the opening of the forest, was still there, the authors who'd been with him on the coach were shaking off their inertia and proceeding along the road and nearly at the peak of the mountain where the conference was happening, and there, thought Daniel, he could see Rodrigo there, Rodrigo the poet from Brazil in his raggedy outfit, bare-chested beneath his dirty white jacket and shivering from the cold, Daniel, said Rodrigo, you're my friend, please slip in a word for me to the chairman of the committee, I have to tell them about my two sons, they have no one else, please, Daniel, you must, you see the state my writing has put me in, I don't have the money the regime is demanding for me to get my sons out, my friend, help me, I beg you, I'm your old friend Rodrigo from Brazil, remember, but just as Daniel started to approach, the poet fled, running into the shadiest patch of forest while still yelling at Daniel can you help me, my friend, can you, and then he heard nothing, just the sound of birds in the trees and the murmurs of the authors walking to the conference along the gradually darkening road, and Daniel was thinking that soon it would be night and he'd not be able to make out the ravishing colours of the forest any more just as he and the writers were confronted by a procession of women and men dressed in black and white and proffering candles, pilgrims mourning the poets lost during the preceding year, writers who'd be missed forever, they said, the procession was solemn and non-violent and Daniel decided to follow them as he wondered about the poet whose hair had turned suddenly white, the poet who loved to party and whom Eddy had mentioned in the bar, he remembered having seen the faces of other poets who'd gone missing during the year, their photographs mounted on the red walls of the village house in which they'd been welcomed, and he thought how ephemeral is our destiny, where did they all go, and what about Suzanne, where among the photographs on those red walls was her taciturn smile, and then suddenly the moment came back to him, clear as day, when she had taken his arm as they were walking by the sea, her smile not the serious one that came to her when she was contemplating the beyond, no, she was feeling only happiness, she said, let's go for a swim and then get something to eat, I have so much to tell you, dear Daniel, what a pleasant distraction you are from my husband, always with his nose in his dictionaries, no, her smile was no longer that of a Suzanne pondering the mystery of our mortality but that of an exuberant, radiant woman refusing to give in to her ennui, who wanted no more of the monotony she called her rascally friend and confidant, the joy of life comes in loving, she said, though not always the same creature, and this is how I love you, Daniel, there are so many I love, from my little dog whose head I scratch when I get up each morning, to you with the strong shoulder I lean my head on when we stare out at the sea, you must realize, don't you, that what we're feeling this instant will never return, yes, our destinies are so ephemeral, that's true, thought Daniel, knowing that Suzanne had never left his side and doubtless never would, just as Mère had not, Mère still speaking to him in dreams, still telling him how to act, and, who was to say, perhaps prophetically, or at the very least as a guardian looking out for whatever hazards lay on his path, and Lou thought she'd grown up, that she'd matured, tonight she'd been invited for the first time to a sleepover, a *sleepover* meant to sleep with friends and tonight she was going to sleep at Emma and Juliette's house and Ari, her circumspect father, reminded her not to forget anything from the general pile on the floor, nor to leave anything out of the oversize backpack at her feet, it might be time to get rid of that, he said, or first the silk pyjamas and the bathrobe she'd never worn, gifts from Ari she'd tossed into the abiding chaos of her room, you don't care about appearances, do you, said Ari, usually girls your age like to doll themselves up and be cute like Emma and Juliette, you're lucky to be going to their place, just wait and see, your school chums from L'Étoile de la Mer live in a nice house by the sea near a canal the girls swim in every day, there's a tennis court and a magnificent garden, your girlfriends' father is an architect and he's seen to every comfort for the family, as much space for games and recreation in their house as there is for study, now don't forget anything, Lou, and remember to shower and maybe take your silk pyjamas, this is your very first sleepover, make it a good one, these people have class and we want them to know I've brought you up right, Lou, maybe when you go to your mother's she doesn't make you shower every day, you're always saying you don't have the time and that you swim in the sea instead, but showering is an indispensable part of your education, you must be clean, and perfectly so, especially for a *sleepover*, do you hear me, but Lou was stuffing her overnight bag full of books, video games, and movies, and wasn't listening to her father at all, I'll go there the way I am, thought Lou, Papa's always preaching about the necessity of being clean and obedient and polite but all Mama said is first and foremost have fun with your friends and don't forget to wash your hands before dinner, you'll have been running on the beach and playing ball so it would be nice for their mother if you washed your hands and brushed your hair, Lou had forgotten to shower but splashed her forehead, cheeks, ears, and blue hair with cold water, it matters, said her mother Ingrid, Lou was wearing her brother's jeans and his tie over a shirt that said, I LOVE LIFE DON'T MESS WITH ME, she'd pulled on knee-high boots, which, her father said, I just don't get in such a hot climate, and she got on her bike and was about to leave, helmet on, guitar strapped over her shoulder, and her huge backpack in the basket, when her father said, hey you, going off to your first sleepover without giving me a kiss are you, how can you forget to kiss your father on such an occasion, which she did with a minimal brush of the lips, excited and perhaps even a little nervous about this first sleepover with the girls, and she thought, geez, I forgot to kiss Mama, and Lou saw the oh-so-refined Emma and Juliette and their oh-so-refined parents on the doorstep of their house with the gorgeous garden, and it felt as if they'd greeted her a little coolly, that they were looking her over from head to toe, and Emma, the elder of the two girls and already a long-legged teenager, was wearing shorts with a floral pattern and said, oh, you came without changing out of your dirty clothes, and her mother told her to get out of her shorts and into a dress, tonight was a special event and it would be better for her to wear a cotton dress at dinner especially, Daddy liked that his girls were well turned out, no swimsuits or skimpy shorts, those were the house rules, and Lou thought this was not at all like in her mother's house, Ingrid whom she loved so much and whom she would resemble further on down the road, except that she'd be a boy, true, her mother already had a son, Julien, whom Lou also loved because he let her borrow his ties, sailing caps, he was really a sweet brother, and Lou would come to resemble him too, Mama would have two sons, Lou really only feeling true to herself when she was in her boy's skin, oh, said her father, how I miss my little daughter Lou, the girl who really was my little one, when you were five years old you were still so feminine and such a beauty, really, but Lou told Ari she couldn't remember that far back and her father said, now I was really proud of that little girl, she went everywhere with me, she was my little darling, my little Lou, but I'm still me, Lou said to her father, even if I do wear Julien's ties, here we go, said Ari, that's your mother's influence, I've always said she wasn't strict enough with you, Lou, really, I don't know what we're going to do with you, though you are still a child and you'll change later on, and Juliette said to Lou, look at you, you're just like you are at school, do you have any pyjamas in that disgusting bag, no, said Lou, just the video games you like, plus books and films and my iPhone to call Mama, and Lou was thinking, one day I'll make films too, she felt like everyone was ganging up on her, even Emma and Juliette's parents scolding, it's true, no pyjamas, nothing, I mean you should know how to dress when you come for a sleepover at our house, well, I just don't like pyjamas or bathrobes, said Lou, aware of the sobs rising in her throat but that she'd not let them out, they'd stop right there, like a stifled cough, and what was Emma and Juliette's mother saying now, really, I think this girl is just too different to be spending the night with you, go back home, my dear, she said to Lou, perhaps you can come some other time when you are more presentable, my husband and I realize your parents are divorced and that explains the difference, we do understand, but I think it would be much better if we postponed your night with your friends till later, but Mama, said Juliette, she hasn't done anything wrong, adding, if she doesn't want to be too different then I have pyjamas she can wear, and okay, she can't stay up and watch films all night in those boots, so maybe we can teach her something, but, realized Lou, Emma and Juliette's parents had already decided, irrevocably, to turn her away from their house and suddenly the door was closed on her, on her *difference*, and though she didn't know what the word meant yet, a lead mantle was weighing down on her shoulders, yes, she was different, but why, and different from whom, it was as if someone had precipitously declared she was ugly, oh dear, it was time to phone her mother, I'm different, Mama, can you believe they said that when I look like you and Papa too, and Lou thought about how sadly her first sleepover had ended, and that the quicker she became a boy, the better she'd be able to defend herself against *difference*, but how was she different, why was she different, what had she done, was it the tie, her blue hair, but what was more natural than that, and Lou thought about the slogan I LOVE LIFE DON'T MESS WITH ME printed on her shirt, the pressure still constricting her throat, *different*, she pondered, they said I was too different to spend the night and shut the door on me, different, she thought, different. And what of these conversations he'd been having with Claudio in various cafés, thought Fleur as Claudio conducted his *New Symphony* with such disarming intensity, the cacophonous and hoary sounds of the music apparently no problem for him at all, okay, Claudio said to Fleur, you weren't brought up in any religion, Andrew, so you don't know how strong my family's ties have been for generations, we belong to a denomination of the church and adhere to a doctrine that must strike someone like you as absurd and compliant, only why does it trouble you so, being born into the Christian faith is not for everybody, and shouldn't it be music that matters to you most of all, the weakness of Catholic doctrine lies in the church not knowing how to deal with those living outside its fortress walls, and in the cafés in which he was conversing almost absent-mindedly with Fleur, Claudio glanced at his watch or cell phone from time to time because he was a musician with little time to rest and who described himself as a careerist, as someone who'd actually done far too little to develop his spiritual side though perhaps, he said, posing the question rhetorically, spiritual practice was an innate aspect of his art, and then he pressed his cell phone to his ear, the call was from Morocco where he was to conduct a concert soon, and he asked his caller if the choristers were prepared, there'd not be much time to rehearse, and Fleur heard the voice of Wrath telling him they'll all be chased from the temple, every one of them and their presumptions, when the Great Beggar comes, know that the inquisitors will be there hunting down the heretics and leading them to the stake as always, and when the Great Beggar appears in the city of Rome, then you'll see, Fleur, because you're young, you'll see, that at first he'll be in the guise of a prince but then suddenly a king, a prince who will take off all his clothes and place his crown and sceptre in front of everyone with such humility it will make them tremble, yes, all the prelates in their gold-embroidered sacerdotal vestments will tremble and I, Gabriel Wrath who lives in hiding, I'll be sheltered from the Great Beggar's gaze, which is not of this world, he'll arrive barefoot, with neither whip nor rod, and by his gaze alone will he cast them out, you'll see, Fleur, they won't know where to run, what woods or forests to flee to, they'll hide the strongboxes stuffed with all the money they have stolen from the poor under their robes, but suddenly these will weigh heavily on them and they'll buckle under the spoils of their larceny, their ill-gotten gains stashed in ornate buildings and in caverns, yes, the whole secular edifice of their stockpiled fortunes will disintegrate before the gaze of the Great Beggar, will tumble, oh, said Wrath, this will come to pass, and suddenly Su, frail in a buttonless coat, emerged from the shadows saying, don't listen to him, Fleur, he's delirious, the old man's a nut-job, he's cold and he's hungry, it's the winter damp getting through our clothes and into our bones, outcasts have nothing to do but howl words like his so, Fleur, don't you listen, Wrath is raving, but Wrath's rancorous voice soon eclipsed Su's, Fleur, listen to what I'm telling you, said Wrath, it will happen just as I say, the Great Beggar, with neither crown nor sceptre, will address all who govern this earth with unforgettable humility, he will say to lords and kings, cease your decrees and all that makes your glory, be done with all that and follow me, for where I go no one has a kingdom, and Su said again, don't listen, Fleur, don't, the man is demented, cold and hunger and the infernal damp of the rising river waters have suffused his clothes and made the man demented, please, it's the cold and hunger speaking, don't listen, Fleur, and did you know this man Wrath saved my life more than once, I was dying from an overdose and alone on a bench with my head dangling back and unable to wake up when he came to me, oh, yes, I was near gone, said Su, and then Wrath, as if he'd momentarily forgotten his rage, said in a disconsolate tone, Su could hardly breathe, it was so cold that night I had to lay my chilled body, flaccid and wasted and useless as ever, over the poor rag that with all his addictions Su had become, and I was able to warm him, the poor lad, despite being so cold myself and, it was a miracle, I heard him take a breath again and then, shivering, he begged me for a cigarette, his first of the new day, oh my dear Fleur, such are the base miseries of the world, and as Claudio conducted his *New Symphony* in the Rome concert hall Fleur thought about how the conductor's innocence had been maintained, likely because of the naïveté of his Christian belief, for he'd never needed to contend with Wrath, or the ambivalent nature of evil of which Wrath was at times the incarnation, for, as Wrath said, should not everything be incarnate on this earth, the beautiful and the brutal, everything, absolutely everything, he said, was this not the enigmatic will of our absent God, that we should all be tossed into the abyss for Him to see how sadistically we react in the mix, would some be saints and others demons, or the lot of us no more than His ordinary creatures, what or who would we be, asked Wrath, and at the prospect of our being unremarkable and neither saints nor demons, Claudio would have replied that each of us has room for improvement, always, and that our striving for perfection eventually humanizes us, take the sounds of instruments in an orchestra, he would have said, chaos and incoherence manifest themselves everywhere, but in an orchestra we are always working toward harmony, toward perfecting some kind of harmonious polyphony and it is this chaos, this incoherence, that is the discomfiting leitmotif of Fleur's music, that is his inspiration, and how thrilled Fleur was that Claudio understood this instinctively and conformed to his music's demands, and then Fleur thought about Alfonso, the priest Alfonso, who, from the isolated reaches of the New England parish to which he'd been relegated, endeavoured to bring the cardinals who'd been the subject of allegations against the Vatican for so long to justice, the cardinals not excommunicated as Wrath had been, they weren't living under bridges, no, but ignoring all the allegations forwarded to Rome by various plaintiffs, they'd retired to distant places, to Britain or Scandinavia, who knew where they were, but they'd definitely not been defrocked, and it seemed to Fleur that Claudio was ignoring this scandalous and hidden face of the church he supported when, with his wife and daughters, he went to Mass on Sundays, and, thought Fleur, as was the case with so many artists engrossed solely by their art, was there not a certain cowardice in Claudio's fealty, the priest Alfonso had for a time been a friend of Fleur's mother, helping to conceal the identities of immigrants they sheltered in churches or at Martha's, the house in the mangroves by the sea where Fleur grew up, and did not Alfonso, who'd been banished to New England and to silence there, insist that the cardinals should be hunted down and prosecuted like war criminals, which, Wrath would have admitted, in a way they had been, though did not Wrath, who never denied the role he played in the cardinals' abduction of children, also say that Alfonso was his own worst enemy, no longer protected or defended by the authorities of the Vatican, in truth he was just another fallen man and his own worst detractor, for the toughest sentences, said Wrath, are the ones we inflict on ourselves, I killed Tai so he wouldn't turn me in, or at least I thought I did, this confession of Wrath's one Fleur had heard innumerable times but refused to acknowledge, not wanting to be sullied by his criminality, and you'll notice, Wrath continued, that those protecting the cardinals never mention rape or murder, crimes of which we are all capable, even when those misdemeanours go back a long way, even if they happened twenty or thirty years ago, their crimes not dying with the passing of time but, oh no, these hypocrites refer instead to victims of inappropriate acts, or to the children simply as victims, in ecclesiastical cases the terms *rape* and *murder* are never used, they adhere to a sort of criminal reticence, said Wrath, in which the word *victim* replaces the word *child*, we are liars, Wrath would have said, and Fleur was sure that were he ever with all of them in hell's antechamber, in the fog on the wharves by the river where Wrath waited in his filthy overcoat, he would never hear the confession Wrath had made, never hear Wrath admitting that he'd killed Tai because he thought he was about to be betrayed, no, he never thought he'd hear it. And there they were, Daniel saw, laughing in a mountain clearing, the girls in high heels who'd been celebrating Daphnée and Peter's betrothal that afternoon, they'd all come together to buy one of Daniel's books and have him sign it, and now he was blushing and they were all laughing because authors did this, wasn't it bizarre, they said, how writers who were welcomed to the village with such enthusiasm and warmth tended to blush, but despite the reddening of his cheeks he signed the book, why call it *Strange Years*, asked one of them as she held out the book, wasn't every year in a life strange, this one's for Daphnée, she said, it's her wedding gift from us, what a night it's going to be, a beautiful evening for us to listen to you all, to the readings you'll be giving in theatres all over the mountain, if we get bored then we'll go for a walk along one of the trails leading through the wonderful countryside, yup, that's what we'll do if we get tired of listening to you, and then off they went, thought Daniel, like sparkling fairies, they could have been Mai's big or little sisters, off to the banquet and dancing a bit as they advanced toward the tables, and as the cooks and servers carried steaming plates, and others brought candelabras to the tables, Daniel noticed that one of the first writers to rush headlong toward a server to secure a huge helping of meat was none other than the author of *Esthetic Eternity*, he who'd been preaching about diet and food restrictions all day, yet here he was, the diminutive, sour man stuffing himself with the meat of animals caught and killed the day before, biting into the bleeding flesh of a deer, then a boar, Daniel stepping back as though he were witness to a scene of the hunt such as he'd seen in the paintings at the hotel and in the bar, it was that repulsive to watch him wallow in the feast, clearly the man had been lying all day, the better to sell his proselytizing vegetarian books, was this some sort of impromptu joke or was it, as Mai said, that given their fecund imaginations writers were simply predisposed to lying, but Daniel was disgusted and it offended him that innocent animals had died for the dyspeptic little man, dishonest on top of it all and a money-grubber too, and Daniel was thinking along these lines when he saw Eddy wandering his way and holding the writer of erotic fantasies by the arm, the bestselling author was looking quite lost at the moment, Eddy clutching him so he'd not get away, here we go, said Eddy, and then, to Daniel, this young fella had some bad news today, he had a sense of just how ephemeral success can be and wanted to end it all, I'd gone to his room with the bottle of whisky he'd ordered and saw he was on the point of, well, I'll say no more, don't want to upset you, Daniel, but it would have been a shame if he'd carried through with it, bad for the hotel's reputation and, well, for him too, I'm going to have to leave him with you so I can wait on the tables, said Eddy, most of the authors are fine with the buffet but others prefer to be served, and then he released the young man's arm and joined the ranks of the other servers and chefs in their white jackets and black ties, so now what have you done, Daniel asked the woebegone author, and the young man took off his huge glasses so that he could dry his eyes and said, I've been humiliated, defeated, it's all over, I'm no longer on the bestseller list, I'm nothing, my publisher said the erotica I write is too subtle, that I have to be more vulgar, but me, vulgar, I can never be that, now I'll just be like one of those down-and-out Balzac characters in their filthy rags, an opportunist and a loser, those who are successful will look down on me, I even bought some good, strong rope, and Daniel said, enough of that, stay with me, I'll keep an eye on you, you've had too much whisky, maybe, said the boy, then we've got to get some food into you, said Daniel, we should go find the chapel for poet-suicides, the young man said, sure, I'll take you there, but stay close, okay, and he said, I'd like to pray for them all, the author who had remained anonymous till now confiding, I'm Henri, like the German author Heinrich von Kleist, who died at thirty-four after killing his fiancée and turning the weapon he'd used on himself, von Kleist was the one who said, and I'll never forget it, *Immortality, now you are mine*, isn't it extraordinary that he should have been so lucid and unforgiving of himself in his final hour, this great poet about to win everything he desired in an act that was murderous, yes, but that demanded courage, in effect he concluded his life by marrying the woman he loved in a spectacular wedding, and betrothing himself to eternity, but Daniel's response to Henri's speech was hardly exultant, he said, let me tell you, Henri, if a good angel such as Eddy had been there, the awful deed would never have happened and the couple would have lived happily ever after like so many others, no, said Henri, no way, they'd never have been able to, suicide's in our genes and its hour comes around, that's all, *Immortality, now you are mine*, repeated the young author, it's a beautiful and noble phrase, and Daniel said, don't let go of me, you've not sobered up enough, and what about your paper, are you ready to deliver it, sure, said Henri, in fact it's about suicide, which I say is the destiny of feeble creatures such as myself, but we're supposed to talk about world peace, said Daniel, well, said Henri, they're connected, I mean living in this world is insufferable and begs the dignity of suicide, that or activism, only I don't have the stomach for either, just for writing, and now my publishers aren't interested in me anymore, they've found someone more exciting, someone more explicit, I wanted to keep my erotic writing from being boring, to give it a literary quality it doesn't usually possess, and now just look at how I'm treated, dumped from my publisher's list, yes, he said, blowing his nose and sobbing, *dumped*, and Daniel heard himself say something he'd not at all expected of himself, in a curious way you remind me of my son Augustino, he said, who knows, maybe I'll find him somewhere in this extraordinary gathering of writers we're a part of tonight, but Henri was muttering, I'm nothing but a joke, it's over, it's all over, and then, I bet your son's way more interesting than I am, what's his name again, oh yeah, Augustino, hey, everybody knows him, Augustino's the toast of my generation and I'm nothing, said Henri, and Daniel, with a measure of penance in his voice the young author did not notice, said, well, you're my son tonight and I'd really like to rid your heart of all this doom and gloom, and Daniel thought to himself, here I am with Augustino, thinking that he really needed to save this desperately romantic young man with a penchant for dark thoughts, but was it even in his power to save him, had he even saved his son who was now who knew where, consider how finite our lives are, said Henri, when I was a child and forced to take naps because I had such a weak constitution I said to myself, Henri, how will it all end for you, and what I could not foresee that I see all too clearly now is how, once we stop living, the body ends in a conflagration of fire and ashes, I can't bear the thought of being cremated, much less my buried body being putrid with worms, oh, how can we entertain such thoughts and yet this is what will become of us, and Daniel said, sure, but long before we get to that lamentable point you'll be writing more books, you'll be enjoying your body and, a lot of the time, with great pleasure, you'll love lots of women, but no, said the young man, all that's over too, you saw how surrounded I was by assistants and agents, all of them so attracted to my success, I was a kick for them and now they're all gone, every last one, though Henri nevertheless recovered very quickly when he spotted a young woman among the people he knew, she's a friend of mine, he said, no, she's more than that, I'd like to sleep with her before the conference is over, do you think I'll manage it, Daniel, I mean the thing is, Henri said, she could really inspire my next book, and there's the truth of a writer's life, he said, temptation quickly trumps all thoughts of suicide, oh boy, what a buzz, I have to talk to her, I'll see you later, and Daniel wondered how he was to keep an eye on the lad if he was already off and running, how could he have compared him to Augustino, thought Daniel, Augustino would never have been so frivolous, even if frivolity is often the companion of despair, Henri seemed to be engaged in a duel with celebrity when fame could so easily get the better of him and his aspiration to wealth, when that wealth was likely to diminish as unpredictably as it had arrived but leave him worse off, and Daniel would continue to worry on behalf of the young writer locked in an existential fight that, no matter how lightweight, reminded Daniel what a crazy business writing was, Daniel then wandering among the white-topped tables to look for Rodrigo but not finding him, no doubt he'd been turfed out of the conference, Daniel would have given the poet his jacket and shoes or anything he had for Rodrigo not to be humiliated so, and he thought of the writers they were still expecting whose arrival was increasingly belated, no news, what about the other writers from Niger, where were they all, what circumstances were delaying them, and Daniel imagined the deafening roar of a plane crashing in some fog-obfuscated pasture on the Irish coast, he thought of poets humiliated and tortured and their books pulped and censored, and now he was struck by just how solemn the procession of writers appeared, dressed in black and white and standing among the trees, along the alleys, and under the luminous reflection of the candelabras set on white tablecloths, they were so homogenous that Daniel could no longer distinguish the men from the women, all so alike and sharing a common language and speaking in voices Daniel could hardly make out, voices that melded into a uniform, subdued chant, yes, here they were still waiting for the writer from Niger who was meant to open the conference, and as he looked for the women writers from the afternoon's roundtable whom the critic of Proust had insulted so gratuitously as they were leaving the coach, he remembered the vision he'd had, if it was that, his vision of Mélanie, mother to young Augustino the writer and this undoubtedly the reason she appeared so triumphant in his dream, Mélanie among a crowd of women writers and poets, all of them able and intrepid skiers making their way down the slopes of a mountain, or were they skiing down from its very summit, cutting through the snow sparkling in the sunlight, when each of their names was illuminated in the blanket of white, and Daniel was dazzled as he watched them all skiing toward him, and delighted and won over when he woke up from his dream, one of them had said it's the end of the new moon, the new moon beneath which words disappear, it's the end of, look, the sun's rising on the snowy slopes, what a pity, thought Daniel, that after being so stirred and overcome by a dream in which the triumphs and future achievements of the female authors he'd witnessed at the roundtable took on such a glittering and symbolic hue, that a disturbing one should follow, yes, how upsetting it was, the nightmare he then had being one of the most persistent and recurring of Daniel's dark dreams, the one in which he was ordered to carry out the execution of his great-uncle Samuel, defiling the glistening snow with his blood and, worse, ordered to do so by a Nazi officer in Poland in a time long passed, and yet suddenly the past felt so much more real and immediate than the present that all time became a seamless whole subject to none of the usual laws, so that in his dream the fate of Daniel's great-uncle Samuel was always a part of Daniel's own polymorphic destiny, and when he awoke from his reverie, Daniel saw the mountain in the twilight, saw the dark azure colour of the sky and that there was no snow here yet, someone had lit a blazing campfire as night was falling and passing authors were stopping to warm their hands, holding their palms out to the flame, it would be an exhilarating evening, thought Daniel, though he was still dissatisfied that his presentation was unfinished and aware that Mai had written a message he'd not yet taken the time to read, and then he wondered where the young author he'd been minding had gone, and when he would next see Augustino, and suddenly Daniel found himself in the middle of the procession of writers, walking with them in a parade beneath the stars, and as he did so words he'd written in the morning came back to him, every writer among us has a debt to redeem with humanity, yes, every single one of us. Invited up onto the dais of the university stage to accept his Poet of the Year Award, Adrien opened his arms, ready to receive the bouquet of flowers offered to him by an admiring young student, Amanda, so evidently moved, a creative writing student with whom he'd been corresponding for several years and who'd subsequently become dear to him, Amanda, Charly, they were all dear to him, the nature of their charm being that they would always be vivacious and desirable whereas he, well no, better not go there, he thought, Adrien instead concentrating on just how impressionable the girl seemed, not as forbidding as Charly, though he was aware that Charly's coolness is what attracted him, and now Amanda was climbing the couple of steps to the dais, she was breathing rapidly, thought Adrien, how moving this was, and now here were the flowers, white roses, oh dear, I don't like those, at least one is a pale pink, Suzanne would have liked them, but white roses, what does whiteness represent, he mused, snow or something I shall not name, though white is also the colour of hope because nothing has yet been inscribed on it, and Adrien leaned toward the young student more than he did flowers, she was a slight thing, full of life and breathing so heavily, so much emotion, he thought, so much emotion there, and then here's me who's forgotten how to feel anything at all, it was her, little Amanda, that he'd really have liked to squeeze in his arms, but instead he bowed humbly and accepted the bouquet, thank you, he said to the assembly of professors and students, and then he turned toward the dean and bowed once more and again offered thanks for the flowers scratching his cheeks, and Adrien decided that Charly and Amanda stimulating his desire was proof that he too was still alive, he should discuss his poem "The Reckoning" with Amanda by email, though perhaps he was better off destroying it and writing another, or why not send her "Feast Day," far more passion in that poem's lines, yes, I'll send her "Feast Day," that's the one for today, thought Adrien, no question he was happy, almost deliriously so. Lou was walking with her parents to a new school where she would never see Emma or any of her family again, her backpack was hanging down almost to her ankles and rubbing against the leather of her boots, and she was thinking of those snobs who'd not let her sleep in their house because she was *different*, they were worse than snobs, they were disgusting, thought Lou, Mama was walking to one side of her and Papa on the other, the two of them hopelessly estranged, though they'd agreed their daughter would change schools without admonishing each other so maybe there was a hint of reconciliation in the air, thought Lou, she was off to the Academy of Arts and come summer would be a student in the theatre school and play the part of the devil in a musical comedy written for schoolchildren, she'd only been given the role because she was the biggest in her group, but what excited her most was that the director of the theatre school would let her build sets for the play and paint them however she saw fit, and really she would have liked to take her mother Ingrid's hand but that would have upset her father Ari, staring straight ahead and showing only a stern profile to Ingrid, true, she was smiling more but that's how things were, thought Lou, she loved her daughter so much, her father did too, so why did they not make up, Lou wondered, she wanted them to join hands, but Ari wouldn't have liked that, that's how he was all the time, quick to anger, and besides, how could she possibly convince her parents to join hands when her father had mistresses, I don't get why you have to wear Julien's tie on the day of your registration at a new school, said Ari, we're giving you a new chance, so you'd be better off behaving well, said Lou's father, but in a gentler, more appeasing tone her mother said, this isn't a day for scolding, really, said Ingrid, she can dress how she likes here, isn't that so, Lou, you know how proud of you we are, Lou, both of us are, but still they were not looking at each other, nor would they speak for weeks, it's over between them, thought Lou, the fire of their love has been put out, it's extinguished, dead, they just don't love each other, and even Lou, who felt so torn because of it, would never be able to get them back together, still, the main thing, thought Lou, was that she would never see Emma or be humiliated by her parents again, she was starting at a new school and at last would see no more of Emma and the family that had so shamefully refused her staying at their house for her very first sleepover, yes, they'd all be punished and she'd never ever see them again, thought Lou. Angel still had a touch of fever, Lena said, but just a touch, and there was a surprise waiting for him at dinner, and it was true, just as Brilliant had promised him, tonight they'd all be going out to sea because the winds were calm, and if Angel was coughing, said his mother, it was from nerves, the house was brimming with excitement in anticipation of the surprise, sad Lena said to her son, so how about waiting outside on the deck chair with Misha, Orange, and Night Out, you'll actually be closer to your surprise that way, but Angel could also smell mango cake in the kitchen, and Angel, the birds on his shoulders, and Misha, who was following behind, all wanted a taste of it, but his mother said, no dear, you have to wait, Dr. Dieudonné is coming for his daily visit, of course, but especially for the surprise, everyone's going to be here, said Lena, Brilliant, and Lucia, who loves nothing better than to make you forget your worries, but Mama, they aren't worries, it's just that when I cough it hurts deep down here in my chest, said Angel pointing under his white shirt, but, Angel's mother interrupted, as the doctor says, you're on your way to being cured so now we're going to celebrate, yes, it's time for the surprise, and Angel said, you know, Mama, the two yellow hibiscus flowered overnight so we can put them in your hair, when we go out with Brilliant and Misha you'll be the most beautiful of all, said Angel, rushing into his mother's arms, he didn't want her to be sad today, often she was, because he had trouble showing affection or cried so much, you say it hurts when you cough, said Lena, kissing him, but you shouldn't let it worry you, the doctor says like all young patients you need more rest though you do hate that, don't you, but Mama, said Angel, I'm waiting for your surprise, let's go out on the veranda, Misha, me, and the birds, we're all ready, Mama, and he looked at her silently expressing the gratitude that was also her own, as if he'd said, with wonder, every day you give me life, Mama. And as the phantom figures of Fatalité and Herman danced in the pre-show video playing on the screen, Yinn called everybody on stage, saying, girls, up there in the booth Jason is about to reveal all of you with the genius of his lights, Victoire, don't worry about messing up your moves, I'll be directing you from the wings, and Victoire looked at Yinn realizing she was no longer so alone though still she worried how her debut performance at the cabaret would go, but there Yinn was with all the queens, so professional and expressive, and Victoire could feel their teasing and their support, because you can't live without laughter, said Robbie, watch the Fatalité and Herman video if you need proof, they're always laughing and making fun, oh, said Robbie, their laughter was unforgettable, how they loved to ridicule themselves and to lampoon bigoted, prejudiced, and homophobic people, that made them socially and artistically defiant, and isn't that how we'll always want to remember them, tonight's the great event, he said, and when the red velvet curtain lifted, Robbie himself was standing on the stage next to Yinn in his white robe and finery and introduced Victoire, timid Victoire, to the audience of the evening, here is Victoire whom all of us admire so much, Robbie began, Victoire, our transsexual companion who's emerged victorious from a furious battle of her own as tough and distinguished as any she faced as a soldier, please, let's welcome Victoire to the Porte du Baiser Saloon cabaret tonight, and Petites Cendres watched as the group around Victoire burgeoned, Yinn, Robbie, Cobra, Heart Triumphant, all of them, crowned with garlands of flowers, opened the red velvet curtains and applauded Victoire, Victoire is in the house, they shouted, and Petites Cendres was also yelling, Victoire, welcome, we love you, Victoire, and was Victoire's courage and triumph not also his own, thought Petites Cendres as he tried to banish from his mind, yet again, the excruciating image of his aged father pushing a cart down Bahama Street, that pile of junk with his Bible and violin, the old man muttering and insulting his son so vilely saying, you, Petites Cendres, I renounce you, don't come near me anymore, and Petites Cendres, galvanized by the echoes of the other voices in the Saloon, thought yes, Victoire, welcome, oh yes, her victory was also his own. And Daniel noticed that even though they were still waiting for the marquee writers from various countries whose absence was sorely felt, really, he wondered, where were they all, that despite their absence a few of the authors were nevertheless proceeding to the stands with their speaking notes in hand, so calm and collected, and Daniel headed off in the direction of the forest and a sign pointing to the location of a chapel situated in the heart of a castle in ruins, a shrine in the apse not particular to any sect but dedicated to the poet-suicides of the previous year, where on a wall of grey stone above the second altar, long abandoned, were photographs of the writers shimmering between flickering candles, the authors seemed alive, thought Daniel, and he felt Suzanne's wry and tender gaze upon him, and under the picture it said,

ASSISTED SUICIDE, ZURICH, though even if nothing at all was written, Daniel would have been profoundly upset by the words, as he was from the immense grief of having lost her, and he felt sad for Adrien too, believing that he was also living through a time of great sadness, and suddenly Suzanne's gaze seemed to light up, to be incandescent with irony, come on now, she seemed to be saying, think of what's left, my friend, didn't I teach you joy during my time on earth, have you forgotten everything, and Daniel was about to leave the shrine, feeling moved by Suzanne's gaze, when he spotted Henri praying in a corner in shadow, he would have walked over but decided to quietly exit, and would he not have done the same if it had been Augustino in the corner, without a doubt he would have been every bit as bashful and discreet and would have left his son to his morose meditation, and then Daniel noticed another chapel sheltered under some birch trees, this one dedicated to the memory of poets who'd been shot, and he remembered how he'd recounted to Augustino, when he'd been in his teens and just starting to write, brutal tales of executed poets because it seemed to him that his writer son needed to be familiar with these terrible stories, needed to know what an ignominious stain on history they were, unspeakable cruelties that he thought belonged to the same cycle of horrors of which the execution of his great-uncle Samuel and the rabbis was a part, all of them kneeling in the snow, and the snow itself seeming to run over with the tears that had not frozen behind their half-open eyes and on their pleading, terror-struck faces, here in the chapel the poets who'd been shot would never be forgotten, or, wondered Daniel, was it that memory owed them this respect and veneration and that his own life was wedded to this everlasting memorial to the martyrs of literature, to the sacrifice of the poets on the altar of wars and revolutions, to the butchering of intellectuals, of the most exalted of souls, wasn't the oppression of thought always the aim, a tyranny instituted by Stalin, as tomorrow it would be by other dictators, and culminating in the terror of the night of August 12, 1952, when thirteen poets were shot on the orders of bloodthirsty Lavrenti Beria, poets accused of what, Daniel asked, poets accused of plotting an insurrection and subjected to endless tortures in prison, they who were poor and hungry and who possessed only words, and now in eternity the sadistic Beria would have to confront those he'd killed, who knows, perhaps, given the mountain of his crimes, he'd not even recognize his victims, and as he left the chapel by a foggy path, Daniel heard terrifying shouts and screams and wondered along which winding route and from which field behind the mountain they had come, and suddenly he noticed tanks and trucks and the same horde of masked youths he had seen that morning, they were wielding machine guns and shouting threats, their voices loud and wild, screaming that they would take the writers to the Hill of Crucifixions, here they were again, howling and yelling vengeance and yet none of the writers walking to the stands for the conference seemed to see them, why did they not also see the fire, the flames of campfires spreading to the spruce and pine and rising to the sky, why did they not see the deer and boars running across the transparent shimmering of flame, why, wondered Daniel, did no one see anything, and then he remembered the message from Mai he'd not yet opened, and read her words, Papa, say to everybody at the Twilight Celebration, is that what should loom above us, a nuclear twilight, yes, Papa, tell them all that we, the young, say no to the nuclear twilight, we say no no, and that they must stop defiling us and violating our future, will you say that, Papa, will you be strong enough, Papa, and suddenly he realized that this was how he would begin his speech, he would read out Mai's message, or perhaps, with more conviction, he'd share again the memory of the two little girls, one Palestinian and the other Israeli, yes, these two young girls, the pair of them victims suffering the same cardiac arrest, killed by bombs because armies are blind and unable to identify their victims anymore, no, thought Daniel as he walked toward the lectern, they don't know how, and now here's your surprise, said Lena to her son, and when Angel's mother lifted up the sheet all of them were there screaming with joy around the egret pond, Kitty and her mother and brothers, this was the day of Kitty's visit Angel had been awaiting for so long, and as Orange and Night Out flew free from his shoulders to the pond, Angel thought how much he would have liked to be able to fly like them, to Kitty and her family and Brilliant and Lucia, but the moment left him serene and as he descended the steps of the veranda with his mother, it was clear to him that the social worker had found Kitty and her family a home of their own, from now on she wouldn't be off in some distant motel, I have Kitty, thought Angel as Misha pushed him along, I have a friend, and with Orange and Night Out I have a family, as Mama says, we'll go see the cosmonauts later, Mama and me, yes, thought Angel, amused that Kitty was still wearing her brother's oversized sweater, Kitty, she's finally come to visit, and this is so much better than my father who never comes, yes, better than anything, thought Angel, this is happiness but, as Mama says, I mustn't get too excited, no, I mustn't, because I could lose everything, like when you tip over a basket of fruit without meaning to, Misha's nudging me about and Mama's complaining and today life is beautiful, my colour's back, I'm feeling better, and Brilliant's friend Jöe is readying the boat at the Atlantic Boulevard Marina and Brilliant will take me in his arms and carry me up the gangplank and together we'll sail the islands and watch the sun set over the sea, thought Angel as he slid his hand over Kitty's in the oversize sleeve of her sweater.

Once again, much love for their patience and support to Marie-Claire, to my sons Antoine and Olivier, and of course Carol Scott-Lanctôt. In difficult and death-defying circumstances, Matt Williams, Maria Golikova, Noah Richler and everyone at Anansi have shown very special support and patience, and for that I owe them much thanks indeed.

—N.S.

About the Author

Photo by Jill Glessing

MARIE-CLAIRE BLAIS is the internationally revered author of more than twenty-five books, many of which have been published around the world. In addition to the Governor General's Literary Award for Fiction, which she has won four times, Blais has been awarded the Gilles-Corbeil Prize, the Médicis Prize, the Molson Prize, and Guggenheim Fellowships. She divides her time between Quebec and Florida.

About the Translator

NIGEL SPENCER has won the Governor General's Literary Award for Translation with three novels by Marie-Claire Blais: *Thunder and Light*, *Augustino and the Choir of Destruction*, and *Mai at the Predators' Ball*, which was also a finalist for the QWF Cole Foundation Prize for Translation. He has translated numerous other works and films by and about Marie-Claire Blais, Poet Laureate Pauline Michel, Evelyn de la Chenelière, and others. He is also a film-subtitler, editor, and actor now living in Montreal.